David —

A
Cupboardful
of Shoes

And Other Stories

*Best wishes from
Colin
25/5/2012.*

A. Colin Wright

Order this book online at www.trafford.com
or email orders@trafford.com

Most Trafford titles are also available at major online book retailers.

© Copyright 2012 A. Colin Wright.

All rights reserved. No part of this publication may be reproduced, stored in a retrieval system, or transmitted, in any form or by any means, electronic, mechanical, photocopying, recording, or otherwise, without the written prior permission of the author.

Cover design and Author photo by Andrew Wright.

This is a work of fiction. All of the characters, names, incidents, organizations, and dialogue in this collection are either the product of the author's imagination or are used fictitiously.

Printed in the United States of America.

ISBN: 978-1-4669-0098-1 (sc)
ISBN: 978-1-4669-0097-4 (hc)
ISBN: 978-1-4669-0099-8 (e)

Library of Congress Control Number: 2011962830

Trafford rev. 04/21/2012

 www.trafford.com

North America & international
toll-free: 1 888 232 4444 (USA & Canada)
phone: 250 383 6864 ♦ fax: 812 355 4082

CONTENTS

About the Stories	ix
A Cupboardful of Shoes	1
Queen's Grill	12
A Pregnant Woman with Parcels at Brock and Bagot	22
Night Train to Cologne	28
The Bells of Khatyn	46
Ghost Stations	57
Unknown	72
Only Fair	78
Wedding	95
Distantly from Gardens	102
Frank's Girl	116
The President Reminisces	130
The Jump	140
The Trouble with Saints	152
Make Someone Happy	168
Seven Minutes' Silence	179
Bethlehem	190
White Nights	204
The Comedy of Doctor Foster	217

Also by A. Colin Wright

Sardinian Silver

Mikhail Bulgakov: Life and Interpretations (non-fiction)

For Mary Anne, Andrew and Nicholas

About the Stories

"I'm a librarian and I kissed a film star once. I touched her nipples too. At least, I think I did."

So begins "Queen's Grill," the second story in this collection. Horatio Humphries (one of several "unreliable narrators") strikes up a brief friendship with a movie star on a rough Atlantic crossing, but his "twin" brother doesn't believe him—particularly when Horatio claims she visited him the following night.

The title story, "A Cupboardful of Shoes," is told by a woman, but others have male or universal narrators, using either a third-person or first-person viewpoint—except for "Distantly from Gardens," whose subject demands the use of the second. The most "experimental" story, this is a variant on the theme of the "double" found in Russian literature, presenting a man with a split personality, inhabited by two narrators representing different periods in his own life.

In "A Pregnant Woman with Parcels at Brock and Bagot," an unnamed woman may or may not have an affair with a man she met at a party—depending on whether she can get by a woman in front of her.

The collection concludes with a novella, "The Comedy of Doctor Foster," based on Goethe's "Faust."

Other stories, all literary fiction, explore subjects as wide-ranging as disappointed love, violence, sex and war, sometimes with an underlying religious theme, while "The President Reminisces" is satirical. Some are told in the present tense, some in the past—serving to illustrate Wright's eclectic style and literary interests. They are set in North America and those European countries the author knows well from his fluency in six languages while living in Canada. Most have been published in literary journals.

I wish to express my gratitude to Elizabeth Barrett, Venus Taylor and other editors at Trafford Publishing for their thoughtful suggestions and corrections to my manuscript. I should also like to express my appreciation to my wife, Mary Anne, for her assistance with proof-reading and her patience during the writing of this and many other works. For their encouragement and enthusiasm my thanks are also due to my sons, Andrew and Nicholas.

ACKNOWLEDGMENTS

"Queen's Grill Bar," *Descant*, 29, 1 (no. 100, Spring 1998), 285-92

"A Pregnant Woman with Parcels at Brock and Bagot", *The Fiddlehead*, 177 (Autumn 1993), 93-97; *The Whig Standard Magazine*, 8 August 1992, 11-12. (Winning entry of Kingson Literary Awards, Kingston Regional Arts Council, 1992)

"A Cupboardful of Shoes," *event*, 13 (1984), 45-53

"Night Train to Cologne," *Journal of Canadian Fiction*, 33 (1981-82), 5-17

"Only Fair," *Dalhousie Review*, 60 (1980), 405-14

"The Trouble with Saints," *In All Directions: Short Story Anthology* (Canadian Authors Association). Toronto: Fitzhenry & Whiteside, 2000. Pp. 145-56.

"The Jump," *Quarry*, 40, 3 (Summer 1991), 31-39

"The Bells of Khatyn," *Waves*, 13, 4 (Spring 1985), 29-35

"Seven Minutes' Silence," *Storyteller*, 4, 4 (Spring 1998), 34-37

"Ghost Stations," *Stand Magazine* (UK), 32 (Spring 1989), 66-74

"Unknown," *Waves*, 12, 1 (Fall 1983), 37-40

"Sketches of Natasha," *Captains of Consciousness Journal*, 1, Issue 2 (2002), 12-22

"Frank's Girl," *Green's Magazine*, 18, 1 (Autumn 1989), 69-80

"Distantly from Gardens," *NeWest Review*, 17, 6 (August/September 1992), 27-30, 38

"Bethlehem," *Dalhousie Review*, 63 (1983-84), 593-601

"The President Reminisces," *Acclaim* (UK), 4, 19 (March-April 1996), 28-31. (Short-listed for Ian St. James awards, 1995.)

"The Comedy of Doctor Foster" (novella), *paperbytes*, imprint of Paperplates Books, published on Internet 1999 (www.perkolator.com); and *paperplates*, Spring 2000

A Cupboardful of Shoes

"Mother! How ever many do you have?"

She looked up at me, touching the fine golden hair that floated across her forehead. "Don't tell Beryl about it, will you, Heather? I don't want Beryl to know."

She was down on her knees, trying to stuff the shoes into the cupboard, which must have held thirty pairs. As she jammed the new ones in, others fell out: a pair of brown patent leather ones, and then—when those were thrust back in—a whole pile fell from the other side. Two white sandals, two snakeskin shoes with pointed toes, and a single knee-length boot.

"Here, let me . . ."

We finally managed to get the doors closed, and she turned the key in the lock.

"Now let's get the kettle on for a cup of tea. That really was lucky. Beryl will be home any minute now."

Still in her outdoor coat she filled the kettle, put it on the stove, and then opened one cupboard after another to find a box of matches. I sat down at the table, smoothing out a wrinkle in the brown felt that covered it, thinking I never really would understand this family I had married into. She looked in her handbag too, and I glanced as one of the letters fell out—the same handwriting as always—but she crammed it back in.

"When's George coming back from Edinburgh, did you say, Heather?" she asked, giving up the attempt to find the matches. "It's better without the men sometimes, isn't it? I really enjoyed today; thank you so much for coming with me. Oh, but"—it only now occurred to her—"I hope you didn't mind not going on the pier with the rest?" She shook her head and frowned at me. "Only don't you go and tell Beryl we were there all day and never even saw the sea! She'd never let me live it down."

We'd seen nothing but the inside of shoe shops.

As my mother-in-law chatted away, I needed only to nod my assent from time to time. Shoes, then, were another of her little vanities. Hats were, too, although if I'd been born with hair like hers, I never would have wanted to cover it up. It had faded since her youth, yet the golden strands seemed to float around her; and sometimes she would pat it, interrupting her constant stream of words for a few seconds of daydreaming.

"Heather," she'd said to me a good two weeks before George had left, "why don't we have a day out together? The Mothers' Union is putting on a bus trip to Eastbourne. I haven't seen the sea for a long time. Just the two of us. We won't tell anyone. It'll be a secret."

Almost everything in the family was a secret, I had discovered, revealed later only if it were whispered. On this occasion Beryl had found out, and had commented sarcastically about some people enjoying themselves while others had to work.

From the hallway came the sound of Beryl's key in the lock. The door never opened for her on the first try, so there were always a few seconds of jiggling before she trotted into the house.

"Hello, Mother. Heather," she sniffed, looking worried. As always, she had a cold. "Gracious me, no tea made?"

A Cupboardful of Shoes

"The kettle's on."

"But you haven't *lit* it. Oh dear, Mother, it's gone six o'clock. And Arthur and Sarah are coming for tea as soon as he gets home."

She lit the burner from a box of matches she'd found behind the stove and then took off her coat and laid it over a chair.

The crowds were terrible tonight. And Mr. Camps wants me to stay late tomorrow because there's that new girl . . ."

"I'll just cut some bread and get it buttered."

I looked on helplessly. Even now, after all these years, the mention of buttering bread reminds me of that old house on the outskirts of London, with its darkened kitchen where the only thing I can ever recall happening was bread getting buttered inexorably. The process took an hour, which I can't now explain. They were always buttering busily without ever seeming to finish, and then there was never enough, just a few meagre slices. The house has other owners now, and I haven't been there since Mother's death, but even if I went back I'm sure I'd be greeted with "Come on in, we won't be long, we'll just get some bread and butter on."

Beryl reached into a cupboard to get the teapot. "Well, did you enjoy your gallivanting today?" She meant it humorously: the Holdaways never really understood the difference between sarcasm and humour. "Did you go on the pier?"

"Oh, yes, and we even paddled in the sea," Mother answered. Then she added vaguely "The water wasn't very warm, though."

I saw again those tiny feet pushing into pair after pair of shoes.

It wasn't exactly that Mother was afraid of Beryl. Rather, she was uneasy in case somehow Beryl *mightn't like it*. It was almost as though the entire family were involved in an unspoken conspiracy to protect Beryl— although what she needed to be protected from wasn't entirely clear.

3

It wasn't long before Arthur and Sarah arrived with their two children, and we assembled in the dining room for our routine tea of bread and butter, cold meat, tomatoes, and lettuce, with a bottle of Heinz Salad Cream. These family gatherings tended to depress me. It was worse when George was there, for he felt obliged to put on a show of bonhomie and would joke—sarcastically—about my silences. Without him I was free to stare round the walls and fantasize over the pictures: three stylized illustrations from the *Rubaiyat of Omar Khayyam*. Or, if we were being informal, sitting stiffly in armchairs back from the table—as we were today—I could play endlessly with the heavy brass fly whose wings lifted to reveal an ashtray and then dropped back with a little click. I hated that fly, but no matter where I sat it always seemed to be within reach.

There was another flurry of activity when Father came home. Like Cromwell, Father had a wart on his nose. For some reason I never discovered, we always referred to him as Ga, sometimes with surname added: Ga Holdaway. Freeman of the City of London and fourth-generation pianoforte maker. Whenever there was a concert by a celebrity, he was the one who would give the piano a last fine-tuning. He couldn't play, though, and never showed any interest in music or, as far as I knew, in anything else.

"Evening, Ellen," her husband grunted. "Evening, Beryl." He only nodded at Arthur, Sarah, and myself, and ignored the children. He picked up the newspaper and read it, as always, while he ate. Usually he'd then go into the living room and read until he went to bed. This evening, though, he decided to make a pronouncement.

"I finally got the tax on my investments sorted out," he said to no one in particular, putting the paper aside.

He must have had it on his mind. One of the convictions of the Holdaways was that part of the immutable order of things was for a man's salary and financial dealings to be a private matter, on no account to be

A Cupboardful of Shoes

revealed to the womenfolk. I hadn't the slightest idea what my husband earned, although it was all solemnly entered in huge account books.

"I got the people from Harrison and Company to come in and do a proper audit," Ga said. "Cost me a few pounds, but it was worth it."

I took hold of the brass fly and lifted its wings. I hadn't been married very long, and little things like this still hurt me. "But George could have done it for you!" I said. He'd just qualified as a chartered accountant. "He's your own son, after all. He'd do it for nothing."

This was greeted by an uncomprehending silence. The Holdaways believed that there were certain ways of doing things and that whatever they did, however stupid in the eyes of others, was irreproachably correct. I put the fly down again, closing its wings carefully so as not to make a noise.

"Have you any smelling salts, Mother?" Beryl asked. "This cold of mine, really . . ."

Mother grabbed for her handbag and dug to the bottom, scattering its contents over the table. Three of the letters fell out and lay there in full view. I almost hoped Ga would see them. I was still angry enough that I would have liked to see him shaken. But Mother just picked them up, holding them tightly, and crammed them back into the bag. There was no indication anyone else had noticed. One advantage, I realized, of living in a family with principles was that no one would for a moment have considered so much as glancing at Mother's private correspondence, not even Beryl. And with their habit of denying the very existence of things that didn't fit in with their particular concept of propriety, they probably hadn't even seen the letters.

"Heather and I had such a nice day at Eastbourne today," Mother began as she handed Beryl the smelling salts. "We walked on the beach, sat and enjoyed the band in the public gardens there, went on the pier . . ."

"Bloody women," Ga muttered as he retired again behind the paper.

5

A. Colin Wright

*   *   *

For a long time I thought George's family looked down on mine. My father didn't make much money and gave almost everything to my mother to manage, keeping only a few shillings for tobacco or the odd flutter on the horses. Once, when he'd spent more and lost, he had to borrow from George because he couldn't tell his wife about it. And my mother had been three months pregnant when they married, which I never mentioned to the Holdaways, even after I knew them better, because somehow I expected their reaction would be incredulity that such a thing should be physically possible.

George's father, at one time, had been the stern Victorian. George told me of how, as a young boy, he'd often had the back of a knife rapped smartly across his knuckles if he dared say one word out of place at the table. His mother, too, sat demurely, anxious not to do anything to displease her husband. But by this time in his life Ga's authority had diminished, and Mother chatted freely with Beryl, me, and the other wives, while he either glowered at us or, more often, ignored us entirely. He was in any case awkward in company. The boys all took after him, having his tendency toward baldness and skin diseases in about equal measure.

Beryl, supposedly, was the sensitive, artistic one. She played the piano and sang, accompanying herself. Never in public, but just at the old upright piano in the living room, filled always, it seemed, with the smell of grape hyacinths. I had difficulty keeping a straight face whenever she sang "We'll Gather Lilacs"—I kept imagining her substituting "We'll gather grape hyacinths." Her other favourites were "Solveig's Song" from *Peer Gynt* and "God Be with You till We Meet Again." Beryl had had a boyfriend once, but nothing had come of it. I'd first met her at dances George took me to, after which, to my fury, he was never able to take me home because he had to take Beryl home instead. I eventually told him he'd have to choose between her and me, and shortly after that he proposed.

6

A Cupboardful of Shoes

Once, after George and I married, Beryl invited a man round. More bread was buttered and a cake with caraway seeds was bought for the occasion. He was a violinist in one of the London orchestras and had been visiting the vicar of the local church.

For some reason Ga decided he was going to impress him, trying—not very successfully—to show his knowledge of London musical life. Several times he said things like "After all, we musicians have something going for us."

"We musicians," Beryl had said disdainfully afterward. "Since when has Dad been a musician?"

Anyway, the violinist never came a second time.

As the years passed George and I decided not to have children, or rather he decided and assumed it was a mutual decision. Marriage was dull, but I had given up expecting it to be any different. We still lived down the street from the old house, still had our regular teas there. Mother still chattered on, bought shoes, while Beryl assumed even more the air of a harassed martyr.

"Tell me," George's mother asked me once, "how is it you have a brother so much younger than yourself?"

This was after my brother Eric, now a young man, had started visiting us.

"Well," I began, wondering whether it was really a fit topic for the Holdaways, "after I was born, my mother had something wrong with her and couldn't have another child. So for years and years she and my father never needed . . . to take any precautions. Then one day—this I remember—she was putting up curtains and fell off a ladder, and felt a terrible pain in her back. The next month she discovered she was pregnant."

A. Colin Wright

"Oh no!" Mother clapped her hands. "And the fall put right whatever was wrong?"

"Apparently. I was fourteen then and was horrified when I knew my mother was going to have a baby. I thought it was disgusting, and I was jealous too. I remember I threatened to kill him with a kitchen knife. But then when I saw him . . ."

Mother was quite delighted. "How wonderful, how wonderful," she kept saying. "Your parents must have been very much in love." She reached for her handbag and touched one of the letters. "Here, let me tell you . . ." But then she stopped, became flustered, and said, "Do you know there's a sale of winter coats on at Hetheringtons?"

Ga, now retired, had by this time become almost totally withdrawn, couldn't stand being surrounded by women, and spent most of his days in a small room upstairs that had been rearranged as a bedroom and den combined. He seemed to like me better than the others, and once took me up to his room to show me his desk, just an old piece of office furniture that he'd bought in a junk sale.

"Yes," he mumbled, "I spend a lot of time doing things at this desk of mine."

"What does he *do* there?" I asked Beryl later.

"Oh nothing," she said with her usual impatience. "It just makes him feel important."

"Like George."

The greatest desire of my husband too was to feel important, and his greatest tragedy was that no one took the slightest notice of him.

A year or so later, in an ultimately unsuccessful attempt to relieve the monotony of our marriage, George and I left England for Canada. Our first return visit was at the beginning of Ga's illness. I remember going up to the West End with Mother on another of her shopping sprees, and when

A Cupboardful of Shoes

we returned, exhausted after battling the sales, we must have been going on about the crowds.

"*You're* complaining!" Ga said suddenly. "You don't know what *I've* been through."

We didn't take any notice of him at first, until he repeated it a little later. But he wasn't going to tell us any more until we bullied the story out of him.

It turned out that he'd had an accident. "Shit my pants," he growled. "God, what a mess. Had to clean it up all by myself. Stank to high heaven. All day I've been running there . . ."

"Why didn't you get Beryl or George to help you?" I asked. "They were here."

"Oh, Beryl . . ."

"What did you do with your underclothes?" Mother asked.

"Tried to wash them out. But they wouldn't come clean, and I didn't want to have my hands in all that mess. So I buried them in the garden."

Mother looked at me and we both tried not to laugh.

"Just as well perhaps that we weren't there," she said to me later. "I don't know I'd have had the stomach for it."

On our next visit, over a year later, Ga was dying. He was bedridden, incontinent, and tearfully ashamed. With Beryl and George's brothers' wives all working, I ended up looking after him a lot of the time. Mother—always the cheerful one of the family, never worrying about the things the rest fussed over—just went to pieces. She couldn't cope at all. And not because of grief, but because she couldn't bear to look at him.

"You see," she explained to me when it was all over, "after all these years of marriage I've never actually seen my husband naked." She

9

A. Colin Wright

patted the wisp of hair across her forehead and then laughed as though she expected to be scolded for it. "You wouldn't believe it, would you?"

"And what about . . ." I wasn't sure what word I should use. "Didn't he ever, then?"

"Oh yes," she said. "Almost every night, until the last few years. It's a wonder we haven't more children than we have. Being pregnant, though, when he never touched me, was the only time of rest. But always in the dark, grunting and groaning away, he was very passionate. Only I wished sometimes that—" She stopped. "I wondered sometimes what he *looked* like. But for me to take off his clothes, when he was ill . . ."

"Mother," I said, "I've never asked you. About those letters you used to get?"

She smiled vaguely for a moment and then shook her head.

She lived for a number of years after that, although I saw her rarely. I'd fallen in love with another man and felt guilty toward George's family every time we went there, because of the affair I was having. Mother died quite suddenly, and I recall being in the house—only Beryl lived there now—after the funeral, feeling I didn't belong, wanting only to get back to my lover in Toronto. She had died in the living room, and it seemed to me that the smell of grape hyacinths was there only to cover the smell of death. Since then, I can't bear to have them anywhere near me.

It's been over two years now since Beryl died in a nursing home on the south coast where, it seemed, she lived a life totally devoid of any interest in anything or anyone. She insisted that people come and see her, and then she had nothing to say when they did, either pretending they weren't there or managing to express a deep resentment toward them. Some ten months before her death she tried to kill herself, or so it was thought, simply by walking out to sea. She was found by some boys, lying in her soaked clothes among the rocks, and taken back to the nursing home. No

A Cupboardful of Shoes

one missed her after her death, not even George it seems, despite all those times before our divorce when we went back to England and we had not just to visit Beryl, but to visit her *first*, before the other relatives. She might not have liked it otherwise.

I dream of that family occasionally, and in my nightmares I can't escape the weight of the Holdaways' terrible respectability.

I had been with Mother the day the last letter arrived. She opened it and read it in the kitchen, something she'd never done in front of me before, while I lit the gas for the kettle, which she'd forgotten to do.

She read it and said nothing.

Then she went to the cupboard, unlocked it, and grabbed the first pair of shoes that fell on the floor. "I really should wear some of these."

She put on the shoes—they were the ones we'd bought in Eastbourne, I think—and walked around the house in them, admiring herself in each mirror she came to.

Beryl saw them immediately when she came sniffling into the kitchen. "More shoes, Mother?" she said scathingly. "However much do they all cost you?"

"Yes, more shoes," she said defiantly. But she took them off. And started to cry.

Queen's Grill

I'm a librarian, and I kissed a film star once. I touched her nipples too. At least I think I did.

A holiday, the kind where you fly to New York and return to England on the *Queen Elizabeth 2*. With my brother Arnold. He hated it, but since my divorce there's no one else to travel with. I've looked after him since . . . well, since you died, Mother. He has to come. This film star . . . well it would have been better without Arnold in my cabin. I like exotic places, libraries like in New York, would have toured the one in Washington if there'd been time.

You'd like her films. Hélène Martin, pronounced the French way, I learnt enough of it in school for trips to Calais, for the duty-free. It happened on the ship. Where there's a library too. Not that it fits in that fantastic world, not what I'm used to either. I mean, why get a book for entertainment with so many other things to do, like meeting famous people? My British Library is for study, I fetch the books for scholars.

Before I met Hélène I spent my time strolling round the ship, in awe at that whole new world of floating elegance between sea and sky. Watching for shearwaters—I'd read about them in the ornithology section, flitting over the ocean, never coming in sight of land except to breed. Arnold, meanwhile, stayed sleeping in the cabin—we might be twins but we're not identical. He's not too bright, poor Arnold. I mean, when there's luxury food day or night, even for those paying the lowest fare like me! Easy to gorge yourself and get indigestion like I nearly did but managed not to. Good entertainment in the evenings too.

I didn't read a single book. Five days at sea and a film star were escapism enough after managing with Arnold in our old East Croydon house . . . well you remember how some people, who might have bought it, called it unpleasantly musty when they didn't.

Exploring decks and their different levels, discovering you can walk the length of the ship on some while others stop at a staircase or a lift . . . that's how I met her. I'd wandered up two flights of stairs to the balcony with its expensive shops overlooking the Grand Lounge. Then forwards towards the Queen's Grill Bar, off limits to the likes of me. You see, Mother, the wealthy passengers have a restaurant of their own, even special seats upstairs in the cinema . . . like a private club where they can remain anonymous without appearing in the public rooms. Except in the casino, the best place for seeing the rich and famous, with slot machines I'd sometimes risk a pound on and green gambling tables. Not that I'd make a fool of myself with things like that. The night before I met Hélène, I'd stood watching a TV personality playing craps. Didn't say a word, of course. He'd never remember me afterwards, not like Hélène.

She was coming out of a first-class cabin. The corridors in the higher part of the ship are no different from those below, nothing to stop you pretending you have a cabin there, provided you don't go too far, to the Queen's Grill Bar itself. She turned to look at me, and with my democratic principles denying special privileges to the rich I told myself I had a right to be there. That I'd no desire to mingle with the upper classes, and that, walking around the boat deck, you could see into their windows anyway and might glimpse a celebrity if you weren't afraid of staring.

She was in tears, genuine as in her first film, *Love in the Morning*. Seeing me—like the fantasies I make up for my brother Arnold, I still can't quite believe this happened—she flung her arms around my neck

A. Colin Wright

and sobbed. No explanations, Mother. I didn't say a word. I didn't know where to put my hands and was tempted to hold her like I would to calm my wife, but that had ended badly and I wasn't sure it was the thing to do. Someone might follow her out of the cabin, and how would I explain it?

"My God, I'm sorry," she said artistically.

She was less glamorous than on the screen, I wouldn't have paid much attention if she hadn't been a star, with wispy blonde hair falling across a face . . . well somehow anonymous, except that everybody knew it.

Did I really invite her for a drink? I'm still in awe at the enormity of it.

"Coffee," she said. "Not in the Queen's Grill, though." (As if I'd ever suggest a place like that!) "I can't stand it another minute! Somewhere else. It'll be an . . . experience!"

With other passengers looking on, I paraded her proudly down the glittering metallic staircase through the Grand Lounge to the Lido Bar behind. Sitting at a comfortable table with views of sea and open sky, with the swimming pool outside and glimpses of an occasional shearwater skimming by between the waves—it was a place I loved. A waiter in white gloves took her order.

I didn't dare ask why she'd been crying, so I asked her name instead. Knew it already, of course, but not whether it was correct etiquette to say so. Bad enough not having a dark suit for dinner, which would have done for our Mauretania Restaurant, but I'd only brought a decent pair of trousers with me, plus that corduroy coat you made me years ago.

I'm not sure she was offended I didn't let on I'd recognized her or relieved. "Hélène," she said . . ." Martin."

"I'm Horatio Humphries."

She laughed. I've never liked my name.

Queen's Grill

"My husband says he doesn't want us slumming with the other passengers. He's the director, Brandon Phillips."

I knew that too.

She told me they were travelling to England to make a film, and Brandon assumed in his usual shitty way (her words, I'd never say a thing like that) she wanted to relax without her fans. So they kept to the Queen's Grill and surrounding rooms, except for going to the casino like they'd done each night, and yesterday she'd lost nine hundred dollars.

The waiter, bringing our coffee, was just as nonchalant serving a celebrity as a complete nonentity like me. If I were famous, I told Hélène, making her laugh, I 'd still have eaten in the Queen's Grill up above—why not enjoy being acknowledged by other important persons too?—but would stroll in public rooms as well, where ordinary people would recognize me. Make me feel good. I don't get much recognition from my fellow humans since you died, Mother, despite working in the library. And Arnold might as well not exist, for all he helps!

I explained I was sharing an inside cabin with him on a lower deck, leaving him asleep in the morning ("Like my husband!" she laughed) while I walked around the deck to welcome the wonderful new day at sea. And when I returned late at night, unwilling to miss something and go to bed, he was already tucked in and dreaming.

I hesitated, "I'm a librarian, you see."

People mostly respond with a bored "How interesting" to that. But she exclaimed "Heavens!" with that touch of drama that reminded me she was an actress. "It's what I always wanted! I *love* books. If I hadn't been forced to do what my parents told me, I'd have gone to library school and never even entered a cinema. My God, I hate it!"

"And if I hadn't been forced to do what *my* parents wanted," I blurted out, "I'd have gone to acting school."

15

A. Colin Wright

An actress who wanted to be a librarian, and a librarian who'd give anything for just half her fame! Her parents, she told me, had been music-hall comedians in France; while you, Mother, were a schoolteacher and Father was a city clerk in Walthamstow. That was the difference. I said I'd acted in plays at school, but not that my greatest success had been playing the grandmother in one of Chekhov's. But I was good! Then I described my work at the British Library, which she thought she'd heard of.

The ship gave a roll, and a wave of anxiety spread through the Lido Bar. The water in the open-air pool slurped against the side.

Hélène said "It's going to get exciting."

I thought the same. On my trips across the Channel, I secretly enjoy the rocking motion and being out of reach of land. I felt a rough sea might be fun, though Arnold is afraid, and calls me morbidly romantic when he knows I'm listening.

"My husband keeps on saying 'If only it doesn't get rough!'" Hélène reached over the table and took my hand. "Horatio—wasn't that Nelson's name?"

"Battle of Trafalgar, 1805."

"Let's walk round the ship, Horatio!"

We struggled along the deck against the wind, under the lifeboats hanging solidly above. Up the steps at the front—battling the gale, we could barely lift our faces towards the bow and the grey waves ahead—and then down the other side, the wind pushing behind us now as the deck rocked and pitched beneath. This was where you could see into the windows of the Queen's Grill, but now my celebrity walked beside me, her steps veering from side to side like mine, shortening or lengthening erratically. Round the rear of the deck to a sullen, threatening ocean without a shearwater in sight. On our next circuit, they'd closed the steps up to the front—high winds, a board across them warned—so we had to go inside again.

Queen's Grill

Back to the bar, where the white-gloved waiters were collecting crockery. Hélène laughed excitedly. "It's so different! Normally I'm hanging around the set, waiting. The same thing time and time again. This is real!"

I thought of the world of books, my usual escape from the gloom of a deserted suburban house and a twin brother whose only existence is watching TV. This was real life, which I was sharing with a star!

I found her more and more attractive. Since my divorce, I've sometimes thought about remarriage, but no, Mother, I'm not that unrealistic. A brief affair, though. Don't film stars have them all the time?

"*There* you are." The voice wasn't pleasant, nor were the possessive eyes and unnaturally black hair of the man staring down at us.

"Brandon, my husband," she introduced us. "Horatio Hodges."

"Humphries," I corrected her.

He stared at Hélène without acknowledging me. "I couldn't find you."

She burst into immediate, impromptu tears.

"We've got work to do," he said, unmoved.

She glanced at me and started to rebel. But suddenly the ship heaved deeply, a more effective ally than I could ever be. With the same sarcastic sweetness she used in *My Darling Lover* she said to him "Brandon, you've gone quite white!"

I don't get sick, except for a slight nausea if I bend down to retrieve a penny from the floor. But her husband turned, his hand across his mouth, staggering between the tables as the whole bar plunged then rose again.

Her hand touched mine, and she gave a little smile, reminding me of that famous scene with her and Leslie Mann.

17

A. Colin Wright

We spent the day together, partners in a new aristocracy now, of travellers who were free of sickness. We'd cannon into each other, grab for rails or furniture, exploring places she hadn't been, screaming like adolescents on a roller coaster. We won a pile of coins in the slot machines, then lost them all again. With six or seven other passengers in the Theatre Bar we attended a lecture on how not to gain weight on board, and then went to lunch at an uncrowded buffet, heaping food onto our plates and carrying them precariously away. I took her to the library—no books about her that I could find—and then she even showed me the Queen's Grill Bar above! Where we sat sipping Scotch in solemn silence with a wealthy couple I didn't recognize.

At dinner we ate in my ordinary Mauretania Restaurant, where the waiter served her cheerfully, not showing any surprise that she wasn't my unattractive twin. Later, in an intimate audience, we watched a comedian performing on the Grand Lounge's tilting floor. A fairy tale! I loved her sitting next to me.

"It really is more fun," she said.

I escorted her through the still heaving corridors to her first-class cabin. We hesitated, and then kissed goodnight. Hélène Martin, the star—for a moment her tongue lingered in my mouth.

Then she was gone.

"See you tomorrow," I said, as the door shut behind her and the snoring husband I could hear inside.

Back through the corridor, past the shuttered shops overlooking the now empty Grand Lounge. Imagining, Mother, how without Arnold in the way, I could have taken her to my cabin. Down the staircase to the dance floor, lingering on it like the entertainers who performed each night. Would she, without her husband, have invited me to her cabin too? Out through the casino, downstairs again, past the library, bouncing with happiness and the motion of the ship. Into the Lower Lounge, with its dark

18

Queen's Grill

windows on either side and a splashing sea beyond . . . to a luxuriously padded chair, where my yearning soul could revel in the memory of that kiss.

I'd failed her, though. Should have taken her away somewhere, like in her films. Hadn't been dashing or romantic enough, and she'd returned to Brandon. But what to do? In all this luxury there was nowhere we could go, and the weather was too wet and cold for the open deck. Although if it cleared tomorrow . . . perhaps a romantic walk with the moon shining on the sea.

I didn't want to go to bed, not yet, but the next day would come sooner if I did. I set off down a different staircase from the ones I knew, and then walked along a corridor I didn't recognize, until I came to a double L-turn in the middle, where we could have stood in a tight embrace, drawing apart if someone came along. I might have slipped my hand inside her dress to feel her trembling breasts.

Arnold, under his blanket, was awake. "Where you been?"

I felt like murdering him. Knowing I wouldn't be believed, I told him: "With Hélène Martin. You know, the star."

"Right!"

Kissing her, I thought. Why, Mother, does he always make fun of things I long for?

Next morning the storm had died. Passengers strolled on deck, in public rooms, laughing over how sick they'd been. A final day with Hélène, before arriving in Southampton the next. A walk on deck at night . . .

All day long I looked for her. Walked the corridors and made circuits around the boat deck, where she might see me from the windows of the Queen's Grill. Queued for a buffet lunch and lost my place because

19

A. Colin Wright

I thought I saw her strolling by. Then sat waiting in the Lido Bar, watching flocks of shearwaters in their lonely ocean world.

In the evening I saw her playing roulette with her husband. I risked a smile. She glanced at me and then whispered in Brandon's ear. He gave an explosive chuckle as the teller called a number. She laughed as a pile of chips was pushed towards her.

The deck outside was dark, there was no moon. I could hear the calling of the sea below.

I cried myself to sleep that night. Silently, so Arnold wouldn't wake. Slept badly. Half dreamed, half imagined, Hélène on her movie set, lonely, bored, while other people thronged around her. Interesting people who talked to me, included me, thought me interesting too. Then I'd turn over, angry at such confused fantasies of what could never be.

Sometime in the night I woke up. At least, I think I did. The cabin door was partly open, and in the half light from the corridor stood Hélène. I looked for Arnold, but for once he'd left. She closed the door behind her and I could sense her moving towards me in the darkness. Then she was on top of me, her lips pressed onto mine, her tongue flicking in my mouth. Not saying a word, she took my hand and placed it inside her nightdress, where I could feel her nipples growing firm. She moaned as she had in *Romantic Interlude*, then held me tightly until we fell asleep.

When I awoke, I saw the same mysterious light, the door still half open. Arnold, in his usual place, was talking about me in his sleep.

In Southampton I watched her go ashore. She looked at me with that well-known smile from *Passion without End* and walked away with Brandon.

I've seen all her films by now. Always the romantic heroine, idealized, glamorized, no longer mine. In the library I've searched the

Queen's Grill

catalogues—credits, husbands, leading men. Love ever after, lasting from one film to the next. They say now she's divorcing Brandon too.

I don't know her address. At the studio they have a system for screening telephone calls. All I can do is watch her on video . . . remembering. And imagining . . .

"Dreaming of your film star again?" my brother will sometimes ask sarcastically.

I hate him, Mother. Trusting only in prosaic truths, Arnold doesn't believe a word of it.

A Pregnant Woman with Parcels at Brock and Bagot

She started to run on the far side of the Market Square, by City Hall. Now, fighting the crowds, she pushes her way to the traffic lights. Crosses King Street first, since it's green in that direction, and then, still running as the light changes, crosses Brock as well. Two blocks up Brock to the bus stop on Bagot, but it's across the street, and buses often leave early to stay ahead of the traffic at this time in the afternoon.

While he is walking fast out of habit. Perpetually busy, he's forgotten how to take his time even when there's plenty of time to take—and now, from the other side of Queen, he strides along Bagot to get back to his car, parked on the lower part of Brock.

Their paths will intersect at Brock and Bagot, in front of the office supplies store with its entranceway cut diagonally across the corner, inside a pillar that supports the upper storey. But all things (except blind fate) considered, they're unlikely to recognize—or even see—each other as they pass.

They'd never seen each other since. Had forgotten all about it.

She runs past the gourmet food store without a glance at its coffees and exotic spices, although the musky aroma of groceries often entices her inside. I must get home! My husband away, and no reason for haste except

A Pregnant Woman with Parcels at Brock and Bagot

a guilty feeling of obligation to explain to him when I'm late. She dashes unseeing into the sun, unaware that other possibilities could be drawing her on.

At Queen Street, by the empty lot, he misses the traffic light. Too many speeding cars to risk crossing against it: a circumstance that might change his future (but will it?) by delaying his arrival at the corner. Had he known this, he might have contemplated the purpose in life of trivial details such as traffic lights; of buses to be caught; of strangers and pregnant women who block your way with parcels. Instead he waits impatiently, remembering he promised to discuss holiday plans after supper before he can immerse himself in work.

Unable to find her again, he'd left the party and returned to his wife, who'd stayed home that evening looking through household catalogues.

Might I do something daring instead of going home? She glances at a window full of tartans suggestive of Scottish mists. Perhaps even buy a picture, something she hasn't done since leaving college. She runs past the gallery just the same. But the sun's in her eyes, she's tired (it seems she always is), and she can't bear the thought of having nothing to fill in the time downtown.

The host had interrupted. Dragging her away to introduce her to someone uninteresting, whom she'd later married and no longer knows why.

Relieved when the light turns green, he crosses the street, driven along Bagot by the gratifying thought of how busy he is. Once there was a hotel here, he recalls, but its foyer was turned into a shopping mews long ago and only the cocktail lounge remains: a bar with warm red lighting. He strides on by, tempted by memories of easy pick-ups and intoxicating music on those (rare) occasions when he has a convention out of town.

Men's clothes, a gift-shop for that man who has everything. Do I care what my husband's doing on his weekend away? Oh shit! Passing a trust-company office, she collides with a parking attendant writing a ticket.

A. Colin Wright

Doesn't notice the car, although in days to come (if things go right) she may find herself eagerly waiting for it to arrive.

Conventions are a small consolation for work that isn't great or even all that interesting. Again he stands at a traffic light, in front of his bank, which used to offer a sense of deserved security. Diagonally opposite, the bookstore now attracts him more, with works on African birds, astronomy, unknown lives.

He'd been about to invite her to dinner; and she to comment on his sensitive hands and inquisitive eyes, which she'd felt an irresponsible urge to satisfy.

Hurry, hurry! She takes her life in her hands (why shouldn't she, after all?) in a quick dash across Wellington Street. Barely a minute left: what if I miss the bus? Nothing much will happen, of course. My world's not likely to change. Is it?

He hurries over the main street to the boarded-up corner, with its walkway under the scaffolding. Where, in the discount drug store, I used to buy condoms when I was young. The building hasn't been rebuilt since it was destroyed by fire, and the new one will be different, I suppose.

Hell, I'll never make it. A red sports car turning into the parking garage blocks her path. Determined still, she skips round the back of it into the road and then starts to run again. Why is she in such a rush? she wonders.

An evening long ago; another lifetime, perhaps. A crowded party who knows where, and a casually playful flirtation over martinis and canapés.

For a moment he slows down, glancing wistfully at the bookstore across the street. There's no real need to work this evening: but better that than boredom, family obligations. A book, perhaps, would do as well.

She pauses to catch her breath, clutching the fence round the sidewalk café in front of the hotel. It's crowded, cheerful: why shouldn't I eat downtown? But she presses on. I'd feel self-conscious sitting there alone, knowing no one, desired by no one, loved by no one.

No, he thinks. I'm too busy. And an approaching bus has blocked his view of the bookstore window. Passing Zeller's Bagot Street entrance, he comes to the office supplies store with its sterile desks and filing systems.

That's not entirely true, she thinks. She starts running again, past Zeller's Brock Street entrance. My husband loves me, I suppose. The office supplies store with its blur of paper and artists' equipment gives her a momentary, sensuous pleasure—how I used to love to write and paint!— but out of time, she flings herself towards the corner. Then ahead of her, against the sun, she sees a pregnant woman carrying bulky parcels.

It wasn't the right time, perhaps.

Instinctively he accelerates his pace. Would have explained this by his recollection that his car is overdue at a parking meter.

She can't push by the woman with her parcels. The bus will be leaving on the other side of the street and with no time to wait for the light, she'll have to dodge across the road in front of it. It all depends on the pregnant woman. If she goes straight ahead I can cut through the entranceway inside the pillar on the corner.

When, coming from the other direction, he too will see the waddling figure emerge and fill the corner in front of him. He too will take the short cut inside the pillar of the office supplies store.

Behind the pregnant woman, she'll swerve to the right.

Decisively, he'll turn in to his left.

She can't avoid him. Out of breath, she'll barely manage to stop.

He can't avoid her. Protectively, he'll grasp her arms.

Each about to apologize, they'll look at each other:

Recall another lifetime, or an evening long ago. A crowded party who knows where, and a playfully casual flirtation over martinis and canapés. He'd been about to invite her to dinner; and she to comment on his sensitive hands and inquisitive eyes, which she'd felt an irresponsible urge to satisfy. But their host had interrupted, dragging her away to introduce her to someone uninteresting, whom she'd later married and no longer knows why. It wasn't the right time, perhaps. Unable to find her again, he'd left the party and returned to his wife, who'd stayed home that evening looking through household catalogues. They'd never seen each other since. Had forgotten all about it.

Now, in the shock of this breathless physical encounter, in their blind haste that has driven them together, there's no time to think of normal proprieties.

"I know you . . ." he starts to stutter.

"I too . . ." she starts to reply.

And in an instant they're kissing, unaware that the pregnant woman, stopping at the traffic light, has turned around and, seeing them, dropped her parcels; that another man, also trying to take the short cut, has moved aside and taken the long way round the pillar instead.

Crazily she finds herself spinning in the air as he lifts her to him. Lips and bodies pressed together, forgetting the others who throng about them, they decide that . . . she'll miss her bus.

They'll have a drink together, and have dinner too, at the sidewalk café in front of the hotel. Laugh at the parking ticket when they return to his car. Stop to leave the fine at the collection box by City Hall as they drive away. Ten dollars, after all, is a small price for a happy-ever-after ending—or rather, for a happy beginning to the game they're about to play. Who knows what the future might bring? An affair, divorce? It won't be easy, for passion never is. That's the real price they'll have to pay. But does it matter? For a while, they'll be playing life's game as it's been offered to them: by chance, by fate, or by their own haste to participate.

A Pregnant Woman with Parcels at Brock and Bagot

If the pregnant woman with parcels goes straight ahead, that is.

But perhaps she'll stop. Step inside the entranceway to the office supplies store to rest, unaware that other lives depend on where she goes.

Yes, I can get by her now, and the light's green. She can go straight ahead and cross here after all.

About to cut through inside the pillar, he'll find his way blocked by a pregnant woman laden down with parcels. For a second he'll hesitate before taking the long way round instead. Almost (but not quite, for he'll manage to stop) bump into a younger woman emerging from Brock Street ahead of him as she runs to catch the light. He thinks he recognizes her from somewhere.

She catches her bus, signals to the driver before it moves away. Smiling now, she thinks of the pregnant woman, who fortunately (she thinks) hadn't delayed her.

She didn't see him. The sun was in her eyes. She'll return to someone uninteresting, whom regrettably she'd married and no longer knows why.

While he'll stride on down the street toward his car. Curse silently when he sees the pink ticket on its windshield, for he hates being caught out, unfairly, in the wrong. He'll work that evening, once he's discussed the family's dreary holiday plans. Yet there's a momentary nostalgia for something he can't identify: the younger woman, perhaps, whom he thought he'd recognized.

Where is it, he thinks, that I've seen her before?

Night Train to Cologne

"You're odd." Susan opened her eyes, smiled at him, and went back to sleep.

With his head thrust stiffly into the angle made by his seat and the window—softened only a little by the hanging folds of his jacket—Brian could feel his whole body vibrating to the motion of the train as it plunged through the darkness. He looked at Susan. At the three other shapes sitting opposite, squeezed between her and the sliding door into the corridor. She'd wanted to fly, or at least get a couchette; had let him have his way, though, with tolerant amusement: "You mean you actually *like* sitting up in a train at night?"

Now, the sides of her mouth were turned down and a wave of brown hair bobbed in front of her face. Forced against her armrest by a solid Hausfrau clutching two string bags, she twisted in vertical discomfort.

You're odd. Brian repeated her words to himself. He didn't mind the pressure from the other passengers, as long as his one shoulder was assured of the window, so he could have his unobstructed view of the dark, passing countryside. Easier now that they'd turned out the light, and a sinister blue bulb provided only shadow vision of the others in the compartment. Timbered farmhouses, the lights of villages, cars standing at crossings waiting for the train to go by: all were carried past in remote anonymity, their individual voices silenced by the roar of the train. Soon

Night Train to Cologne

he might sleep. It was all part of the ritual—to try to sleep, perhaps actually lose consciousness for a while, so you could then reward yourself with the long watches out of the window. Relax now, though, enjoy the sensation of speed over the track below. Each time you open your eyes a little, you can see the two thin metal plates below the window, their words indistinguishable at this angle. *Nicht hinauslehen*, they say. *Do not lean out. Ne pas se pencher en dehors. È pericoloso sporgersi.*

Frances. The same, sudden feeling of anguish, diving to his stomach, told him that the train was taking him back to England. With Susan. Taking him away.

He frowned. A journey like this meant less to him than it had in his youth, when being tired held none of the fear of later exhaustion. He remembered his first train journey by night, his excited awareness of rows of seats hurtling through space, of only thin, transparent walls separating him from the unfamiliar landscape on either side. Years ago. If only Susan could share that kind of enjoyment with him. But she would list it among his other oddities, which she loved him for and yet which remained mysterious to her: like his sudden enthusiasms for things such as astrology or writing poetry no one would ever read. Important to him, she knew, but never as urgent as mowing the lawn or tidying the garage.

"God help me for marrying a mystic," she'd been in the habit of saying, with a kind of puzzled respect. Until the children had picked it up and thought it was part of his job. "Daddy's a mystic," the younger boy had told several people before it was possible to stop him.

Yet Frances understood. With immediate admiration—undeserved, really—she'd told him of her unshakable conviction that there were ordinary people, who lived in comfortable, box-like worlds, and extraordinary people, who didn't.

He closed his eyes, no longer resisting his memories. Frances, whom he had seen three times in Stuttgart while Susan thought he was at the art gallery. Frances, he thought, as he slipped into rhythmic unconsciousness,

29

A. Colin Wright

who was the cause of this frightened emptiness inside him as the train carried him farther and farther away.

"Was that Frances?" George turned to Brian with startled eyes under his jet-black hair, then laughed and tried to shrug his shoulders.

Brian wished they hadn't seen her. "It doesn't mean much."

"No." George screwed his long face into a grin, although he couldn't manage to convey his usual quiet humour. "No, it doesn't really."

Below them were the lights of the town and, standing out against the dark band of the river, a single row of lanterns leading across the old stone bridge to the clusters of villages on the farther shore. They walked slowly back from the terrace, through one of the partly ruined towers, and across the castle courtyard. The music from the Great Hall told them the ball was still going on.

"Romantic, isn't it?" George said. "Just right for our last night in Heidelberg."

There was nothing Brian could say. He, too, felt angry with Frances even if, in the casual pairings of a school holiday, it was George who had been her devoted companion for two weeks. It was unkind of her to spoil it for him now.

They walked into the bright lights of the hall, with its dancing couples and long tables of young people huddled noisily around bottles of wine. A girl with long hair and a blue vein in her forehead got up to meet him, expecting him to ask her to dance. Brian followed her onto the floor, but as they moved languidly to the music he found himself looking around in case Frances should return. Too late he had realized she was the one girl who really interested him, but in the initial shuffling he had become paired with Jill, whom he kissed and fondled before saying goodnight because a holiday wasn't a holiday without romance. Which meant, in his naïve code

30

Night Train to Cologne

of honour in those days, that he saw himself as committed to her until the end of the holiday. In any case, he could hardly have abandoned her for George's girl, since he was a friend. It angered him all the more, though, that Frances was now outside on the terrace kissing the German boy she'd been dancing with.

Later that evening, when she had returned and was sitting at another table with the Germans, Brian approached her with determination.

"We were so young then, weren't we?" That same woman, who had been only a vague image in his mind, laughed lightly. The lines at the corners of her eyes deepened.

It had seemed like a whim, no more. He would almost have been relieved not to find her. But now they sat facing each other in her cluttered apartment.

"I read about your concert in *The Observer*," he said. "That's how I knew you were in Stuttgart."

"It's extraordinary. To see you again after all this time. Why, it must be . . . twenty-five years."

He had remembered her fair hair, now tinged with grey, and her determined chin, but not her manner of speaking with her hands which, he noticed, she'd run unconsciously over the keys of her piano when she passed it. He thought that the unobvious, sensitive beauty of her features had been there before, although he mistrusted his memories, aware of having perhaps romanticized her on the rare occasions he'd thought of her.

"You're not married?" he asked.

"I was," she said. "Briefly. You?"

"For twelve years now."

"And have you ever heard any more of . . . Jill, was it? Or George?"

31

A. Colin Wright

"I don't know what happened to Jill. We never did write. George went to work for a bank, but I haven't seen him in years."

For a moment they were silent, and he found himself staring at the metronome on top of the piano, panicking in case they could find nothing to say.

"You remember the little lecture you gave me?" she asked quietly.

"Yes." Her question took him by surprise because he'd wanted to ask the same thing himself.

"You told me off for treating George badly. To my face, as we danced."

"What an idiot I was." He recalled her expression of perplexity, which had immediately put him in the wrong for saying anything. "And you said there was nothing between you and George. I really was a terrible prig."

"It wasn't very kind of me, I can see that now. It was rather nice of you. I was furious then, of course. It was none of your business. But I felt even then that you were just a little different."

"I think I was as disappointed as George to see you kissing someone else."

She got up. "Come and talk to me while I make coffee." She took his hand to lead him between the music stands and piles of sheet music into the kitchen. "I'm afraid you'll sit down on one of my violins or something otherwise. I don't mind what you say or do as long as you don't break my violin."

"May I just try it? I can still play, you know."

She looked for a moment into his face and then at his hands.

* * *

Night Train to Cologne

A sudden jerk of the brakes and then a long grinding sound startled him back to reality, bringing a few seconds of fear lest the train would not stop in time for any danger on the line ahead. Susan nodded but remained asleep. Outside were the lights of marshalling yards, oil tanks, factories with German names in large neon letters. Slower and slower, until the spur of a platform appeared, and then the dim illumination of a station. An echoing, muffled voice: *"Wiesbaden! Wiesbaden! Achtung Gleis vier!"* Another shudder and the train stopped. For a while he heard trampling outside the door as passengers struggled aboard with their luggage. Then there was silence again, except for one person's footsteps echoing in the corridor.

He looked out of his window at the two rails alongside and the next platform beyond, where a solitary official strolled up and down. An empty track, leading back. He still had a journey to look forward to, with memories to be indulged in, but soon even that would be over.

He recalled the two afternoons with Frances in her living room, with its piano, music stands, and violins. One that he had played badly, and she'd been anxious but had tried not to show it. Even the bedroom, on his third visit, had been full of all the accessories of music, and she had left the record player on. For him now making love would always be associated with Mendelssohn's Violin Concerto, with its contrasts of anguish, melancholy, and unbelievable joy. But that was two days ago. As he stared at the cold rails, the train started to move once more, almost silently gathering speed until the station lights disappeared and the outside darkness descended.

"Susan." He shook her knee. "We're nearly at the Rhine. Do you want to see the Gorge?"

She opened her eyes, stared at him for a moment, and closed them again. "Too tired . . ."

He watched, waiting for the first glimpse of the river. Suddenly it was there, flat and dark beyond the vineyards, with a hint of hills beginning on its farther shore. Then they were streaming alongside it, faster than its current, so that if you kept your eyes fixed on the water, you could imagine it flowing backwards. Look ahead and you might just make out the sinister shape of the Mouse Tower on its island.

The train shrieked past the town with its shops on the one side, their lights blazing forth; past the river on the other, swelling against the outline of distant barges. The windows rattled as they sped through the station. Nearly there. The train plunged beneath the hill, cutting short his view, and emerged abruptly in the village, shaking the old, crumbling houses along the line. An illuminated sign, *Hotel Post*, a name on the station that there was no time to read, and it was gone. One village of many along the Rhine, special only because it held memories of one afternoon years ago.

On the way back, their group had spent an extra night and day on the Rhine, in Rüdesheim. That final afternoon the others had gone up the chair lift, but Frances, George, Jill, and he decided on a boat trip instead. Plunging through the waters of the river—past the Mouse Tower with its legend of a cruel bishop; past the ruins of the Ehrenfels, where later bishops too had collected river tolls—the small boat brought them to a tiny landing stage. The village was their own discovery. The streets were almost deserted, with restaurants and inns so dark inside they could hardly see. Just a happy afternoon, romantic because they were young. They sat on a bench overlooking the river, watching the barges and the pleasure boats, while the hills opposite steamed in the heat of the afternoon sun. If you looked carefully through the haze you could see the two castles of Rheinstein and Reichenstein under the hill. George read aloud the legend of Helmbrecht and Gerda, and pointed out the Klemenskapelle where the lovers lay buried. On a higher hill stood Sooneck, fortress of a robber baron.

Holding hands with Jill, Brian felt closer to Frances since that pompous speech to her. Yet when the holiday was over Frances had become no more than a vaguely romantic memory.

Night Train to Cologne

I wonder why, he thought. Would it have made any difference if I had loved her then? He had almost forgotten her in the thrill of going to university and the assurance of a brilliant career afterwards. Life at that time was exciting.

None of them spoke much that afternoon. Walking back to the boat, they tried to sing German romantic songs, but on the return journey they again fell silent, looking back at the river behind them in the early dusk. A few hours later they were on a night train to Cologne.

He looked out, now as then, at the shapes of hills belonging to legend. They were well into the Gorge. Cologne, it seemed, was still a night's journey away, rather than the hour or so shown on the timetable. He looked at Susan again, sleeping soundly, unaware of the river outside. Home, he thought, and family, a secure job, possessions, love . . .

Anger arose within him. "It's unreasonable," he said mentally. "Unreasonable for you even to suggest that I give that up."

"Yes, it's unreasonable," Frances's quiet voice replied.

"And there'd be so many problems. Storms. Tantrums."

He turned towards the Rhine again, dark and mysterious. Tomorrow it would no longer exist.

"But you can't expect to avoid the tantrums of life!"

He had tried to avoid them, always. All his life he'd sought what was safe, regulating his passions and desires because of what others might think. Rebelling only in words. "Why is so much in your life *unthinkable*?" Frances had asked him. Unthinkable that you should ever go back on responsibility, allow conflicts to wrench at your commitments. All his life, he mused, he'd stopped short of true experience, limiting himself to what was consonant with worthy, publicly expressed attitudes. Even his love affairs had been that way. Distant, kept in tight compartments in other

A. Colin Wright

towns. Sufficient for him to feel he was still free, but with lids that could be shut down resolutely at the mere suggestion of impropriety.

Now, as he stared at the river, he knew he was frightened because of the new feeling that there could be a commitment to Frances. For the first time in his life a woman had grasped immediately at that man of intuition within him, that man of belief in a life that was different from the everyday of houses, jobs, possessions. "Not things you've chosen," she said, "but which others have chosen for you. Yet you've allowed it." Now his fear clung on to those very possessions. For days fear had gnawed at him, twisted his bowels to produce almost constant diarrhoea. It wasn't just the German food and change of water that Susan attributed it to.

You're going back home, he told himself, and that'll be the end of it. Easy enough to rationalize, do the right thing. Say you'll never go back on your commitment and that Frances should be left on the sidelines of your life. Put in a box, like your other affairs, to be taken out furtively the next time you go to Stuttgart. If there is a next time. What everyone expects of a good husband . . .

Except that what was called doing the right thing was no more than an easy way out. Fear, not morality, was taking him home to his family. He'd found his pearl of great price, but was afraid to sell all he had in order to possess it. He wanted instead to keep it all. Frances wouldn't fit conveniently into a box. She kept popping out again, saying annoyingly "I love you and I know you love me, even if you deny it." Those last words— even if you deny it—had spared him the necessity of *actually* denying it, and he was grateful because he couldn't have denied it anyway. But was everything else to be given up? There was nothing wrong with his marriage, nothing wrong with Susan. She was different from him, that was all. One of the normal people.

Frances, like himself, was extraordinary.

Extra-ORD-inary, extra-ORD-inary, extra-ORD-inary. The wheels beat out their rhythm as his eyelids closed on the Rhine with its

Night Train to Cologne

rising wall of cliffs. Not high, but sloping like the sides of a tub—or a magic cauldron, perhaps, with the moon reflected on black water, which could be emptied through the whirlpool where the Lorelei combed her hair and enticed enamoured sailors. Fanciful, of course, and it was rocks and not a whirlpool by the Lorelei—but he opened his eyes to check how his fancies corresponded to the view through the window. Barges, ships, islands floated in the cauldron, which had ledges running around it at water level, with model houses, lights, and even, on the other side, an immensely long model train running in the other direction.

Extra-ORD-inary, extra-ORD-inary, extra-ORD-inary . . . Again he forced his eyes open to look at the river. At Susan. Dear Susan. Asleep.

His back ached, and it was a relief to sit forward and peer with greater determination out of the window. A voice in his mind, Susan's voice, told him: "You're not extraordinary. Just a little different, and I love you for it. People like you for it, as long as you don't start arguing too loudly."

Another voice, Frances's, whispered: "You are extra-ord-inary, extra-ord-inary, extra-ord-inary. We're both extra-ord-inary, extra-ord-inary. But we can never tell them, they'll never understand. I know it, you know it, I know it, you know it. But your fear of them is ordinary, ordinary, ordinary. You'll end up being ordinary, ordinary."

He nodded forward and his head hit the window. *Nicht hinauslehnen. È pericoloso sporgersi.* It's dangerous to lean out. Sit back again. Forget. Still a long way to go before Cologne. Unless in Cologne . . . He leaned forward again. Can you make such a decision? Ordinary, extraordinary, ordinary, extraordinary, ordinary . . . Long way to Cologne. Long way, long, long way to Cologne.

*   *   *

A. Colin Wright

It had happened before. Trivial, it seemed now. He hadn't exactly planned to stay in Germany after that holiday. Yet he had hated the thought of going home to the routine of school and then university entrance exams; there was a strange, recurring feeling of doubt about it all. That last afternoon the thought had come to him as a startling possibility: Why not stay? He had only to decide, and no one could tell him to do otherwise. They'd think it odd, that was all.

On the train—a slow one, stopping more than this—he dared himself to get off at the next station. Several passed, but finally he really did get out, stood on the platform watching the train, waiting to see it go. Then he started to think of the others worrying about him, his luggage still aboard, and Jill, who expected him to share their final journey together. At the last moment he climbed back on. More sensible to wait until Cologne, where he could collect his luggage and at least tell someone.

In later years this memory embarrassed him, until he forgot it altogether. Until now, when he wished that just for once in his life he had done something irrational. But there was more to it than that. It all somehow had to do with the mystery of life: that life which lay beyond the everyday and was mostly unattainable, except when it suddenly intruded through events over which you had no control, and which demanded a choice you were unprepared to make. Something had happened during those two weeks in Heidelberg, although whenever he remembered those feelings, he usually dismissed them as the romanticism and sentimentality of youth—like his earlier conviction, when he'd been just sixteen, that *The Student Prince* was one of the world's greatest love stories.

It had started in *Der Rote Ochs*, one of Heidelberg's well-known inns, one evening with the group. Looking at an ordinary beer mat, for a few moments he was intensely aware that he was *seeing* it. He saw the glasses, too, the solid oak tables, the collection of amusing signs purloined from various places and now decorating the walls. *Kein Wasser unter der Brücke lassen*—don't pass water under the bridge—and he saw the *K* as a strange letter, the word *Wasser* as having a deeper significance than mere

Night Train to Cologne

water. Then he laughed to himself, for in that particular context that was indeed true. He saw vividly, on the table in front of him, hands with tiny but distinct pores and hairs. He saw the colours of the room around him as an artist might have spread them on canvas. He saw George's dark eyes and the ironic, shy twist of his mouth. He saw the prominent blue vein on Jill's forehead. And looking at Frances, he was almost aware of the air as it passed over her moist lips. He caught her eye, and she smiled, looking at him intently.

Inside him he felt an anguish of doubt, which lasted for only a moment, a deep awareness of the futility of everyday life compared with *this*. Later, he tried to explain it to George, who passed it off as an excess of alcohol, but appeared troubled too. Several times during those two weeks the same feeling returned, but he could never quite seize it and knew only that it was important.

Sometimes in trains he could almost recapture it. Now, in the dark carriage, he told himself to see the river. To see the plate telling you not to lean out of the window. To see the shapes of the passengers and Susan, asleep in her own world. It was still a long way to Cologne. Nights like this, when he could look out over a broad river normally absent from his life, passed with pleasurable slowness. In the pit of his stomach a decision waited, but even his doubt and fear were pleasurable.

Frances. If this were some kind of second chance, he was still unprepared. She had been an unexpected gift of fate, which it would have been ungrateful of him to refuse. All because an uncle of Susan's had died, leaving enough money for a holiday in Germany, and a copy of *The Observer* that he'd read on a park bench, with a review of a concert. Frances Gracey: at first he hadn't recognized the name. "Her extraordinary performance," "real talent," "accomplished solo violinist." When he realized who she was, his first reaction had been anger.

"Anger? Why anger?" she asked. Her breast was nestled in his hand, while his lips brushed the back of her neck.

39

A. Colin Wright

It sounded petty when he tried to tell her. "Oh, from envy. Resentment. I felt cheated that you'd achieved something I hadn't." As though, he thought, she'd been outside on the terrace again while he was dancing with the wrong girl. "After all, a career in business doesn't give you time for much else. I'm not even successful in that. At least, I never seem to have any money. I dabble in other things. But you heard how I can only scrape at a violin now."

Even now, he didn't understand it. He'd expected to find her superior, successful, too busy catering to the applause of her admirers. How had she known of his intense inner life, his reading, his dreams that meant more to him than the world around him? Her warm body pressed against his. For her he'd turned out to be someone she immediately respected and believed in.

"Why? I can't do anything." He saw the wisps of golden grey hair in front of his eyes.

"I don't have to explain. You judge by intuition rather than reason: use it now. Have faith in yourself."

He saw the ceiling above, ordinary squares of plastic tile.

"And you still play the violin." She turned over to face him and kissed him. "Oh, not very well, but you told me you do write poetry."

"It's amateur." He saw her grey eyes.

"Art's not achievement. It's the way you look at life. You have to live your own life, that's all."

"What I should have done years ago." He saw the fibres in the one sheet that covered them. "Only now there are all kinds of difficulties."

In his arms she said: "You need courage if you're one of the extraordinary."

*   *   *

40

Night Train to Cologne

Extra-ord-inary, extra-ord-inary, extra-ord-inary. The Rhine was flowing straighter and more sluggishly, no longer hemmed in by the hills. Susan was still sleeping and the compartment was silent except for the monotonous hum of the wheels beneath. Two barges, barely visible except for their lights, groped downstream in the blackness. He could still turn around in Cologne.

The unexpected sliding of the door startled him, and with a click the white light in the ceiling went on.

"Alle Fahrkarten, bitte!"

Susan opened one eye, squinted, and left it all to him, while the other passengers hunted in their pockets. He handed over the tickets and asked the arrival time in Cologne, which he knew already, but it was one last opportunity to speak German. The official told him, looked at the other tickets, and then with a curt *"Danke"* put out the light again and pulled the door closed behind him. There was a quieter rumbling and a slight thump as the door to the next compartment was pulled open.

Almost at the same moment, like an echo, Brian felt a rumbling in his bowels and the quick beat of his heart. Fear told him it was unreasonable for Frances to expect him to give up everything. He had to think. Decide. Before he got to Cologne.

The train crossed the river, visible only through the iron girders of the bridge, and passed into the dimly-lit barn of the station. Outside his window large square letters—once they had been Gothic—announced KÖLN HBF, and a hollow voice also proclaimed their arrival. The light was snapped on and the compartment became a sudden shuffling of coats and suitcases.

Susan yawned, stretched, and took her time. They stepped out onto the platform. "You're sure there wasn't a through train to Ostend?" she asked.

He checked the board with its printed sheet of departure times, and then lifted cases and led the way down the stone steps.

"There's a while to wait, I'm afraid," he called back to her.

Up to another platform and the cavernous restaurant, full of people drinking coffee or slumped heavily over the tables. Susan must have wondered why he went to a table in the opposite corner instead of one closer to them. She said nothing. They sat down.

He ordered two black coffees.

She glanced at him strangely. "Dear, you know I don't like black coffee."

Of course. He called to the waiter again.

As he drank, he looked at the door. Soon George would come back to say they ought to be going if they wanted seats on the train. Jill, Frances, and the others would get up to go. He'd go with them as far as the train. He'd say goodbye to them there, stay the rest of the night in Cologne, and then go back. But where? The sudden freedom of choice overwhelmed him. The time came and he still wanted the company, the security of the familiar. The more reliable course was surely to go along with them, he could always return later. There's always another day, as his parents were fond of saying. He sat down with them in the train. An hour later they crossed the frontier.

He looked around the darkened carriage. He was the only one awake; the rest were nodding heavily. No, Frances was awake, staring out of the window. She turned and looked at him for an instant, and then stared outside again as though she hadn't noticed him.

"You're not tired?" he asked.

"Yes. But I don't want to sleep."

Night Train to Cologne

He nodded. "I don't either. I love travelling. For its own sake. That's how I'd like my life to be. A constant exploration. Through art or literature perhaps."

"Like music," she said. "Everywhere you go there's music."

"Don't you mind, though? To be going home?"

She was puzzled. "But I'll come back someday, if it's important enough."

"So shall I." He didn't know then that it would be twenty-five years later.

"Brian," he heard Susan's insistent voice. "Brian, dear!" She touched his arm. "I thought you were falling asleep." He looked at her. "I was afraid you'd spill your coffee. Isn't it time we were going?"

Habit, what was expected of him, took him through the motions.

The cases weighed him down as he dragged them up the steps. Why did Susan always have so much luggage? They stood on the platform, waiting. Then at last there was a light bearing down on them, and he saw a solid dark-green electric engine with its square letters "DB" on front: *Deutsche Bundesbahn*, those mysterious words so much more suggestive of possible fulfilment, even now, than the shabby familiarity of British Rail. A green, square carriage slowed in front of them, with its board announcing in bold letters *Köln—Oostende* and a list of names: *Aachen (Aix-la-Chapelle), Leuven, Bruxelles Nord, Gent, Brugge . . .*

A crowded compartment again, but they got window seats. After settling Susan down, he went back out and stood on the platform. He looked towards the rear of the train and imagined an engine being coupled on to take it in the opposite direction. But only he could take charge now.

Can you do it, Brian? Here you are in Cologne as you were twenty-five years ago. At that time to stay was just a whim perhaps, and you were right to go home. But now? "It's your life, to do what you want with,"

A. Colin Wright

Frances had said. "If you want me, I am yours. Just come and take me." The woman he'd expected to be remote had appreciated him, loved him now. No, she'd said, you're not odd, but extraordinary. Weighed down, though, by the ordinary. He stared at the long green wall of the coach in front of him. If he ran towards it fast, from the far edge of the platform, he'd have to swerve in one direction or the other. Or he could toss a coin—but had he the courage to follow the coin's decision? Family, children, a whole life, was he really going to abandon that? For the typical other woman?

"No, Brian, not for the other woman. I'll never be the typical other woman. For yourself. For the destiny you've never quite managed to catch up with."

Put one foot on the step of the train. Between his feet is the tiniest of gaps, too small for escape. Others would never understand. Could he do it this way, just walk away? "It's that simple," Frances would say.

He heard the announcement for his train. Passengers to climb aboard and close the doors. Decide, for God's sake decide. There's no more time. A whistle in the distance, shouts to get in, an irate official approaching . . .

The train slides through the lights of the station and into the dark of a riverless countryside, heading relentlessly towards the Belgian coast. An hour later it crosses the frontier. Border officials are unconcerned and Susan sleeps on, unknowing. What if you are alone, Susan, you who have never hurt anyone, never done anything to deserve being abandoned? Has your husband the right to forsake you even, as he sees it, to receive a hundredfold and inherit everlasting life? You will not see it like that, but only as a man putting away his wife for another. Should not life be fair to you too?

Sleep on, dear Susan, for everything is as it should be in a well-ordered world, and you are not alone. You remain unaware that fate could

Night Train to Cologne

have ordained otherwise. Or could it? Was there really any decision for Brian to make?

Wanting to sleep now but unable to, he stared out of the window. Tomorrow they would be home, and trains along the Rhine and a woman he loved in Stuttgart would be as unreal as they had ever been. Susan would know nothing. But, he told himself, he could always come back. Save for another holiday, find Frances again. There was always another day. Always.

Since it was too dark for anyone to see, he allowed himself the luxury of tears, which rolled down his cheek and off his chin, one falling on the heater under the window with a little sizzle of steam. He opened the window and leaned out into the night in a futile burst of defiance. But the wind took his breath away, and he soon drew back inside.

"Close the window, dear," Susan murmured without opening her eyes.

The Bells of Khatyn

In the memorial village of Khatyn*, a bell tolls every thirty seconds from one of the twenty-six symbolic chimneys. The twenty-six symbolic gates do not open. The cottages are missing, the names and ages of their former occupants etched into plaques of marble.

A bell . . .

. . . and Gerhardt Schiller, B.Sc., Dipl.Ing. (construction company in Toronto, Ontario), surveys the empty desolation of a vast clearing in the woods. And thinks

It wasn't like this. It wasn't like this!

—The stones we're walking on mark the main street. Imagine the happy villagers, youngsters playing. However often the guide repeats the words, she can't control her anger for the people she might have known, for the children who, had they lived, would now be her contemporaries.

Slavs: like wasps, you thought then. You felt no hatred, just anger. But my God it was *fun*, was that it? Like spraying a wasps' nest in your garden, and still they keep flying, so take aim individually, waiting for

---

* Khatyn should not be confused with the more infamous Katyn. K and Kh are different letters in the Cyrillic alphabet.

The Bells of Khatyn

them to fall. Sometimes you finish them off with another burst as they writhe in the grass. Sometimes—since they'll die anyway—you don't bother. But remember: some will sting if you don't do it properly.

A weak sun shines on the peaceful concrete and marble commemorating the absence of a village amidst the mixed forests and undulating grassy fields. Gerhardt Schiller's eyes, like those of the rest of the group, are moist. Might have been then, only it wasn't like this.

A bell . . .

. . . because

—In the three years of the occupation, two million two hundred and thirty thousand citizens of Soviet Byelorussia perished: one in every four of the population . . . Her voice, a little sanctimonious like Soviet newscasters you've heard, falters as though in disbelief.

They sounded the same in Germany then: the same sincerity, the same outrage. And shit, all you wanted was for life to be exciting, different from the dreary integrity of your parents in an age of changed ideals—of your father, maligning as hoodlums your brown-shirted friends. But be like others, an innocent tourist now, and admire through your tears the stark symbolism of a huge cemetery complex. Eternalizing the memory of

Snow, melting in the heat. Of night, of anger. A time when Gerhardt Schiller, with all the rest, shrieked different words. Anger, power, was that it? Drive them into the barn (meeting hall, church, whatever). A woman won't go, points at her kids, shouts words you don't understand. Kerchief on her head, thick padded coat, a face that has potato blight. Hit her with your gun. It's war. Think I want this either? Move, bitch, move! Captain's watching and I'm desperate for promotion, shit, woman, get it over with. Fire in the mud at her feet, she grabs the kids and moves.

A bell . . .

. . . because of

A. Colin Wright

—Nine thousand two hundred villages destroyed (her statistics go mercilessly on): one hundred and eighty-six of them together with *their entire populations.*

Were you here or not? So many villages: who can remember all their unpronounceable names? Hating us because we're young, the new race who'll rule mankind. We need their bread, their cows, their horses, the booty for ourselves to make our sacrifices bearable. Fuck them all for getting in our way. I've a family as well, two children I adore: Ilse, blue eyes, the Aryan ideal; Jürgen, tough little bugger, sentimental like his dad. It's them I'm fighting for, and my warm-bodied wife Liesl, in a land that's proud again. What are *my* chances of getting back? Think you're not angry when your pals fall to the partisans? Teach them all a lesson, it's us or them—Slavs, inferior as everyone knows.

We walk on. Small groups of architects, construction engineers: a builders' convention on its afternoon excursion from Minsk. Lamenting the destruction with pompous professionalism. In Canada, it's said, one man in ten beats his wife. Where I sometimes wake, trembling, from a dream . . . that I murdered someone. Where, since my divorce, Ilse, Jürgen and their children know me as an aging, kindly introvert, pottering in his garden. But there's

A bell . . .

. . . because of

Tent caterpillars. What else can you do but burn the nest?—while the children on the street come running to watch them writhing in the flames. Wood burns easily, of course: grenades are quickest, or put straw around and drench with gasoline. Don't ask me to have pity when my friend Heinz . . . my best friend Heinz . . . but then, he got promotion and I didn't.

Now Rudi, sure, enjoys it, when I think I've had enough. Loves to hunt, pheasants, duck, anything. Somewhere it was in daytime and we're

The Bells of Khatyn

driving them into a barn (meeting hall, church, whatever) and a kid, a girl, runs away. Look at her, Rudi says, just like a jack-rabbit, lets her get past the cottages almost to the trees, then bang and she's down, two more to make sure of her. Rudi's always loved sport, still hunts occasionally; me and the boys and my beer, has slept round too in his time. I take a couple of shots so they won't think me odd, show I'm a man like the rest, and Captain Schmidt's watching again, his fat belly quivering in a mirthless laugh.

A bell . . .

. . . where

—To your right is a symbolic barn of black marble. There, on 22 March 1943, all in the village—every man, woman and child in Khatyn—were herded together, straw was placed round the barn, soaked in gasoline and set alight. One hundred and forty-nine souls were burnt alive. Soldiers surrounded it to shoot any who escaped.

And where were *you*, I think at her defiantly. Confusion, cries of infants, insults, shots for those who can't make it. Move, damn you! Out of your houses! Carry those who can't walk. All into the barn (meeting hall, church, whatever). War purifies, they say, and we're the bosses now. On the banks of the Rhine, in the sun, we grow grapes: in the new Germany to be, reborn from the defeatist chaos my father's decency led to. To avenge Versailles, we reminded them. And yet . . .

Gerhardt Schiller remembers the statue at the entrance to the memorial complex. In the hundred-metre walk towards it from the buses he'd tried not to look, while its jagged bronze towered above: a man, haggard, scrawny, with staring eyes, carrying a dead child like a drooping letter M.

A bell . . .

. . . because

A. Colin Wright

—They were largely the women and children, the old, the sick, the helpless. The young men were at the front . . . She's almost crying too, not *for* them but sentimentally, at the idea of it.

And the others, are they watching, wondering about Gerhardt Schiller, B.Sc., Dipl.Ing.—who has a construction company in Toronto, and understands that it was terrible? SS Corporal Gerhardt Schiller screams inwardly that it wasn't like that. They were our enemies, sheltering the partisans, hindering our work, our great ideal. It was only a small massacre after all, no worse than thousands since the world began. Sure we're murderers, who isn't? Ordinary people, justified, angry. Was your Russian Civil War any better, the Americans in Vietnam, the French in Algeria? The British in Cyprus, and now the Israelis—as if the Jews haven't made fuss enough!

Slav peasants they are, that's all, not like you. They force you into it, make it difficult by resisting, hitting back. And then, well yes, it's *exciting*, I admit.

A bell . . .

. . . as she shows us

A black marble wall with openings like prison cells. Commemorating those from each town or village who died in the camps. No names, just figures. Beyond this a cemetery for every village destroyed, stretching out of sight: the graves three metres square, with an urn, a red flower, a black stone. Each village's name in the angular backward capitals of an unreadable alphabet:

СТАРИЦА, НОВОСЕЛЬКИ, БЕЛАЯ ЛУЖА,

ЗЕЛЕНЫЙ ЛОГ, ЛАДЕЕВО, ДРЕМЛЕЕВО . . .

. . . In September 1942, drunken SS soldiers—she spits the words—drove into Dremleyevo. They forced everyone into a cowshed, plundered the cottages, then set fire to everything. Two hundred and

The Bells of Khatyn

eighty people were burnt alive or shot, including a hundred and twenty-five children. Only three escaped.

What did I tell you?—it was only a small massacre in Khatyn. I knew all about the thousands killed, the burning piles of corpses. And the Gestapo, they got my father too . . .

A bell . . .

. . . because

Such, you see, were my orders. Captain Schmidt, his eyes glistened, his belly heaved as he read them.—Pity, sympathy, nerves: no place for them in war! Kill every Soviet Russian, old men, women, girls, boys, all of them. Animals. That way you'll save yourselves and assure the future of the glorious Aryan race. Schiller, repeat!

—Imagine the barn as it filled with smoke, the despair as they realized they'd never get out alive . . . (An involuntary, uncomprehending shudder.)

You repeat without question. He thinks you've a stake in the culture because your name is Schiller. So be zealous like the rest, don't stick your neck out, that's how to get promotion. Like Heinz, whom I loved as a friend, and hated, hated, when he made it and I didn't.

But the squealing disturbed me at first. Even of the pigs when we slaughtered them. I'm sentimental, you see. The first time I heard children trapped in the flames I nearly threw up. But others were watching.

A bell . . .

. . . commemorating

—The sacrifice made by those one in four who fell to the Fascist barbarians—she'd translated the plaque where we'd got off the buses. No mention of those ordinary people who suddenly discovered they'd been

A. Colin Wright

murderers all the time. No memorial marks the passing of Gerhardt Schiller, who also died in Byelorussia. Or earlier. Dear God, I didn't mean it!

Remember how, as a child, you loved staring into a fire, imagining a different world of cities and flaming buildings? When a cottage burns you see a flickering in the doorway and windows, until the whole inside's alight. It flames up around the jambs, through the roof, and suddenly it has a hold on the walls, the flames shoot higher, so beautiful; the wind carries the sparks into the sky, the heat scorches your face, the snow's already melted. Later, there's nothing but the brick stove and chimney, a desolate, accusing finger in the smoke. Now, from another symbolic chimney

A bell . . .

. . . tolls.

You lie with the others as the barn blazes, the heat searing your eyes, the blood throbbing in your ears. Shoot anyone who gets out. Some always do, children crawling between the adults' legs. Their clothes on fire, so they're better off shot anyway. But sometimes, if no one sees, you let the others do it. It's that way now. You hear the shots but keep your eyes closed, thinking how it's really a shitty job and not even exciting any more—praying you'll somehow survive and get back to Liesl and your children.

—Schiller! Fire!

Open your eyes and there's this man walking straight at you, burning like an avenging god. Ageless: grief, suffering, dirt makes them look all the same. The dead child he's carrying could be four, or six, or eight.

A bell . . .

Oh God it wasn't like that it wasn't like that it wasn't like that. You tried—once—to condemn the Nazi excesses, but what's a Party without discipline? You had your share of ordinary pride and patriotism. The Führer

52

The Bells of Khatyn

well in secret we could make fun of him but it stirred us just the same when Europe shuddered at our might, while old-fashioned liberals shook their frightened heads. Just ignore the fanatics, stay clear of the Gestapo you know full well is necessary. Some have to be sacrificed for a new and greater society. The power and the glory, the soul-stirring marches, the thousand-year Reich, the mass rallies in a common cause: it brought tears to your eyes. When was it that the excitement, the intoxication, the glory, gave way to lassitude and despair? To realization . . .

But if you still want promotion go along with everyone else.

A bell . . .

. . . recalling that

—Only one man escaped alive from the barn.

(Meeting place, church, whatever.)

The Captain's alarmed.—Schiller! Fire, damn you!

You can't. He lifts his pistol, points it at you, you're terrified, think you're going to die, he shoots it into the ground so that the mud splatters against your face.—Fire, Schiller!

Close your eyes and fire. Then open them.

It's as though he hasn't noticed. Still he comes on, clothes on fire, staring ahead of him, the child hanging limp in his arms.

A bell . . .

. . . for the times you try no longer to think. That play by Shakespeare: You are in blood stepp'd in so far that, should you wade no more, returning were as tedious as go o'er. So many terrible things it's too late to change, nothing you'll ever do can be worse. So shut your eyes and shout with the rest that someday it will be different in the new society most of us no longer believe in. Grab what you can, make the most of your power. Some still enjoy it. Rudi, Captain Schmidt. It's exciting, you see, the adrenaline, the blood pounding in your veins. Then, if it has to be done, get it over with.

A bell.

—Again!

You fire. Still he comes. Again, and now you're firing crazily, while the bullets just don't seem to touch him, why won't he die? On he comes, you fire again and again, another moment and you'll turn and run. But he stops, barely five metres in front, falls to his knees, still holding the child; sinks over it, collapses, and Rudi goes to finish him off with his rifle butt.

A bell.

—In Lesiny, she tells us, they grabbed all the children who weren't in the barn and threw them down a well.

The simplest way. And somewhere else a spring flood washes up the bodies buried in a ditch. Over three thousand, and we have to go out in boats and catch them all. Then make the locals bury them again. Later, we're told to dig them up, rotten as they are, and burn them. German efficiency.

A bell.

Snow, night, wind, fire. In Munich, after the war, I meet Captain Schmidt in a beer-hall. We recognize each other straightaway.

—It wasn't like that at all, he tells me. I didn't enjoy it any more than you. I'd have been shot for disobeying orders. And you, Schiller, didn't help. You'd never have got your promotion.

A bell.

You didn't believe him. Whose fault was it then? *Yours?*

The Bells of Khatyn

—When you wouldn't fire I was so angry I could have killed you myself. Only then I'd have had to shoot that man. And for a moment the boy reminded me . . .

A bell.

Butcher, murderer. He believed in it to the end. He shows you photos of his podgy children, a tiny wife, and himself eating candyfloss. He doesn't suggest you meet again. Were you ever like *him*?

A bell.

—Afterwards, she says, in springtime, the storks returned to Khatyn. There was nowhere for them to roost anymore

A bell . . .

. . . and they circled, puzzled, before flying away for ever.

A bell.

Why am I here in the wilderness of Byelorussia?

A bell

It wasn't like this

A bell tolls

It wasn't

A bell tolls, a bell tolls, a bell tolls

. . . so that, dear God

—It should never be forgotten or forgiven. And we, in the Byelorussian Soviet Socialist Republic, have solemnly sworn . . .

*   *   *

55

Gerhardt Schiller, builder, of Toronto, returns with the group to the waiting buses.

The radio blares forth its news about the brotherly assistance the Soviets are giving the Afghan patriots. The guide explains she has a brother in the army there. She believes, as I did; as they all do, wherever they live.

—It's so terrible for them, fighting for freedom. So that this—she looks back towards the memorial complex, where the bells still toll—will never happen again.

Soon, thank God, you'll be home again. A peaceful man who, in a new country, finds solace in his garden and an understanding Canadian second wife. While your grandchildren, with Ilse and Jürgen, visit you unsuspecting in your flawlessly decorated house. A civilized neighbourhood, respectable friends paying off mortgages and lamenting the sex and violence on television.

The buses leave, turn onto a road you must have patrolled many times, watching for partisans. A solitary accusing finger-like sign points back to an empty clearing in the woods:

ХАТЫНЬ

Now it's a major highway and, since we're an important delegation of builders, we're preceded all the way to Minsk by a medical vehicle with a flashing light, warning oncoming traffic to move to the side of the road.

Ghost Stations

The train slows in the tunnel before emerging into a station I know will be dimly lit and abandoned, its name in black Gothic letters on grimy boards that have been hanging there since the thirties. I stand by the doors, anxious to catch each detail in the seconds it takes to rattle through. Stadtmitte, the signs read. I glimpse the wide steps leading down from blocked-off corridors above, and again we're carried past a little booth in mid-platform that would have been for some controller in bygone days. Perhaps even now someone is sitting there, silently observing these ghostly trains from another world. But we pass too quickly and I can't be sure.

An anguished female voice comes from behind me in German: "Why aren't we stopping?"

I turn in surprise. The other passengers, long used to travelling these dingy tunnels under the communist section of the capital, between the modern and brightly-lit stations of the West, sit with their normal indifference. This woman, though, drab and sixtyish, looks as though she'd intended to get out.

"We're under East Berlin," I explain, something I know perfectly well although I haven't been on this line before. "The western trains still go beneath it"—we pick up speed as we plunge into the tunnel again—"but without stopping. The stations are all closed."

A. Colin Wright

I'm a collector of underground railways. I know all about them. The London Tube, the Paris Metro, the New York Subway, and even the modern Russian ones: such systems have fascinated me since I was a child. I learned German so I could come to Berlin, with both its underground proper, the U-Bahn, and the elevated city railway called the S-Bahn, which in places goes underground too—and with all the peculiarities of their operation caused by a divided city.

"But they always stop," the woman contradicts me. "I've lived in Berlin all my life. We stopped at Kochstrasse, didn't we? Then there's Stadtmitte, Französische Strasse, Friedrichstrasse, Oranienburger Tor, and the Stettin Station."

"They call it North Station now," I correct her, but she doesn't hear. "And there's no station left there anyway."

"I had to change at Stadtmitte for Alexanderplatz! Oh no!" We slow again and pass without stopping through the next station, as ghostly as the first. "Is there an air raid or something? But"—she's puzzled—"that only affects the overhead railway, not the underground."

"You can't change at Stadtmitte anymore." I show her my map. "You could in the old days, but the other line's in the East. You see." I point to the key in the upper corner. "A white box means 'stations where the trains don't stop.'" And haven't for more than twenty years. "We're going from south to north under East Berlin, where the old city centre sticks out in a huge spur, until we come back into the West, here, at Reinickendorfer Strasse."

She doesn't understand. "I suppose I'll have to change at Friedrichstrasse and take the S-Bahn. And at least"—her fussy anxiety gives way to a sudden relief—"I didn't see Kurt on the platform at the last two stations. Did you? But the trains always stop."

We're slowing again before I can point out that this obviously isn't the case.

Ghost Stations

"You see," she says. "What did I tell you? We *are* stopping at Friedrichstrasse."

Triumphant, she looks into my eyes. If she's a Berliner, how can she not know what is a commonplace, that Friedrichstrasse is still a major interchange station for the whole system, a little enclave of the West under the centre of East Berlin? This U-Bahn line and an underground section of an S-Bahn intersect here. Overhead you can take the other S-Bahn back to the West or, from a different platform protected by a high metal barrier, to the East, as long as you pass through the checkpoint first. It's this line the woman will have to take to Alexanderplatz.

"Of course," she continues, "if he's on the platform here I won't have to go any farther."

The doors open and she disappears in a surge of other passengers. Crazy, I think, wondering if she'll get through the checkpoint. I've been into the East, so I know the procedure. Join the queues in front of doors of frosted glass marked variously *For foreigners, For citizens of the Federal Republic, For West Berliners*; have your passport examined; receive a one-day visa for five marks; and then exchange a further compulsory non-refundable twenty-five marks. It all fascinates me. My interest in transport systems and the like started in England, when my grandmother died and we had to spend several days at her house in London. Bored and lonely while my parents rummaged through her possessions, I drew maps of the Underground lines and learned the station names by heart; and sometimes my parents would give me the odd shilling so I could take a trip and be out of their way. Now, the woman gone, I return to my contemplation of the ghost stations, three more of them, eerie and abandoned like fossils of an earlier age, before we pass somewhere under the Wall again and into the mundanely efficient western stations.

Two days later I see the woman again, on the platform of the S-Bahn this time, where it drops below the surface at Anhalter Station, once the busiest terminus in Germany but now no more than a crumbling

A. Colin Wright

façade with a weed-covered wasteland where the main-line trains used to stand.

"It's terrible, terrible." The woman doesn't look at me, and I'm not sure whether she'll recognize me. "They must have come in the night. I used to think the British were decent people, but they're monsters, monsters. Why are they dropping bombs on innocent people?"

I peer down the track to see if our train is coming and then ask where she is going this time.

"Alexanderplatz," she says. "I meant to get on at Gleisdreieck, but they said the line was closed"—she's right, it was shut down completely where it crossed over to the East—"and that it would be simplest to walk to the Anhalter Station. Which was when I saw what those monsters had done to it. I'll have to change at Friedrichstrasse, or Potsdamer Platz."

"Better Friedrichstrasse again," I advise her. Potsdamer Platz, once the Piccadilly of Berlin, is a barren wilderness in the middle of the Wall zone: one of those places where I climbed an observation platform on the western side to look out over barbed wire, batteries of lights, and dogs being led by guards in drab grey-green uniforms. The S-Bahn station will be yet another relic where we won't stop, and the U-Bahn station it communicated with was turned into a museum by the East Berliners. I ask: "Did you reach Alexanderplatz all right the other day?"

"Well yes," she said. "That's where I said goodbye to Kurt. But I have to see him today. I'm so worried about him since the terrible flooding."

There's been no rain in Berlin since my arrival, but the approach of our train prevents me from asking about the flooding. As I expect, the woman is again dismayed when we creak without stopping through the empty Potsdamer Platz station. At Unter den Linden, she thinks she sees a figure in the controller's booth.

60

Ghost Stations

"Was that Kurt?" she asks, but we've passed too quickly. Was there really anyone there, or were we both imagining it?

When she changes at Friedrichstrasse, I decide to go with her. She leads the way up the steps in the middle of the platform, with assurance at first, but then she gets confused. "No, this isn't right." She won't let me tell her but stops another man, who points the way to the banging glass doors of the checkpoint. It's Saturday and there are long lines. I wonder if she'll know which door to queue at. But an East German guard comes up to her and immediately bars her way.

"But I must get to Alexanderplatz," she says. "I've got to find Kurt!"

The guard is firm, and she soon gives up arguing with him. I ask him if he can't help her.

He's so taken aback that he answers. "She's crazy, that one. She comes here every day. Always the same, never has any documents or she could go through, so she sits down for an hour"—she'd already taken a place on a bench—"then toddles off home again. Don't waste your time on her."

In the busy life of every day I'd shrug and forget her, but the woman obviously belongs to this underground world; and after all I'm on holiday, pursuing—in a way that I admit is a little obsessive—my one and only hobby. I've no wife or children making their demands upon me; my grandmother was the only person I ever loved and she let me down by dying when I needed her. Why shouldn't I indulge myself by exploring these depths, systems that function reliably when the surface holds dangers, obstacles, walls that man's conscious mind has built? I go to sit beside the woman, thinking what a great game this is.

"It's always blocked," she says. "It must be because of the flood."

"What flood?" I ask.

A. Colin Wright

"They haven't said anything? It must have been some accident. I'd said goodnight to Kurt—we're going to get married, you know—and was on my way home on the U-Bahn. I changed somewhere and the platform was full of people bedding down for the night. Actually sleeping in the Underground because the British are bombing us! Suddenly there's a rumbling from the tunnel and a huge wave of water comes rushing in. People are struggling to get up, fighting to get to the stairs. Well, I'd only just come down so I was right there, but I think some were drowned."

Passengers are arriving in front of us, forming perpetual queues, the war years long forgotten in the reality of a city rebuilt but forever cracked in two. I recall how, at the end of the war, Hitler flooded the Underground by blowing up the tunnels under the river, in case the Russians tried to use them to reach the city centre. But how reliable are the woman's memories? Were the trains still running then? I, of all people, should have known.

"And I don't know what happened to Kurt!"

"What did he do? What was his job, that is?"

"*Did*? Why do you say *did*? He's an inspector on the Underground. He travels all over," she says with pride, "but he's based at Alexanderplatz."

The kind of job I'd have liked, if my parents hadn't forced me to go to university.

"He's an invalid of course," she goes on, "or he'd be at the front. He was wounded in North Africa. They gave him the Iron Cross." She looks at me. "You're not really Kurt in disguise, are you, playing a trick on me? No, you're older. He's not very handsome," she whispers. "He even looks a bit like Himmler. But charming, and a real hero." Unexpectedly she starts to cry, as though for a moment something has brought her back to reality. "They always stop me here, but they let the others through. They'd let *you* through. Could you go to Alexanderplatz for me and give him a message?

62

Ghost Stations

Tell him to meet me on the Potsdamer Platz at the kiosk there. He'll know where I mean."

Which is why I again find myself crossing to East Berlin, with a name, a photograph, and an address that may no longer exist: looking for a man from the past whom I'll never find, to give him a message to meet a crazy woman on a square long destroyed and inaccessible, from both East and West, between walls and barbed wire. A game, I think, unable to say why a make-believe excursion into the 1940s should so inflame my imagination. When this woman last saw her lover I was only a child and in a different country, but where bombs dropped just the same; where grandmothers died and parents didn't care, so one sought one's escape in diagrams and underground systems.

The guard in his box compares each detail of my face with the photo in my passport, and then stamps his approval on a card that he hands me in exchange for my fee. A woman changes the currency I'm required to produce, and I press past a throng of people waiting for visitors into the streets of a different if strangely similar world. Up stone steps to the S-Bahn overhead, and I wait on a platform separated by a metal wall from those more familiar trains going back to the West.

She told me to look for Kurt at all the stations, but how will I recognize a man nearly seventy years old from a picture taken when he was twenty-four? So I look at young and old alike, examining each detail of their faces. A train arrives, rickety and old, emptying itself of passengers, who disappear down the steps below. Once it would have continued westwards; now it will reverse—as I get on, the driver walks to the other end—and head back across the Museum Island in Berlin's grimy River Spree. Marx-Engels-Platz, I read at the next station, then: Alexanderplatz. I descend into a modern concrete square with a complex of hotels and shops around the huge pod of the TV Tower that dominates the city.

63

A. Colin Wright

But I must find the world of the forties. "Any of the lines from the Alexanderplatz," she told me. "That's where he'll be." So down again to the Underground, more crowded than in the West, and I wait on the platform, aware that there's one line I can no longer take from here. Somewhere beneath me, difficult to imagine, is ghost station Alexanderplatz, the line I first travelled on, carrying its unseen passengers between the entry points of their own, western world. No, there's no access—I look carefully—and there's no indication of its existence. One can only guess where the corridor once leading to that life beyond has been blocked off. So on to Stadtmitte then, the end of the line since they closed the rest. Another station deprived of its own ghost—and where, I recall, I first met the woman whose fiancé I'm now seeking.

It's futile, of course. No one matches the photograph, though I travel all afternoon, even taking the S-Bahn again as far as Ostkreuz. I've never had a better excuse for pursuing a hobby I find difficult to explain to others.

Only I wish she hadn't given me that address. It's true that she told me not to go there—"That might spoil everything. His parents don't know about me, they wouldn't approve"—except that I really don't think they'd be too concerned anymore. By now I'm ready to take the train back to Friedrichstrasse and the West. It's getting dark, but perhaps at least I should see if the house is still there. I find Köpenicker Strasse on my map, and it's right by one of the closed U-Bahn stations on that western line going through Alexanderplatz.

"I'm Kurt Baumgartner," says the man who opens the door. Frail, old, smelly, but I recognize him from the photograph. Not expecting this, I have trouble finding what to say. "Anna Hofmeier," he says after my jumbled explanations. "Oh, come in, come in."

He leads me up a precipitous flight of steps into a dingy apartment crowded with possessions: antiques, pictures of his family, books and,

64

Ghost Stations

framed on the wall, what is surely an old map of the Berlin U-Bahn and S-Bahn. I manoeuvre myself towards it as he shuffles around. Yes, it's a pocket-sized folder, from the thirties perhaps, a diagram of the system as it was then.

"Anna Hofmeier," he repeats, indicating for me to sit down on a chair he's cleared of papers. "Yes, there was an Anna then. I didn't get her pregnant, did I?"

"I . . . don't know."

He slumps down in an armchair right in front of the map, which I can still see on the wall above him. We're in near darkness, though. "Do you mind putting on the light?"

He turns on a lamp by his chair.

"Yes, that's better." I tell him about Anna as I peer over his head, recognizing easily enough the central part of the system, with the S-Bahn of those days forming a complete circle around it. More S-Bahn lines then, but fewer U-Bahn ones, and their tentacles don't spread out so far.

"Said I was going to marry her?" he said. "It's possible. I told most of them that. No one could be accountable for anything then." The loose folds of skin on his face move to form a smile. "Oh yes, there were plenty. All the men were at the front, but I'd been sent home, a hero no less. One lived for the moment before being blown to pieces the next. And I had my moments when I was young. You'd never think it now."

I try to follow the lines on the map behind him. I'm embarrassed by confessions of love affairs. Friedrichstrasse in the middle, Alexanderplatz to the right of it.

The memories make him talkative. "I got one girl pregnant. And now, well the desire's still there, but as for the means to do anything about it . . ." He shakes his head.

65

Is there any way he'd part with the map, which sparkles in the light from the lamp? What a reward for me, I think, for helping a crazy woman.

"So there's one who's alive," he goes on, his eyes shining. "I'd like to meet her. After I got married in 1946, I had to be careful that none of them turned up! My wife's dead though now, and the children don't care. It might give me something to live for again. See if I've any of the old charm left. Anna Hofmeier, you say?"

He rattles on, imagining he's young again, while my eyes follow the line I've now located from Alexanderplatz to Stadtmitte, and then on to where it's now closed through Potsdamer Platz to Gleisdreieck.

"You're looking at my map," he says suddenly. Accusing me? But no, he decides to tell me about that too. "They couldn't trust me to pull a trigger anymore, so they told me to punch tickets instead. I had that map with me on the night of the flood. Can you see the water stains?"

"That's when you last saw Anna," I remember to say.

"So that's the one," he says, smiling again. "Gorgeous red hair, and a figure . . . I thought she'd drowned. Before I even managed to get her into bed with me!" He shakes his head. "Then there were the Russians, the occupation. All one could think of was survival. Now, though, it would be nice to see her."

I remind him: "You were telling me about the map."

"Yes. Well, I was nearly drowned. They say the Führer did it. All those people, I'd never have believed it then. I was a different person, I suppose." He sighs. "But I managed to swim to an exit. Afterwards I found that map in my wallet, and I thought, well, if it had managed to survive with me, perhaps it had brought me luck. So I dried it out and kept it. Later I had it framed. Superstitious maybe, but I feel that as long as nothing happens to it . . ."

Ghost Stations

But I want it! He couldn't know how marvellous it would be for me to have a map like that. "You wouldn't sell it?"

He doesn't hear. "Does Anna still have the same figure, the same red hair? No, of course not."

"I'll give you a hundred marks. Two hundred. West marks."

"I'd like to see her. You tell her that. She can visit me. They can now, from the West." He whispers, confiding, "I've still got the double bed. No fear I'll get her pregnant now, eh? "

It's revolting, I want to shout. Forget her, she's insignificant. Only things are important, reliable. See how the Underground still works, while people you love are either dead or crazy like your Anna? I check my wallet. "Five hundred marks!"

"Or"—he still ignores me—"it might be possible for me to go to the West. They don't care once you're too old to work anymore."

"Look, I'll have to go back to my hotel and change more money, but I can come back tomorrow. A thousand marks."

He waves his hand, understanding my words at last but not what I'm saying. "Tomorrow? Who knows if we'll still be here tomorrow? I don't need money. Just tell Anna to come and see me." Suddenly triumphant, he points to a telephone sitting on a pile of books. "Or she can phone me. It's only a local call, they tell me, from West Berlin to East. It's considered an international one from here." He pulls himself up out of his chair. "I'll get something to write my number on."

He disappears into the bedroom, where I can hear him shuffling. I eye the map. If nothing happens to it, nothing will happen to him, that's what he meant. But that's nonsense, and now I know it's fate that's brought me here. Why else would I do stupid things for a crazy woman on the Underground? Today, I realize gleefully, could be the culminating point of my life, from the days when I was a child and the stations on that

A. Colin Wright

map were real, not the ghosts they are today; from the days when I was secure and happy with my grandmother. Now I've found it at last, all I was searching for, on that wall in front of me. Easily portable under my arm, if the old fool would only sell it. Or perhaps I should just take it. Only how to remove it without him noticing?

He returns with his phone number on a scrap of paper. "Here you are, Herr . . . Even if she's not too well"—he taps his forehead—"get her to call me. Or write. Then she can visit me. It gets so lonely nowadays."

I'd like to help, I really would, if he'd just let me have the map. Things like that don't abandon one. Didn't it save his life in the flood? "Two thousand!" I say.

"Anna Hofmeier," he says, again taking no notice of my words. "Why, little Anna. The one who got away. Well, perhaps I can make up for that."

I can't stand it any longer. "Give it to me!" I shout, pushing by him so that he topples backwards into the chair. I grab the map from the wall. He puts his hands on his head and groans, but he does nothing to stop me. "Here." I take what money there is in my wallet and throw it at him.

"Our Father who art in Heaven . . ." He clasps his hands and starts to babble, which makes me angry. When did a heavenly father ever do more than an earthly one? Then I see he's looking between his fingers at the telephone. I step over him to reach it first and yank the cord out of the wall. Aware now of how much he smells, I push past him to the door, while his gaze follows the map I carry under my arm. Then I rush down the narrow staircase, almost falling in the dark, out onto the street below; stopping only to take the map in both hands, in case it should fall and be forever lost.

The nearest station, quick! To the Friedrichstrasse crossing before he calls for help. (Or Potsdamer Platz will do, where that crazy woman waits.) I consult my map in its handy frame: Heinrich-Heine-Strasse at the

68

Ghost Stations

corner here, then the S-Bahn from Alexanderplatz. But where's the station? I look around. Could my map be wrong? Looking as I walk, I hurry on. I reach the river. Still no station, but on the other side I can already see the S-Bahn overhead. Of course. I check my map. Jannowitzbrücke, and I needn't change. Over the river then, and up the steps. A train comes straightaway. Three stops (time to admire my map again) and out onto the platform at Friedrichstrasse. Down more steps into the street below, to find the modern building—the glass house, I've heard it called, or even house of tears—that conceals the entrance into West Berlin.

The guard compares each detail of my face with the photo in my passport, probing my inner secrets. I hold my map beneath my arm.

"What's that?" he asks.

"My U-Bahn map."

He grunts, returns my passport, and opens the barrier for me to pass. I'm still uncomfortable, walking on. Will they think it suspicious when I hesitate over which corridor to choose?

The S-Bahn overhead, I decide, and I mount more steps to the place I just arrived at, except that now I'm on the other side of the metal dividing wall.

Waiting for a train, I notice a border guard patrolling on a footbridge high in the roof's arched dome, where he can look down on the whole station, both its eastern and western halves. Another guard joins him, bringing the message perhaps about the theft. What if they see me here with the map under my arm? This is still the East, for all the Westerners passing through. Can they stop me now? Cautiously I move behind the refreshment stand and then back into the passage. I'll take the other S-Bahn, which is underground here and out of the view of the guards. And of course—I check my map—I can go straight to Potsdamer Platz, where I'm to meet that crazy woman, little Anna, at the kiosk on the corner.

69

A. Colin Wright

On board the train I feel safer. We rattle sharply round the turn into Unter den Linden—but something's wrong. We're not stopping, yet we always stop! Just an empty platform, lights burning dimly, blocked-off steps leading down from above—and in the controller's booth a figure observing, watching me. I'm carried past. It's another turn to Potsdamer Platz where I'll get out, but—I don't believe it! We only slow and keep on going. And again a deserted platform, except for the figure waiting, watching from the booth in the middle.

Quick, check the map again. Yes, we should have stopped: maps don't tell lies as people do. Look: Friedrichstrasse, Unter den Linden, Potsdamer Platz, and next, Anhalter Station. What if we don't stop there either, going on and on, forever and ever amen?

It was the best day I've had in my life. If only there were more like that to relieve the loneliness, the boredom.

I still carry Kurt's scrap of paper, since I didn't give it to the crazy woman. I considered trying to find her by going back to Friedrichstrasse— I'd really like to help—and waiting at the checkpoint. But that's in East Berlin with their border guards, and they could still notice my map under my arm. And then, I remind myself, it would be useless giving her the number, because Kurt has no phone. I disconnected it before I left. She's crazy anyway. Whoever's going to love a crazy person?

I saw her one more time. I was travelling from north to south, on the ghost line that goes under Alexanderplatz. It's my favourite, I've decided. Bernauer Strasse, Rosenthaler Platz, Weinmeisterstrasse, Alexanderplatz—where there's nothing but the silent observer in his booth to remind me of the interchange station where I once stood overhead. Then Jannowitzbrücke—I could change to the S-Bahn if I could reach it—and Heinrich-Heine-Strasse. She stood by the doors, lamenting each time we passed through a station.

70

Ghost Stations

"Why aren't we stopping? We always stop." At Alexanderplatz, her eyes were full of tears. "That's where I should get out. To find my Kurt."

But I knew better. It was Heinrich-Heine-Strasse she needed, on the corner of Köpenicker Strasse. "Look." I proudly showed her Kurt's map as we rattled through. "Look, there really is a station here, it really does exist. Maps don't lie, you know."

It excites me every time, when I remember how once I couldn't find it. I imagine a darkened room in an inaccessible world above, an old man staring at an empty wall. But why tell her? I doubt if he's alive by now.

I clutch my map more tightly. I take it with me every day (when my parents give me a shilling to get me out of their way), following every station on it as we pass. Not that I need to, for I know each twist and turn in this marvellous underground world. For instance, the U-Bahn line: Stadtmitte, Französische Strasse, Oranienburger Tor, the Stettin Station (some people call it North)—shall I go on? Would you like me to list the S-Bahn too?

The main-line trains run on the S-Bahn tracks as well, on parallel tracks, that is. With *Deutsche Reichsbahn*, German Imperial Railways, painted on their side, left like that as though it were still the thirties. Other trains run right through East Germany to the normal world again. Passengers get on at Friedrichstrasse or at the Zoo Station in the West. You used to be able to watch the guards crawling beneath, clambering on the roofs, checking through the trains. I'm expanding my collection to the main lines, too, you see. One shouldn't become too limited, that's what I always say.

I'd like to take a train like that, when I finally leave Berlin. When I'm satisfied they're not looking for me anymore. But for now I must be careful in case they see my map. I can't risk that. What would I ever do without my map?

Unknown

He cried on the day the *General Belgrano* was sunk. We do not know his name for, although history is often made of tears, the shedding of them rarely finds its way into books. For all we know he was one of many. There may even have been others like him among the junior officers of the *HMS Sheffield*. At all events, we may guess that there was little rejoicing aboard. Officers and men alike, for whom this uncomfortable mass of steel was as much a home as the houses and flats in Portsmouth that they sometimes returned to, could feel only a sombre sympathy for their unknown—if apparently now enemy—comrades. All of them could imagine, and yet not imagine, what it must be like.

He cried that day, though, more for the loss of the ship than for the lives. For life, as we know, is cheap and people die all the time, while a ship is a more permanent, historic symbol of the dreams of glory we all have. The Argentinians, he had heard, loved that ship; it was part of their national pride. It seemed wrong to rob anyone of that, and he hadn't thought the British would do it. Two weeks earlier he had regretted that the *Sheffield* had not been in port to sail with the main fleet, so that he could experience the emotion of the occasion, with the crews lined up on deck and the cheering crowds on the dockside. Now he no longer minded: suddenly the fervour, the patriotism, the emotion had turned into a cold struggle with the sea and lurking enemies. Trying to picture

Unknown

the *Belgrano* going down, he felt almost the same as if it had been a British ship. He lay in his bunk, tears streaming down his face. He didn't know any Argentinians and didn't doubt that Britain was in the right, but if the Prime Minister had asked him, he would have handled it differently. She hadn't, and so he was on his way to shoot at people who, oppressed as they were by their leadership, like anyone else saw their lives made more cheerful by the sudden fulfilment of the national aspirations they had been brought up with.

Perhaps it wasn't entirely true, though, that he didn't know the Argentinians, whom he could picture leading ordinary lives far over that changeless horizon to the northwest. At least he knew about them. He was probably the only one on board the *Sheffield* who knew who General Belgrano actually was. To the others, and to most of those in Britain too, he was just some unknown Argentinian general who had happened to give his name to an aging battlecruiser now at the bottom of the Atlantic. By one of life's odd coincidences, six months earlier, just before sailing, he had embarked on a reading of Borges. A collection of Borges's stories was with him in his locker, underneath his own manuscript. And General Belgrano had been a friend of Borges's great-great-uncle Juan Crisóstomo Lafinur, a poet who had written an ode on Belgrano's death in 1820.

He swung his legs down off his bunk and opened the drawer. Put his hand down—lingering a little to touch with pride the three hundred or so pages he had produced—and took out the collection of Borges's stories to check out the information on his biography. General Manuel Belgrano, whose first military experience had been fighting the English in 1806, during their invasion of the Vice-Royalty of La Plata. Principal leader in the Argentinian war for independence, member of the junta after the break with Spain, victor of the battles of Tucumán and Salta. Argentinian national hero, but unknown to the British.

Unknown. As he himself was still unknown. That thought was a continuing source of anguish to him during these too-long years at sea. It would change, but he was weary of waiting. He had a deep faith

A. Colin Wright

in his destiny, deeper than ever after the years of rejection slips that still kept accumulating. Three years at university, another three so far in the navy—which undoubtedly slowed things down, since he could only get manuscripts into the mail during his leaves. Each time he went home and found a whole pile of large brown envelopes waiting for him, and never the longed-for white one with an acceptance, had finally become like a promise of success for the future, for he knew that to become a writer one had to build up endurance. To do something well one had to persevere, accept the disappointments, become reconciled to the fact that no one knew how good you were and what great things you were going to accomplish.

And yet, he thought, if I could have one wish, which would it be: to become a great writer or to raise the *Belgrano* again and stop the possibility of a stupid war? Is what I'm writing about that important, compared with the possibilities of destruction? Thank God that in life one isn't called upon to make that kind of choice. One had only to make the minor decisions—such as whether to take a short-term commission in the navy to earn some money to live on afterwards. All he needed was time. A few more years: just get through this Falklands business, and then return to the normal tasks at sea from which his ship had been diverted, and which at least let him do some writing. Then, after this endless period of waiting, he'd be able to get on with what he was really meant to do in life.

Still holding Borges with one hand, he again touched his novel with the other. Since November he had managed to make many of the final corrections, although he would not have brought it with him at all if he had thought there was a possibility of seeing action. At least, though, he should be able to finish it on the way back. If things went well.

He had no desire to fight, and wondered what he was doing here. What, he thought, turning again to the collection of stories, would Borges have felt about the present idiocy? Would a man who knew England and loved English literature have been one of those jumping around on the Plaza de Mayo shouting in jingoistic fervour "*Los que no saltan son ingleses*"? He thought not, hoped not. Any more than he himself could have read

74

Unknown

without nausea the chauvinistic filth that was apparently now being printed in certain English newspapers. He had seen television pictures of ordinary Argentinians indignant at English aggression, of ordinary Englishmen indignant at the Argentinians and, although he knew where his sympathies lay, they both seemed oddly the same. All wanting something from outside themselves to seize their interest, the consoling thought that brought no tangible advantage except to relieve their boredom: like the little pieces of good news from home, which for him could somehow make bearable the endless monotony of the sea.

I am, he told himself, profoundly depressed. It was odd to read of the gauchos on the pampas, of the roughs of the Buenos Aires suburbs, even of the questioning intellectuals, and to know he might have to shoot at people such as these. That, in fact, some had already died with a ship bearing the name of a national hero. He had turned to Borges more from a sense of duty than from inclination. It was his mother who had persuaded him to read one of the greatest innovators in fiction. But experimentation for its own sake did not interest him, and his novel—that would finally make him famous and now lay, almost complete, in the drawer beside him—was written in the traditional linear manner. Some modern writing left him wondering whether it wasn't just a game, an exercise for Ph.D. candidates to unravel. He had started on Borges expecting perhaps the shifting viewpoints of a Robbe-Grillet, expecting struggles to keep his mind from wandering. Instead, he had found a disarming clarity, a directness of narration combined with a metaphysical questioning of life. And of death and violence. Of human stupidity as well as human nobility.

And, above all, of inevitability. Perhaps that was why he cried: the sinking of the *Belgrano* suggested the inevitability of more to come. He got up, wiped his eyes. It was time to go on duty. To somehow cope with that inevitability.

* * *

A. Colin Wright

By now the reader may be feeling that this is all rather abstract, lacking the tangible details of life on a British destroyer. The motion of the sea, the naval routine, the underlying anxiety they all must have felt. But I have never been aboard the *Sheffield* and, as you know already, never shall. I cannot recreate those last few hours, nor is it my purpose to do so. We know what happened, and that is enough. We have been talking simply of an unknown junior officer on a mission that, at that date, was still not seen as war, which everyone wanted to believe would somehow be prevented. Some commentators even suggested that after the sinking of the *Sheffield*, with each side having lost just one ship, negotiations might become easier.

We have then one unknown officer who will be remembered only by a mother who loved reading and encouraged him to write. And by a girl, of course, whom we haven't mentioned. Who, in later years, will sometimes look at a husband and children and think how strange life is, when it all could have been entirely different for her, had the aspiring writer she first loved not made the apparently minor decision to apply for a short-term commission in the Royal Navy. He achieved, of course, nothing: nothing of what he wanted to achieve. But let it at least be recorded that he shed tears at the sinking of a not really enemy ship named after a general he knew about because his desire to write had led him to read an Argentinian poet and short story writer called Jorge Luis Borges.

He shed tears before he knew that his own ship would be destroyed: tears for the gauchos and the roughs of the Buenos Aires suburbs he had never seen, as much as for the Portsmouth dockyard workers he had.

We do not know his thoughts as he looked over the shoulder of a rating in front of a radar screen and understood what that blip of light approaching far too rapidly must be. Or perhaps it didn't happen that way. Perhaps he was on deck and caught in his binoculars a flash of light as something horrible skimmed over the surface of the waves. We do not even know if he had time to think of Borges's theory that a whole lifetime leads towards that one moment when a man finds out, once and for all, who he is.

The burned-out hull of the *Sheffield* remained afloat for some time. Impossible though it may be, I imagine that somewhere amongst the ashes of a smouldering locker were the charred remains of an unknown manuscript by an unknown author. Probably a very ordinary novel, perhaps not even publishable. We shall never know if it might, just possibly, have been a book that could change an apparently unchangeable world.

Only Fair

Before Bob left on the *Franconia* for Europe, he put his favourite photo of Marie in his wallet—determined that, no matter what other girls he met, it would stay there, and he would tell them who she was if they asked him. It was only fair. To have a good time if the opportunity presented itself was one thing, but to deny that there was a girl waiting for him in Canada, whom he would almost certainly marry on his return, would be spiritual treachery.

As the huge ship steamed past the shimmering grey of the Gaspé Peninsula—where Marie would be standing at the window of her father's crumbling farmhouse—Bob told himself there were many reasons why he loved her. He waved nostalgically at the shoreline, half listening to a couple of French tourists who were leaning over the rail and speaking the clear, precise language of Paris that seemed the epitome of elegance after the harsh, nasal tones of the Gaspésie. He reflected that it was perhaps just as well that Marie wasn't coming with him. She would surely resent Europe, not understanding the more liberal social customs that had been described to him. He needed his freedom to truly appreciate the exciting, different world that awaited him. He and Marie couldn't have travelled together anyway: her father, with his hostility towards all English Canadians and towards Bob in particular, would have seen to that. *"Le mariage, d'abord le mariage!* Marriage first, then you can travel."

Only Fair

Bob glanced round guiltily at some of the girls already stretched out on the sun deck in their bikinis. One with long blonde hair—Marie's was brown—smiled at him, and he turned away to continue observing the monotonous shoreline. In the past he hadn't been without his conquests, even if few of them had been really exciting, unlike those his friends at McGill had told him about. There hadn't been many girls in his physics courses, and the one glamorous one had been crazy over a football player. Bob had got on better with the ordinary ones. Well, there was nothing wrong with that. There were some he liked very much: they were pleasant and fun to be with. But then, on holiday in the Gaspé, he'd met Marie working in a library, and she was most attractive in her shy, unostentatious way. They'd become quite devoted to each other, and she'd hinted that she'd make him a good wife. He knew it was true. And now he loved her: that made all the difference.

The blonde girl, he noticed, was still staring at him, and he smiled back, trying to picture her without the bikini. He would like to have slept with Marie, of course, but it had been out of the question before marriage. Still, she had quite a figure too. She loved cuddling up to him and several times had kissed him with remarkable passion. So when, in the days that followed, he didn't manage to get very far with the blonde girl, he put it down to his lack of enthusiasm and told himself that Marie would be waiting for him when he got back.

"You see," he told the barman in one of his confiding moods, "I love her, honest to God I do. But you know what it's like. I'll be in Europe a whole year. How can I be faithful all that time? Look at the experiences I might be missing."

The barman only laughed and told him how he managed very nicely with a wife in Southampton and a mistress in Montreal.

"Yes," Bob interrupted him, a little unsteady on his feet as the ship rocked beneath him. "But I believe in sincerity, and so does she. It's only fair. It's just that she wouldn't understand my going with anyone else. If I

A. Colin Wright

wrote and told her, there'd be no hope of marrying her. So I'll have to keep quiet about it. But I'll tell her about it when I get back. There'd never be any trust between us if I didn't."

The barman laughed again. "Not much point worrying about it, sir, is there? Not until you've actually *been* unfaithful to her."

Europe lived up to Bob's expectations. He'd left during the summer so he could have a month's touring before term started at London University, where he was to do a year's graduate work. He visited Germany, Italy, and Spain, and in his letters to Marie he was able to say with perfect sincerity that he missed her and there was no one else. He sent her postcards from every town he stayed in, hoping he might interest her in travelling with him someday.

"It must be fascinating to see all those foreign places," she wrote back to him in London. "I'm sure they'll make you appreciate your home in *La Belle Province* even more when you return."

Life in London wasn't the long round of fun and pleasure Bob had imagined, but there was a lot more happening than in Quebec. The theatres were good and comparatively cheap; there were more concerts and exhibitions; and, above all, a feeling of broad culture quite different from the restrictive local one he was used to. And in different moods he could always go to a club in Soho where the girls stripped quite naked and performed far more erotically than in Montreal or Toronto. After such occasions he would go back to his dreary room, with its flowered wallpaper and sagging bed, and imagine making love to Marie—although, since she had never undressed before him or tried to arouse him in same way, he usually ended up visualizing one of the strippers instead.

Why was it, he thought rather guiltily, that the mere sight of pointing breasts, of silky hair revealing two pouting lips of flesh, should be so inexpressibly beautiful, causing a pang of longing not only in himself

Only Fair

but, evidently, in the other men in the audience too? And why was it that such longings couldn't be spoken of publicly, without instant condemnation from people such as Marie's parents? He was aware of a certain bond between him and the strippers. He would sit hoping to catch their eye, expressing his open adoration; and sometimes they would see him and in their further provocative gestures indicate that he'd given them pleasure too. Marie wouldn't be able to understand that.

It wasn't until November that he was actually unfaithful to her, in a minor sense—for although he and the girl, Jill, would fondle each other until they climaxed, they never went the whole way.

She saw the photo, of course, and he told her who it was when she asked him.

"And will you tell her what we do together?" Jill asked.

"Yes," he said. "When I get home. It's only fair, don't you think?"

She looked at him strangely.

"Perhaps I won't tell her," he said, reconsidering.

It seemed too trivial to make an issue of and, in any case, Jill soon left London to go north. He just hoped that Marie wouldn't notice how his letters had been getting shorter and less frequent, while she continued to write that she missed him dreadfully. "It's wonderful to hear from you and know you are still thinking of me and loving me."

"Bob," he said to himself as he read that, "you're a louse." And he reluctantly decided to phone the date he'd got himself for that evening and tell her that he was sick and couldn't make it.

Fortunately, there was no answer. He couldn't get in touch with her and he could hardly leave her waiting on the steps of the National Gallery, where they'd arranged to meet. For Merle proved to be one of the hottest girls he'd ever known, and she surprised him in his room that night with the urgency with which she pulled off his clothes.

A. Colin Wright

"You're very naïve," she said as they rested afterwards in bed, "if you think girls don't want it too."

"It's just that those I've met . . ."

Merle, however, had two other regular boyfriends and told him she couldn't see him again because her fiancé was returning from abroad.

The next day, tired and despondent from the night before, Bob sat down to reply to Marie's letter. He was aware that spiritually she meant everything to him, for he loved her, whereas Merle had been only an exciting distraction. But again his mental image of Marie began to fade as he remembered Merle lying on top of him, her full breasts swinging in his face as she bounced up and down to a climax. He took out the photo to remind himself of Marie's calm beauty, the seriousness in her eyes, and kissed it gently to ask her forgiveness.

For a while after that he didn't meet any girls he wanted to take out, and he thought lovingly of the girl he'd left in Canada. He began to imagine the comforts of married life, with mutual devotion and a home of their own substituting for his drive to travel and seek new experiences. It was, he told himself, time to settle down, and if he couldn't imagine a life of passion with Marie, this would surely become less important after marriage. On those occasions when he felt in need of relief from his books, he'd go to the strip club again, sitting with the respectable businessmen dropping in to pay furtive homage to the animal principle on their way home from the office.

By the beginning of May he realized his year in Europe was almost over. Term ended in June, after which he was to spend four weeks in France and depart directly from Le Havre on a ship for Quebec City. From there he would travel to the Gaspé to see Marie before returning to Montreal. Then he'd have to decide for sure whether to marry her, and have the whole thing out with her father. The remaining months were little enough

82

Only Fair

time for him to continue a relatively carefree existence before he thought seriously of career and family.

Perhaps it was this thought that caused his attraction to Patsy. He'd known her for a long time—she was a chemistry undergraduate, renowned chiefly for the fact that her experiments invariably went wrong. If there was the smallest possibility of an explosion in the lab, it was Patsy who caused it. If she broke a test tube (as happened almost daily), more often than not it contained some corrosive material that she would shower over someone else's books—or her own, for she was quite indiscriminate. Indeed, she would have been pretty, except her forehead was marred from an acid burn she had acquired through getting two bottles muddled. But Bob had never really taken much notice of her until the night after she missed his party.

He'd just got out his books when he heard a frantic knocking at the downstairs door, and there was Patsy.

"I'm awfully sorry for being so late," she burst out breathlessly. "I would have been here an hour ago, I really would, but I was halfway here and I fell off my bicycle—I know it was a silly thing to do, but I'm like that—and it was so muddy I just couldn't come in that dress, and I grazed my knee, so I had to go home and change and wash . . ." She paused, panting. "But where *is* everybody?"

"The party was last night."

"Oh no!" Her mouth fell open. "I'm always doing things like that. Hell! Oh, I'm sorry."

Laughing, he invited her in.

"I'll leave if you want." She came in, apologizing all the way up the narrow staircase to his room, while her raincoat dripped water and smeared mud on the walls.

"Here, have some coffee."

A. Colin Wright

"Oh look, let *me* get it, while you get on with your work!"

Bob had never thought it possible for anyone to ruin instant coffee, but Patsy managed it, and he started looking at her with new eyes.

In herself, Patsy wasn't at all sexy. Life with her just became crazy and exciting because you never knew what she was going to do next. It was amusing, but it could also be annoying, because she'd never remember where they were to meet. Or she'd get on the wrong bus and end up twenty miles away on the other side of London without any money to get back. When they finally started sleeping together, nothing could have been less romantic. It was one glorious romp that would have driven the textbook writers to celibacy, for everything was done wrong. Bedclothes became tied in knots, they'd find themselves in all positions except the recommended ones, and spend most of the night in shrieks of laughter. They never once achieved a climax at the same time, and it was marvellous.

Patsy, of course, knew about Marie and was jealous. And although Bob wrote as dutifully as ever, repeating words of love that he knew, if he considered them, were true, he thought very little now about Marie. He was too involved in his enthusiasm for this scatterbrained girl.

"Do you love me, Bob?"

"Yes, madly!" Said in fun, but with truth in it.

"Oh, that's super!"

"Darling Bob, chéri," Marie wrote, "I can't wait for your return to Canada. I shall be looking out for the ship as it passes our Gaspé Peninsula on its way to Quebec. Will you be on deck as it goes by?"

"Darling Marie. Thank you for your last letter. I too am looking forward to seeing you again. I am writing this in haste, as I'm just going out, so I'll try to answer your questions very quickly. The ship arrives in Quebec in the early morning, so it will pass the Gaspé sometime the previous evening . . ."

84

Only Fair

Patsy: "How can you say you feel for me when you're going to marry *her*?"

"It's true." A quick kiss. "I can't explain."

"I hate her!" Said in fun, with no malice. "Hate her, hate her!"

Bob left for France knowing he'd miss Patsy—although he was to see her once more, since his ship home from Le Havre would stop for twenty-four hours in Southampton before heading out into the Atlantic, and she'd promised to come down from London for a last day and night together.

He'd intended to travel in France, but ended up spending most of his time in Paris. Above all he enjoyed the river, with its stately bridges, the quays one could walk along, and the calm splendour of Notre Dame on one of its two islands. But he loved the rest too: the jumbled streets of the Latin Quarter and of Montmartre, with their bars and cafés, contrasting with the huge department stores and the elegance of the Champs-Élysées. Here at last was a kind of culture that surpassed even that of London. The Gallic temperament gave the city a vivacity, a charm, that he saw his own Montreal was striving towards with little chance of being able to attain. He felt that, without realizing it, he'd been living in the provinces rather than at the centre of the world. And yet Paris, the proud capital of Europe, was still modest compared with the garishness and empty vulgarity of American cities.

He wrote a couple of enthusiastic letters describing it all to Marie, who in her replies talked only of her ecstatic happiness at their coming reunion.

He was uneasy now, wondering how he would manage to tell her about his relationship with Patsy. It might create difficulties between them after all; there'd probably be an awkward period before everything was back to normal. True, he told himself, it was Marie he loved and, when he

A. Colin Wright

saw her again, he'd surely forget this absurd enthusiasm for the other girl. The time with Patsy would remain no more than a pleasant memory, except that naturally he was still looking forward to seeing her in Southampton. Here in Paris, at least, he could rest his emotions. Then there'd be one more glorious day with Patsy, followed by seven whole days on the ship in which to forget her and prepare his mind for loving Marie again.

So when he went on board at Le Havre—enjoying the unfamiliar prospect of a luxury world at sea, complete in itself, for more than a week—he determined just to relax and make no attempt to meet any of the girls amongst the passengers. The first part of the voyage, across the English Channel, belonged to Patsy; the longer part on the North Atlantic to Marie. The only girls he even spoke to were the three seated at his table in the dining room: all French, one about his own age with long dark hair, and two giggling younger ones.

The next morning he was one of the first on deck as the ship steamed slowly between the green banks of Southampton Water towards the towering gantries of the port. He leaned eagerly over the wooden rail, scanning the waving crowds on the dockside for his first glimpse of Patsy.

She wasn't there.

He checked the radio office for any messages and then, when they were allowed to disembark, scanned all the notice boards. Only then did he realize that he hadn't even her address or phone number in London, since at the end of term she'd forgotten to renew the lease on her apartment and had to start looking for somewhere else. Of course she might be late. He spent part of the day on the dockside in case she turned up, and the rest on board ship—unable to turn his mind to anything else because of his frustration at not being able to contact her.

There was still no sign of Patsy as the tugs began pulling the ship away from the dreary dockside the next morning.

86

Only Fair

"It doesn't make any difference," he consoled himself, kicking at the railings as he turned to walk along the deck. "I don't love her as I do Marie."

But at a deeper level he understood that such moments of lost opportunity, however small their ultimate significance, had always had for him the essence of tragedy. And now there would be emptiness, seven days of boredom until they reached Quebec. What a waste, he thought, of this luxury liner, with its panelled lounges, its glassed-in promenade deck, its outdoor pool that soon would be splashing and sparkling in the sun.

He pulled open the heavy metal door into the main foyer. "Damn!" he muttered to himself as he walked down the curving grand stairway to the restaurant. "Why should I make myself miserable? Why not make the most of what time there's left? Don't I have the *right* to enjoy myself after this?"

Finding himself alone for breakfast with the dark-haired French girl, he immediately started a conversation.

Her name was Catherine, and until then he'd known only that she was from Paris. Now she told him she was going to New York for six weeks to arrange for an exhibition of French paintings, but she was stopping first in Montreal to visit an uncle.

"You're travelling alone?" he asked.

She seemed surprised. "Yes. I'm used to travel." She hesitated. "I work in the French Ministry of Culture. The Fine Arts section. Organizing exhibitions and exchanges."

He looked at her with respect. "Where else have you been?"

"Oh, most of Western Europe. I've never been to America before, though. It will be an exciting new experience."

A. Colin Wright

Marie, he reflected, had only once been outside Quebec.

In an obvious attempt to be pleasant, Catherine asked about him too. He answered a little evasively, feeling that his own life, except for this last year, was mundane enough. Instead, he encouraged her to tell him more about herself. As she spoke, he was aware that she wasn't really what he would call beautiful, for indeed there was something in her face that was a little severe, as though she were constantly judging what she saw. But she had an expression of intelligence, and eyes that were both full of life and infinitely sad.

"You must be an artist yourself," he interrupted her as she started to talk of the Impressionist paintings she adored.

"No. I paint a little for fun, that's all. I just love everything connected with art. I'm very fortunate in my work."

They were joined by the two younger girls, who were talking excitedly about a couple of men they'd met the night before. Catherine joined in with them, teasing them, showing she could be as light-hearted as they were—and yet somehow remaining aloof, as if she had problems of her own. Perhaps it was the way she would laugh and then look at him questioningly, as though to ask whether life really consisted only of parties, clothes, and being a giddy success with the opposite sex. Bob frankly admired her, noticing how even with these two girls—with whom she clearly had little in common—she made the effort to adapt and show interest in them. Her self-assurance suggested that she was probably a little older than he was, and he noticed she had a nervous habit of occasionally patting her long hair where it fell around her shoulders. He found himself thinking of her as someone it would be difficult to get to know well.

They spent the morning together, lying on the deck by the pool, feeling the throbbing of the ship's engines beneath them and gazing contentedly at the sky as the swimmers shrieked in the background. They talked lazily, interrupted sometimes by water splashing onto them. Yet he

Only Fair

sensed in her a certain reserve, which made any idea of romance at once more attractive and infinitely remote.

As they were finishing lunch in the restaurant, a waiter came to tell him there was a telegram for him, and he went to the radio office after arranging to meet Catherine for coffee.

It was from Southampton: "TERRIBLY SORRY THOUGHT YESTERDAY WAS TUESDAY EVERYTHING AWFUL LOVE YOU PATSY".

He chuckled, felt a moment's genuine sadness, and then joined Catherine in the lounge.

"Anything wrong?"

He found it easy to tell her about Patsy, and about Marie. He showed her the photo and confessed how he was dreading the thought of telling Marie he'd been unfaithful.

"You seem to have had quite a time during this past year," Catherine said, teasing him. She went on more seriously: "These things are difficult. You can't always think of others in such situations. Love can never become a duty, or it's no longer love. You have to accept your fate and be responsible for it."

"Fate?"

"Accept life and do what you must, without regretting it. That's what I mean."

She told him more about herself: how she'd suffered through falling in love, through her own loneliness, and through her own demands on life. "I put all I have into trying to live a full life, and all I get out of it is suffering." Then she corrected herself. "No, I've had wonderful times, too, while they lasted."

He looked at her with a certain fear, realizing he'd been wrong and that there were, after all, tremendous possibilities for understanding.

For the days at sea, they were together most of the time. Bob found that they were able to talk to each other in a way that almost made them old friends. She spoke of her problems, brought about by her love of travel and her independent mind, which conflicted with a deep desire for marriage and a family. "But by the time I'm willing to give up my independence and settle down, men probably won't find me interesting anymore."

Her frankness surprised him. "I'd like to travel too," he said, "to see the world, to . . . experience life, if you understand me."

"Can't you travel with Marie?"

He hesitated. "I guess so."

She spoke of Paris too. "It's the only place I could ever live permanently. I'm a product of Paris, I suppose. And because Paris is the world for me, almost life itself, there's no contradiction in my travelling and being away from it for long periods."

She liked him, Bob was sure. It surprised him, for he still believed she was out of his reach. She often travelled and was part of the cultured life of Europe. Yet she listened to him and took notice of his opinions, as though it wouldn't occur to her to consider him a provincial from Quebec who'd only just begun to explore the wider world. Here, in the social life on board ship, she was sought after by other men and she would flirt with them with open enjoyment. But if Bob didn't join her, she'd come to look for him and reproach him for leaving her. On one occasion, when she had some ironing to do, he asked her jokingly if she'd like to do some shirts for him, and she took him seriously and ironed them.

Lying in his bunk at night, looking at the mysterious dark shapes of this unknown world—the porthole with its huge bolts, the metal walls, the little nozzles of fire extinguishers in the ceiling—he would think of

Only Fair

Catherine and tell himself that she represented his ideal of femininity. He couldn't really define it. It was as though, conscious of being a woman and intellectually superior to many men, she guarded her femininity by holding it in check. The only thing she had in common with Marie was her deep desire for love and affection.

"But that's a desire I doubt if I'll ever achieve," she told him. "I have too few illusions, I suppose. And then love between a man and a woman . . . Well, you can't order it at will. Love's a gift, from God if you want to think of it that way, and you only receive it unexpectedly."

On the fifth night after leaving Southampton he tried to kiss her, as they walked by themselves on the darkened deck. She laughed, dodged out of his way and, when he persisted, said she didn't play with romance. So they went back to the main lounge and danced. But later they went outside again and, finding that the wooden paddles and disks hadn't been put away, they played shuffleboard with the laughing agreement that he should kiss her if he won. And so he kissed her, and she responded by putting her arms around him and drawing him to her, darting her tongue into his mouth and pressing herself against him. When they said goodnight she admitted that she'd lost the game deliberately.

The next day was their last on the open sea, for in the early evening the ship passed through the Strait of Belle Isle between the tip of Newfoundland and the rocky coast of Labrador, and then into the wide expanses of the Gulf of St. Lawrence. That night he and Catherine kissed more freely, and she was frivolous, joking, as though to contradict her words about not playing with romance. But somehow there was no contradiction. She became more serious when he suggested they go down to his cabin, and asked to dance again instead.

As the ship's band played sentimental late-night music, they held each other without speaking, both of them saddened by their knowledge that the voyage was almost over. When he said goodnight this time, she shook her head without saying anything, and he suspected that she'd been

A. Colin Wright

crying. After another morning in the Gulf, Bob had learned, followed by an afternoon spent passing Anticosti Island, they'd be into the St. Lawrence River. He knew that the next night he'd have to be on deck, as he'd promised, since Marie would be looking out for the lights of the ship from her home on the Gaspé.

After breakfast the next morning, Bob dutifully went to the radio office and sent her a telegram to say they'd be passing at about 10:30 that evening; then he went to join Catherine on the sun deck again. The ship was heaving its way through the rough waters of the Gulf—they were almost out of sight of land again—and Catherine was feeling sick, so he spent much of the time trying to comfort her. But in the afternoon, once they'd reached the sheltered passage between Anticosti and the mainland, the seas became calmer and she felt better. They said very little, just lying face down on their towels, shoulder to shoulder in the sun. When he started to caress her, unobserved by other passengers, she didn't stop him and, as his fingers ran along the top of her swimsuit, she lifted herself up slightly so he could slip them inside and take her breast. She gave a little sigh of contentment and closed her eyes.

Later they had tea together. "So tomorrow you'll be leaving," she said. She tried to tease him. "And this time tomorrow you'll be with Marie."

He joked about it as well, looking with quiet despair at the dark green shores not far away from the ship.

Somehow he knew that Catherine would come to his cabin that night; that she accepted he was probably going to marry someone else and would make no demands on him.

In the evening she accompanied him in his vigil on deck, among the other passengers looking wistfully at the lights on the familiar Canadian shore. It was about eleven o'clock before they came to the Gaspé, for the heavy sea had delayed them, and then they stood for a long time watching the glinting lights of the houses on the peninsula. Bob imagined Marie

Only Fair

somewhere in the darkness: Marie loving him, looking eagerly for the ship, thinking of his arrival the next day. But the lights of the villages all looked the same, and it was impossible to tell exactly where she'd be. She seemed unreal.

He put his arm around Catherine, who said nothing, understanding and respecting his silence. He knew that, even if he confessed to Marie about Patsy, there was no way he could ever tell her about his betrayal on this last night.

They went down to his cabin. Still a little in awe of Catherine, he half-expected her only to lie down with him and let him caress her as he had that afternoon, but after she'd turned out the lights, she allowed him to undress her and helped him with his own clothes. In the darkness he could only make out the silhouette of her body before she came to him. When they made love, her hair hung around her shoulders and across her breasts, and Bob found the woman he had unconsciously been seeking for so many years.

"Men have always liked me," she said sadly. "I've known what it is to love. But there's always been something wrong."

He begged her to stay with him for the whole night, but she refused.

"You've got to sleep, prepare yourself to meet Marie tomorrow."

They said goodbye while still on the ship, moored in the bright morning light at the long quayside below the Plains of Abraham. "Where the English conquered the French," Catherine said, trying to joke. He kissed her again, but for the first time they had nothing to say to each other. Nothing, at least, that could be said in a few hurried minutes before they parted. That evening he'd be in the Gaspé with Marie. Catherine would be at her uncle's in Montreal, and he couldn't be sure that he loved her yet.

93

A. Colin Wright

On the creaking train, larger and slower than those in Europe, with its constant ominous hooting, he took out the photo of Marie he'd kept faithfully in his wallet for a year. He was weary now, but he told himself he still loved her. It would be all right once he saw her again, heard her voice with that quaint, nasal Gaspesian accent. He must allow time for their love to develop again; he must give it a fair chance.

But if it happened to go wrong, would it be in time for him to find Catherine in New York?

Wedding

I was to get married the next day. At twenty-four, I had just secured a tenure-track position at the University, and Elaine would soon article as a lawyer. Young enough, we told each other, to get a good start in our respective careers before having to devote our energies to raising children—which we both wanted to do, eventually.

The wedding rehearsal had gone without a hitch and, secure in the expectation of a memorable ceremony the next day, I departed for the Faculty Club with my best man, Charles Thompson, and some other friends and colleagues. Not for me the traditional bachelors' party!—for I loved Elaine and had no desire to start my marriage with some sordid sexual escapade. As we relaxed in the bar with its large round tables and framed photographs of the University on its walls, I allowed myself to speak modestly of my future plans, with little doubt that if I worked hard enough I'd be looking at tenure in a few years' time. Every so often some other member of the Club would come over to congratulate me, adding to my pleasurable anticipation of what the next day would bring.

One of them was Harry Jespersen, Head of the Comparative Literature Department, a large, wheezing older man close to retirement, who lumbered over just as the party was about to break up. He'd been divorced many years before and spent a lot of time at the Club. In one previous conversation I'd learned only that he'd started his academic career

95

A. Colin Wright

late, in the days when you could still get a university position without a doctorate. Charlie, it seemed, knew him better, for they often had lunch together. When I suggested that the three of us should stay for a final drink, Harry readily agreed.

As Charlie and I started reminiscing over our days in graduate school, Harry followed our conversation with interest.

"I was never in graduate school myself," he said finally. "But then, I had a different kind of training that was certainly as valuable. I was a policeman, you see." He paused before adding: "I made it as far as detective sergeant before I decided to quit."

"What better for an understanding of literature?" Charlie said with a touch of irony.

"Except that some of my colleagues consider me old-fashioned for trying to relate literature to life, rather than only talking about its form."

"What made you turn to a university career?" I asked.

"Now that's the big question." He twirled his brandy round in his glass and sighed. "I loved the police force, actually. Only . . . I always wanted to understand more than was required of me. I got *involved*, which was the greatest offence there was. The others all thought I was odd, and they were right: I didn't have a policeman's detachment."

His voice had the trick of breaking on him in the middle, and his students said that when he was lecturing on Greek tragedy he'd sometimes become almost tearful. There seemed to be a danger of this happening now.

"So you took up literature as a way of understanding it all?" I asked.

"Funny, I never thought of it like that. Perhaps it was in order to understand one particular incident."

Charlie leaned forward, encouraging him to tell us about it.

96

Wedding

"Well, I'd been a detective sergeant for about six months. And of course I'd discovered that for many people life was very different from the respectable type of behaviour I knew in my own family, which was solidly middle-class. I never quite got used to the violence, or to dead bodies and the kind of crude humour my colleagues used as their way of coping with death and ugliness. This particular incident was a double suicide. A suicide pact, as it turned out." He paused, and it was true, tears were beginning to form in his eyes.

I first assumed he was talking of an older couple—a husband with an incurable disease, perhaps, and a wife who didn't want to live without him—but I was wrong.

"It was a death of extraordinary beauty," Harry went on, staring into his glass. "A young boy and a girl hardly into their twenties."

Why was my mind so quick to seize now on the cliché of a modern Romeo and Juliet, preferring death to separation? I was wrong on that count too.

"The girl was at college, and was renting a room with an ordinary family. In a good neighbourhood too. It caused quite a scandal. We arrived less than twenty minutes after it happened. The landlady had gone in to ask the girl about something quite unimportant."

"So if she'd gone in earlier, it might not have happened at all?" Charlie interrupted.

"I suspect they'd only have done it on another occasion. Anyway, it would certainly have been uglier if we hadn't arrived so quickly. Dead bodies aren't usually a pretty sight." He paused, recalling: "A typical student's room, table, bookcases, a few chairs, and a bed in the corner with the covers thrown back. The two of them were lying on top of it, naked in each other's arms, for all the world as though they'd fallen asleep after making love. Side by side, still hugging each other, their mouths almost touching. The autopsy revealed that they had indeed made love

97

A. Colin Wright

immediately before, but their faces . . . well, the only way I can describe it is that they retained an expression . . . of lust, of sheer sensual desire for each other. There was this muscular, well-built young man embracing a voluptuous fair-haired girl in the prime of her youth, with a body that I could have gone crazy over myself. Full breasts, a tight little behind, and her leg was thrown over his, so you could see absolutely everything. Well, I was young then, I'd never seen anything so beautiful. Their clothes had been dropped beside the bed as though they could hardly wait"—he paused, self-consciously—"to screw each other." He repeated: "God, was it beautiful! In other circumstances it would have driven me crazy just to see them like that. I couldn't believe they were dead, so beautifully and so arrogantly, deliberately mocking their surroundings: the comfortable middle-class house, their understanding landlady."

Harry Jespersen, I thought: elderly, respectable professor of literature, whom I would only have described as conventional.

He went on. "They hadn't even locked the door, as though they wanted to be found like that."

"They'd taken sleeping pills?"

Harry shook his head. "Because of the way they were lying, you couldn't see the blood until you went right up to them. And there was plenty, only it had run down between them and soaked into the bed. They each had an arm around the other, and in their other hands they held identical knives."

"But that's horrible," I said.

"Somehow it didn't seem that way."

We were silent. Harry was right: it was an affront to all normal people.

"But *why?*"

Wedding

"There wasn't a logical reason. They were both intelligent—he was a musician—and without any problems we could discover. Their parents adored them. No psychological difficulties. They were crazy about each other, according to their friends. They hadn't known each other long, and she wasn't pregnant or anything like that. Their death was an act of pure, physical passion—the truest crime of passion I've ever seen."

I looked around at the oak tables, the pictures on the walls, the bottles behind the bar: tangible evidence of the type of security to which I was aspiring. The barman, who'd been listening too, shook his head.

"And what," I asked uneasily, "were your conclusions?"

"I really had none. The very selfishness of the act bothered me. No thought of the others who'd be affected by it. But isn't sex always selfish, or self-cantered at any rate? You exclude the rest of the world. And yet passion, which to me is the very opposite of a rationally organized society, is everything that's creative: all that makes life worthwhile beyond humdrum, everyday existence." He took a sip from his glass. "But how can you talk about that to policemen? That's really what caused me to leave the force. I'd always loved reading, and I felt that literature tackled those broader problems that were only touched on in the police reports. I've never had a clinical approach to human life, so it was natural I should turn to literature."

"And did you find any answers?" I asked.

He chuckled. "I found only more questions. It was the police reports that demanded *answers*, in the hope that every crime might be neatly filed away and labelled 'solved.' At least in literature there was a sense of reality."

I was dissatisfied. I thought of my wedding the next day, of how my whole life lay ahead of me. There had to be some solutions.

So Harry had gone to university. After he graduated he thought of writing a thesis on the *Liebestod*: Tristan and Isolde, and the idea of

A. Colin Wright

love expressed in the ideal marriage with death, which, he explained, was a common theme in literature. But it had been done before, and he had a job by then anyway.

"You've published articles on that, though," Charlie said.

"Well, yes. And on the theme of the rebel, who rejects the everyday happiness that most of us consider desirable—where passion's frowned upon because it's anarchistic, interrupting the rational course of events and important things like work and making money." I saw that tears were forming again. "And yet, even if you're religious—and the couple believed in God, although they didn't go to church—you're told to count the world as naught."

"But one has to live in the world, try to make it run smoothly, help others," I objected. "Passion *is* destructive."

Harry wiped away the moisture from his eyes. "Perhaps my couple decided they *didn't* have to live in the world. That they preferred passion, a sacred experience if you like, and death. Hubris, I suppose, bringing its own nemesis. But that's only my idea, of course."

Again, we were silent.

"I should be going," I said. "I've a big day coming up tomorrow."

"Of course." As we got up, Harry added: "Anyway, thanks to that young couple I've spent a lifetime searching for real answers rather than just solving crimes. And I don't think my life's been entirely useless. I'm grateful to them for showing me a strange kind of beauty at a time when I might have lost sight of it in pursuing the practical." The tears were now running down his cheeks, and he brushed them away impatiently. "From my point of view, I don't think their lives were entirely useless either."

As we turned to go in different directions outside the Club, I recalled how Harry had never remarried, and I remarked to Charlie that it must be lonely for him. Charlie, though, explained that Harry had a

Wedding

certain reputation and that, by many accounts, he wasn't always alone in his apartment.

I was still dissatisfied as we said goodnight. Walking through the darkened streets, I found I was depressed by Harry's story and the mystery of why it had all happened.

At least, I thought, from tomorrow on I won't be alone in bed either. There'll be the excitement of my wedding to Elaine, my beautiful— and yes, sensual—bride to be, followed by a lifetime of happiness and success. As for tonight: well, what harm will there be in shedding a few secret tears for that couple, or in picturing their glorious passion that sustained them unto death?

Distantly from Gardens

You should know that I'm a professor of German, and I've been in two minds, as usual, as to whether to open this story—or should I say dialogue?—with a quotation from Friedrich Hölderlin. Relevant it would certainly be, and I promise you I'll work it in somewhere, even if it's in German. But you read German anyway. In English it goes something like this:

The playing of distant strings is heard distantly from gardens; perhaps

Some being in love is playing or a lonely man,

Mindful of distant friends and the days of youth.[1]

Now lying here on your hospital bed, you may as well confess, although you'd never reveal it to the students, that those lines express something about you personally—even if I now shudder at their underlying romanticism. You may, though, convince yourself of my strict avoidance of such sentimentality since your days by looking at any of the thirty-seven scholarly articles and two books listed in my (rather impressive) *curriculum vitae*. And in case you, as a young man, may be thinking of me the older one as some old fossil (it seems you had such ideas), I should point out that

---

[1] My translation—H.W. It should be pointed out that the repetition of "distant" (Ger. *Fern*) and "playing" (Ger. *Spiel*) is in the original.

Distantly from Gardens

I am only fifty-nine and that I won the Student Association's Award for Teaching a few years ago. I am, despite my recent problems, a competent and entertaining teacher.

What's that to do with anything? you say. Well, really, it has . . . But that was typical of you, to interrupt with a damn-fool question before we even started. The purpose of this exchange is to make an excursion into our past, though God knows if we'll ever sort it out.

Bim-bam, bim-bam, shake it, man. You smile. That's when you were younger, of course, or words to that effect that I no longer remember. Or was it entirely that way? I'm not sure my personality was any less divided as a young man than it is now. But let us call the place Rondara, in Spain (for a while you played with the idea of abandoning the Germanic temperament for the Latin one), and:

I am leaning out over a balcony under a sky almost dark. Far in the distance a guitar is playing in the night, sad and yet passionate, as though the interpretation of some tragedy inexpressible in any other form.

To quote, that is, from what you wrote—how long ago? You probably thought of the poem by Hölderlin then, for you'd certainly read it in your first year at university. It had all been so unexpected: that you should have been transported, almost literally overnight, from Bloomsbury, to the Mediterranean. The surroundings appeared theatrical: a white hotel with extensive gardens, a fountain with a cupid, I think, in a fragrant orchard, the guitar playing.

I felt that after an hour or so of acting I should leave by the stage door and wake up to the reality of a journey back to my flat.

During the vacations, you recall, you worked in the London office of a rather exclusive travel agency. On the Monday, the guide in charge of a small group on the Costa Brava was arrested by the Spanish police for smuggling; you left Victoria Station on the 9.30 a.m. Dover train

103

A. Colin Wright

on Tuesday; were in Rondara, after travelling overnight from Paris, on Wednesday. You were to return with the group on Saturday night.

I didn't meet the guests that day—perhaps you'd slept—*but by evening I was indulging in my own loneliness, looking out over an orchard whose white blossoms reflected the lights around the fountain. And somewhere beyond, a troubled spirit was declaiming its grief to the strings of a guitar.*

One expects such romanticism from youth. You listened, moved by a sense of unrest:

As though the throbbing rhythm were part of my being. And as I stood there, the music was prolonged in its dying anguish. Then it ceased. For the first time I was aware of the steady trickle of water in the fountain.

Wanting as always to find romance, you went out into the village, to a café on the square, in the middle of which a small band was playing and couples were dancing. With a desperate yearning to be a part of that strange, exciting life outside you, you went up to two girls and asked one of them if she wanted to dance. They looked at each other and laughed. So after a lonely drink you returned to your room. Went out onto the balcony again, so as to have that image of the garden below to carry in your mind before sleep.

The guitar was playing, less passionately now. Suddenly I felt that this dream, as I imagined it, was real after all, that only now I had an independent existence.[2] *The three days remaining seemed an age, as though they were the rest of life; those beyond them, when I should be home again, a vague afterlife and nothing more.*[3]

I was sitting with the others at breakfast when you came in. You wanted, naturally, to find us all together to introduce yourself. But Eileen, the bright young teacher, wasn't there yet. I'd been telling a rather clever

---

[2] Sounds good. Does it really *mean* anything?

[3] Banal.

104

Distantly from Gardens

joke, remember? About Edith and Mabel in front of Wagner's statue in Bayreuth. Edith says "Look, Mabel, there's Go-thee." Mabel says "No, it's Batch. You know Batch, don't you? Eeny kleeny knack-music. Pom-pom-pom-pom!" There was a roar of laughter from those who understood it—a pity that Eileen wasn't there, but I'd repeat it for her later—and Mrs. Hunt at least pretended to understand and laughed as well: "Oh, Professor Wallace, the stories you tell!"

"And here's our new guide," I exclaimed majestically, in the affable style I use to students on social occasions. "How do you do, sir! Allow me to introduce ourselves. My name's Henry Wallace. Mrs. Hunt, Mr. Johnson . . ." I went round the tables. "And you are?"

You told them your name, and why you'd arrived out of the blue. This man Wallace, you thought, wrongly wasn't interested in you personally, but behaved like a senior executive in polite conversation with an employee. When a girl came into the room, he called to her "Ah, come over here, my dear. I've been saving a place for you. This is Harry, our new guide"—grandly, as though claiming ownership.

She said hello in that brisk, efficient manner that told you, even before I did, that she was a teacher. Glasses, a sharp, attractive face, a possible answer to your loneliness.

I sat down to breakfast—and I quote—*and Wallace started on his professorial jokes again. Eileen had been singled out as his favourite, and she listened with attention. It must have been quite flattering for him, I thought, to hold a girl's attention at his age. Well, his taking charge had annoyed me.*

You little prick. Eventually you made your announcement about the day's planned excursion, apologizing that you weren't as familiar with the district as your predecessor.

"Oh I know the place pretty well," I said. "I'll sit behind you on the coach and give you any help you need."

105

A. Colin Wright

Wallace, you soon realized, was one of those garrulous professors: it's a mistake to think they're all introverts. Eileen sat next to him on the coach. He graciously included you in the conversation, although that didn't mean your having to say anything.

Wallace was entertaining enough. Knew everything and didn't like being disagreed with, which inhibited you (and surely Eileen too?) from expressing your feelings. The coach would come to a beautiful view, he'd point out the geological features that his colleague Professor Crudd would have been enthralled with, give you the name of the village in the distance, reading it from the map in his perfect Spanish accent; saying how awe-inspiring it was. Talking the whole time.

Eileen made rather a good partner for me, laughing and sparkling because she was on holiday. You tried hesitantly to seduce her away from me, with little success, and knowing I enjoyed your failure.

That evening, though, you decided to forget your annoyance and went out with the whole group for drinks. You flirted mildly with Eileen, but she still seemed under the influence of the older Wallace, and you realized how little impression you were making. Despairing at your lack of confidence, you returned to your room thinking that perhaps you wouldn't be sorry after all when Saturday came.

I went out onto the balcony to listen for the guitar, but tonight all was silent and the trickling of the fountain sounded mean and prosaic.[4]

You awoke in your white-walled hotel room with the realization that it was already Friday and that the atmosphere of the first night (guitar, scent, orange blossom) was unlikely to be fulfilled in a way that would justify for you those lines of Hölderlin's about some being in love. (Hölderlin went mad, of course.) When you went down to breakfast it was

---

[4] Oh, for Christ's sake!

Distantly from Gardens

raining and most of the guests were drinking lukewarm coffee, listening to the cold harmony of the sea and the gentle patter of the water splashing on the windows.[5]

Now Eileen. How much should you say about her? For she is, after all, a cipher: any attractive woman one weaves dreams around, without bothering whether these correspond to reality. A partner one conceives of for romance, with all the excitement the word suggests. The girl you desired but who was soon forgotten, like so many others you never approached close enough to love.

You sat with her, desperately trying to find something to say—relieved that she was sociable enough to make it easy. She had a number of stories to tell about the schools she'd taught in, and you were a sympathetic listener—wondering, though, whether you'd ever learn a technique for chatting up women. She gave the impression of self-assurance, making the most of her holiday in a bright, sensible way. And in three months, she said, she was getting married, to an accountant, who no doubt would make far more money than a teacher ever would. She was pleasantly flirtatious, even when she said, looking into your eyes, "Oh, this damnable weather."

"I'm enjoying it," you replied. It was true, for sunshine and beaches made you self-conscious. Perhaps, you thought, some being in love is playing, or a lonely man . . .

You were interrupted by Wallace. He came in talking to one of the maids, who was asking if his extra pillow had been satisfactory. Typical, you thought, for him to make a fuss over a pillow. But as you get older, these things become important.

"*Sí, sí,*" I replied in my lordly, gruff fashion.

"And the señor would like an extra blanket too?"

---

[5]   *Ibid.*

A. Colin Wright

"*Sí, muy bien.*" I walked over to you and Eileen. I could, you were thinking with your youthful naïvety, at least have said thank you to the maid.

"Good morning to you," I continued almost in the same breath. "And what are we doing at the moment?" You, in your intolerance, saw that as being patronizing.

"Come and join us," Eileen said.

"It's always a pleasure to sit with a charming young lady. I must tell you of when I was in Italy once . . ." Chatting her up, I think the expression is.

You stayed for a while, but then, feeling yourself superfluous in a scene where Wallace and Eileen were again the main actors, you went up to your room, sat staring out of the window at the blurred image of the garden below. "It looked ugly and distorted," you wrote, "because of the rain streaming down the windows, as it would to someone observing it through eyes washed with tears." The ridiculous sentimentality I've always had to fight down in myself to become an objective critic of literature.[6]

The pillows in this hospital are uncomfortable too, though no more so than in the last one.

That afternoon we went by bus to a large city inland, where it was hot and dusty. As we made our way towards the Cathedral, you were talking to Mrs. Hunt, one of the sillier middle-aged members of our group. Behind you, you could hear that Eileen was being given a detailed account of the Arabian influences in Spain. By Wallace, who else? You despised him for being older and yet more successful with her, while you suspected that his supposed erudition was commonplace. Eileen, though, seemed to

---

[6] And note that strictly correct grammar demands a possessive in your sentence: "rain's" rather than "rain."

enjoy his company. Look, I'm more intelligent, more sensitive, I really am, you wanted to scream at her, and this evening's the last one.

We went into the Cathedral and I was ashamed. Through the stained-glass windows there spread a soft glow of coloured light which held the cool, silent air in its grasp; this intruded upon only by the muffled echo of footsteps belonging to no one person but to the vast stone enclosure alone; each one joining the others as the expression of a common admiration and wonder.[7] I walked around, away from the rest of the group, with a consciousness of wanting to let it mean more to me than the others. (Not knowing what to say to Eileen, you mean, and trying to display an imagined sensitivity instead!) *This cathedral atmosphere of melancholy, fear, tension, relaxation, all combined,*[8] *would soon disappear in the sunlight outside. I heard whispered voices all around me: "Isn't it beautiful?" "Just look at those colours!" "How lovely!" Banal, I said to myself, and in my mind I could hear the same throbbing of the guitar, an ideal one, playing in the night.*

Wallace was explaining the architecture, with detailed descriptions of the cornices at the top of the columns. (Capitals, you mean, you young ignoramus. The cornice is a part of the entablature.) Later he orated "It's an impressive thought that there are . . . . tons"—you didn't catch the figure—"of granite in all this." Now *that* he must have learned from the guidebook.

You said yes quietly and moved on. He went with you, as he's done ever since, still showing his knowledge in, you thought, an attempt to hide his inability to feel any of the beauty: indulging in clichés of admiration. You thought he was pretending, like yourself, as if to say I would have liked to feel it but for some reason was no longer capable of feeling anything except the agony of my own lack of feeling. You felt sorry for Wallace, but wanted to get rid of what you perceived as a threat to yourself.

---

[7]   Confusing image, as well as bathos.

[8]   Here I suppose I can agree with you, but you do have a penchant for clichés and rhetoric with little real meaning.

A. Colin Wright

"Can't you be quiet?" you finally said. "Save your explanations for your dreary lectures! Isn't that how you spare yourself from really experiencing anything?"

Put bluntly like that, it would have been inexcusable, but we'll admit we've both forgotten the actual words, which were more subtle. But such was their intent and Wallace moved away.

In reality I was sorry for what I'd said. I wasn't normally impolite, but I was miserable at the consciousness of my own shyness. The Cathedral no longed seemed extraordinary, its atmosphere somehow false, remote. And you, Professor Wallace, undoubtedly felt the same.

I hate this room, the whiteness of the walls, even the whiteness of the paper I'm writing on.

After dinner on the final evening, a number of us went to the large café on the square. The lights, the laughter, the sound of half-understood Spanish conversations, couples dancing again: it was a different, exciting world.

I was unusually quiet. Although I used to make an attempt at it in my youth, I've never been a good dancer, and you realized that. While I sat smoking, commenting on the rather grand cigarette holder I'd bought that day, you took the opportunity to dance with Eileen—not very well, need I say?—and then to seduce her away from me for a drink in the café on the other side of the square. Sometimes you could manage these things if circumstances were right. Eileen—well, Wallace wanted her, I admit. I was never successful with women when I was young, and in my less guarded moments I can still dream idly of conquests (even of some of my students, although I would never allow them to guess it). And I really thought Eileen liked me, enough at least to flirt with me and perhaps even let me kiss her. But no, she was engaged.

You danced, jostling over the square.

110

Distantly from Gardens

More than dancing, you wrote, *it was a wild gesture of defiance in the face of time. It became one of those nights that seem as if they must last forever, as if they alone have any real existence, and yet afterwards seem as if they've never been at all.*[9]

After the music finally stopped, you took Eileen to the beach, walking, running, skipping, scrambling down onto the sand. Youth's foolishness, of course, both pretending at something neither of you believed, but sufficiently under the spell of the night, the music, the dancing to agree to the pretence. Eileen abandoned her brisk, efficient manner, and you your trick of looking cynical, as though you saw through everyone.

In a moment of laughter I tried to kiss her, but she escaped me and ran back to the road as fast as she could, stopping behind a parked car or lamppost to tantalize me, and over the stone bridge, through the little park. But I caught her, kissed her, and we both were so out of breath that we fell laughing onto a bench nearby.

I can't write this without making it sound like cheap romanticism. It was so long ago: the night, the sound of the sea, the wind in the trees. Romanticism is a pretence that entraps us all, even pathetic old Wallace, who'd now gone back with the others to the hotel. As for you and Eileen, it meant nothing, a few minutes of giggling passion and breathless kisses before she stopped you when you tried to feel her breasts. She was, of course, engaged. But there's always a tragic beauty in impermanence. So I used to think.

We walked back to the hotel through the orchard, where the guitar was playing again. As though my very desire had caused it, the notes tearing themselves away from my soul and leaving me exhausted yet jubilant.[10]

You stopped before you reached the fountain. You heard voices.

---

[9]   ?

[10]   Does this *mean* anything?

A. Colin Wright

"Oh, Professor Wallace! The things you say!" It was Mrs. Hunt.

There were more words you couldn't hear.

"You've given me a delightful evening . . ."

Eileen was listening too, and you noticed she was smiling. The guitar twanged into silence.

"Goodnight, Mrs. Hunt." I must have sounded tired.

"Goodnight, Professor Wallace." After a moment's hesitant shuffling, she scurried off to bed.

You heard me strike a match, and then you saw the tip of a cigarette glowing amongst the trees. You walked on with Eileen, who didn't realize I was still there.

"Let's say goodnight here."

You kissed her passionately. She, too, I realize now, with her tongue touching yours. But your thoughts were on Wallace, on his envy as he stood watching. When Eileen left to go in, you heard me turn and move away. You fool! You didn't even enjoy that kiss, didn't realize you could have held her longer, that you'd missed yet one more opportunity in your desire for a cheap victory over an older man. Oh, yes, it hurt, I won't deny it. I was bitterly jealous and tortured by my old, unsatisfied longing. You won, as youth must always win over age. But now it's my turn, since I exist, carrying the burden of my years, it's true, while you do not. Although merely being alive seems a feeble kind of victory.

I went back to my room, then out onto the balcony. Wallace was still below in the garden, sitting alone by the edge of the fountain and smoking the last miserable inch of his cigarette in that ridiculously ostentatious holder. I watched as he extinguished it in the water, and he began to recite, slowly, quietly, to himself. A love poem, pathetically sentimental.

Distantly from Gardens

Oh, no, I shan't quote my youthful, atrocious attempts at poetry. Nor shall I further describe your feeling that night after your deliberate exercise in humiliation—for basically you were a decent fellow, just young.

I recall that I really did want to apologize, but it was too late. I was shy and there was really nothing I could apologize for. There wasn't even a pretext for going out to the garden again.

The journey home was uneventful. On the train from Dover to London you sat with Wallace and Eileen, oppressed by a feeling of hopelessness because nothing had come of it and it was all over.

As Wallace sat talking interminably, I thought of how understanding people was perhaps the first stage towards loving them in the biblical sense and even in the sexual sense too. How all wanted that, but were prevented from finding it by lack of confidence, egoism, and the inability to make contact, so they just played games instead.

What banality. One gets ideas like that when one's young.

Wallace left at Victoria station as jovial and as garrulous as ever. Eileen shook hands, just smiling and looking into our eyes.

You should know that I'm a professor of German, an acknowledged expert on German eighteenth—and nineteenth-century poetry, renowned for the rigour of my critical approach and my ruthless elimination of any subjective interpretations. My God! How could one bear to live if it were otherwise? But wait, I promised you the poem. Hölderlin. I'm even a bit like . . . But no, it's called *Brot und Wein*. Bread and Wine, that's it.

Aber das Saitenspiel tönt fern aus Gärten; vielleicht dass

Dort ein Liebendes spielt oder ein einsamer Mann,

Ferner Freunde gedenkt und der Jugendzeit.

A. Colin Wright

Looking at the first line, you'll notice the enjambment, and then, on the still formal level, the two umlauts, the *tönt* followed by *Gär* . . .

The guitar playing in Rondara.

. . . which produces an effect of not exactly assonance . . . Is comparable to . . . The playing of strings in those fragrant, distant gardens.

Repetition. You're right, *fern*, distant . . .

Where perhaps a being in love was playing; seeking love desperately, playing at it because there's nothing more desirable in life.

What, what? But that's so typical, when we haven't even mentioned the unusual use of the neuter *ein Liebendes*, not a man in love but a *being* . . .

A lonely man. Mindful of distant friends.

And the alliteration: *ferner Freunde* . . .

My God, how can one . . .

What friends? You. I. Eileen, who never knew your loneliness and desp . . .

See Hölderlin, *Sämtliche* . . .

Gardens, fountains, days of youth, of love, of music. Romance.

See Höld . . .

The playing of strings, distantly from gardens. Write it, professor, one more time, before in this white-walled room you take your pills and sleep.

No, not yet. Professor of German, known for . . .

Distantly from Gardens

His despairing dreams of female students. His way of staring, before turning away.

Mein Gott, how can one bear it?

His romantic nature, his *sentimentality*.

Look, you wanted Eileen, right? Any attractive girl to impress, to be loved by and to be romantic with. You're screaming, I know. It's starting again. Let me scream then the things that words can't . . .

Romantic . . .

And so I shout at you, all of you, who've never taken notice of me, never understood, the most important things, that words

No! See Hölderlin can't ever

Sämtliche . . . let me go, let me go

Werke, vol. I scream it louder, louder, louder. Repetition, alliteration, assonance!

Distantly from Gardens, a guitar twangs into silence.

See Friedrich Hölderlin, *Sämtliche Werke,* vol..I (Stuttgart: Kohlhammer, 1946) p.95, lines 29-32!

Frank's Girl

It was entirely typical that the most attractive girl at the reception should have come through the arched doorway with Frank Harding. He gave enquiring smiles all around, certain of recognition, touching his wavy, slightly defiant black hair. Clothes impeccably casual, with shirt open just low enough to reveal promising knots of hair beneath. His girl glanced at him with deep, calm eyes as they parted in different directions, while he nodded in scant acknowledgement and strode over to a group of our fellow students.

"Hi, Harry." I heard his rich, casual voice. "Hi, Julian. Good of the Institute to put on a show like this, eh?"

We were in some kind of assembly hall, distinguished only by its Gothic ceiling and a stage at one end, piled high with folding chairs. I took two more olives, realizing that in France I'd expected something more exotic. The only alternative was celery sticks or raw carrots, and a dip that fell off if you took enough of it to enjoy the taste. For some minutes now I'd been stuck in conversation with one of the middle-aged women instructors. But at least this evening I was making a good attempt to disguise my awkwardness at such gatherings; and to everyone I'd been giving a display of uncharacteristic cheerfulness in the uncertain hope that I might manage to meet some of the girls.

116

Frank's Girl

"So your impressions?" the instructor prompted.

"My impressions?"

Frank's girl, I noticed, was standing by the ornate darkened windows, a lonely figure now that he'd left her. Long chestnut hair, rather untidy; wide eyes; a slight stoop; a pink sweater suggestive of softness underneath. I hadn't seen her in our classes, so she was presumably one of the French students who'd been invited along to meet us.

"Your first impressions of Paris."

"Oh, yes. Well . . ."

Our week there was already half over, and I looked hopefully around the hall, reminding myself that I certainly didn't want another emotional attachment: somehow I always got too romantically involved and it finished by making me miserable. At Cambridge several of my attempts at love had failed because of Frank. He had simply taken over from me, without malice, without boasting, as a natural consequence of his inborn superiority. We remained uneasy friends, but there was no way I wanted to compete with him.

As I struggled to answer the instructor's questions, I was aware that Julian Debrusk had gone over to Frank's girl. After greeting him in short-lived eagerness, she was letting her gaze wander around the other groups of students. Ignoring Frank, who was in easy view, still talking with some of the men. Was she really Frank's, or had they only come in together accidentally? Like myself, he'd never been to Paris before, and I did make too many assumptions about him. The girl was now standing in near silence while Julian beamed upon her. Her appearance of timid intelligence almost made me change my mind about not going over to talk to her.

"You're from London?" the woman pursued relentlessly.

"Canterbury."

A. Colin Wright

Bits of Frank's effortless conversation came to me from across the room. His spoken French wasn't as good as mine but sounded better because of his confidence. I would stutter and not know what to say to strangers, even if I could then say it with grammatical and phonetic perfection. Leaning against a pillar, he was laughing easily with the others. Julian had once told me he thought Frank deliberately posed for the best effect.

It wasn't intentional when, after the instructor finally released me, I found myself beside Frank's girl, and she turned to me in a way that forced Julian, unwillingly, to introduce us. Her name was Lise.

"Martin Strong?" Her eyes dropped to the buttons on my blazer before she looked up again and risked a smile. "Henri Picard was telling me about you. He's a friend of mine."

"Yes, we've corresponded. His thesis topic's related to mine."

Gaining confidence, she explained that they'd gone through the Sorbonne together. She looked directly into my eyes with a shy friendliness. Turned her glance away. Then back again.

Julian interrupted to tell her a joke, at which she nodded politely and then turned to me again. Soon she was telling me of her difficulties getting into a graduate programme and supporting herself in Paris. She came from somewhere in Alsace. When Julian insisted on trying to flirt with her, she smiled at me rather than at him, her brown eyes resting on my own. Frank, I noticed, had now left the men and reappeared, godlike, among a group of girls, who immediately responded to his friendly baritone.

Lise had taken a stick of celery. "Do you want something?" She turned to plunge it into the dip and managed to scoop up quite a lot before holding it out for me to take in my mouth. When some ran down my chin, she wiped it off with her fingers.

118

Frank's Girl

We were joined by Harry Haskill, another acquaintance from my undergraduate days, trustworthy and good-natured, and Julian looked even more disgusted.

Later, I wandered away to chat with others. Sometimes it just happens with someone you're interested in that you don't have to stay close. You can relax and be certain the girl will be waiting for you to return. I don't know why it was like this now. Talking, I was aware of Lise's quick glances in my direction, the occasional smile and half-guilty nod of the head when I caught her at it—just enough to make sure I didn't run away from her. She smiled gratefully when I returned.

Then Frank came back. "Look, the others are going to the restaurant at the top of that modern hotel they've just built behind St. Germain. Why don't we all go? Order some wine, have some fun. Martin? Julian? Harry? Lise?"

Lise turned to me. "Are you coming?"

In the upstairs restaurant—plain enough, with Formica-topped tables, not too expensive—Frank sits opposite me, Lise beside me.

"So, Martin." He looks at me with that expression of interest that he uses so effectively. "What are your plans now that you've graduated?"

I try to respond with the same ease, hoping irrationally that Lise will be impressed by the attention Frank's giving me. I ask about his plans too.

"I'm having a year off first," he answers. "You know"—one of his attractive smiles—"go round the world or something, spend a bit of money, rough it a bit, I don't mind. There's plenty of time for becoming the serious scholar. If I take a couple of years longer getting my Ph.D., so what?"

Julian Debrusk, slightly maliciously, asks about the girl Frank's supposed to be engaged to, but Frank doesn't care and says she'll wait.

119

A. Colin Wright

Lise has been fingering the menu. "You'll be at the banquet the day after tomorrow?" she asks me.

"Yes."

"I'm coming too. I'll see you there." A moment later she adds: "I've been planning a trip to England this summer. Perhaps on the way I could come to see you in Canterbury?"

"Of course."

I talk to her for most of the meal, while Frank has a thoroughly good time being sociable with the others. For over an hour, I realize, I've been totally relaxed.

I offer to take Lise home.

"No, he's taking me." She nods towards Frank, who's telling jokes but says he'll be coming shortly. It comes as a surprise, since by now I've almost convinced myself she isn't his girl after all.

She smiles at my disappointment. I go down with her in the lift, knowing there's something erotic about lifts and that I should kiss her now, even if she's Frank's. But I hesitate too long, and the doors are already opening into the hotel's entrance hall.

"Frank will take you home then?"

"Yes. I'll see you again, though, all right?"

I leave her waiting for him to come down.

In no hurry to return to the loneliness of my hotel, I walk through the jumbled streets of the Latin Quarter and then across the Pont Neuf, where I stop to gaze down at the darkened garden on the tip of the Ile de la Cité with the black river on either side: a moment of silence between the ever-insistent clamour of the city on the two other banks. The Paris of lovers. I still wonder about Frank and Lise. My envy pictures them making love together—he probably met her the first day, when I was sick—while

Frank's Girl

my more rational mind says I'm unreasonably credulous about Frank's ability to effortlessly seduce anyone he wants.

I walk as far as the metro station at the Louvre, so I won't have to change at the Châtelet with its long, dreary corridors. A lonely figure I must appear, in my English blazer and trousers that need pressing. Even if she's with him now, I tell myself as I clatter down the stone steps into the metro, my chance might come later, in Canterbury. I travel on to the Bastille, from where I walk to my shabby hotel.

Then I can't sleep. Why is it that the Lises of this world always belong to the Franks?

It wasn't until the next afternoon that I saw her again. Frank and I had just come out of our classroom into one of the Institute's echoing corridors, and the broad black, red, and green bands of her dress immediately drew our attention as she walked towards us. Her brown eyes met mine before she smiled at Frank.

We went for a drink together at one of the bars on the Boulevard St. Michel. Despite Frank's presence, she was clearly pleased to see me. A comical character passed in front of us and we smiled our amusement at each other; the waiter tore the cash-register slip halfway through as we paid, and she noted my curiosity about customs that differed from English ones. Frank, meanwhile, was grandly casual, and I couldn't tell whether it indicated confident possession or lack of interest.

I suggested having dinner together, addressing Lise and leaving it for Frank to decide whether or not I'd included him.

She was uncertain. "I have a student coming—I give him private English lessons. He's coming to my apartment: I have to go back for him. Could you phone me? He'll be gone by seven." She scribbled down her number for me. Frank seemed to accept that my invitation was intended only for Lise.

121

A. Colin Wright

When we left, we all took the métro together: Frank and I back to our hotels and Lise to the Château de Vincennes, at the end of the same line, since she lived in one of the suburbs to the east of Paris.

"You'll phone me at seven then?" she reminded me as I got out at the Bastille.

Frank's hotel was one station farther on, and on the platform, before their train was carried away, I caught a last glimpse of him bending so she could say something in his ear.

When I phone Lise I know from her first word that she isn't going to come, and that she's going to lie about it.

"Martin, I'm awfully sorry but I'd completely forgotten. Some friends of mine are coming over. I'd promised to see them a week ago."

I say nothing.

She's embarrassed. "Perhaps we can have lunch tomorrow instead? And then I'll be coming on this trip to England in a few weeks. You'll be at the banquet tomorrow too."

"Yes."

"I feel terrible about it, really I do. We'll have lunch?"

"All right."

I don't really expect her to come for lunch either, but I hope she will if only so I can make light of it and not let her think I'm upset. I could perhaps have asked Frank straight out whether he's interested in her, only he tends to be secretive about his women and is, I think, rather compulsive about being able to have any girl he wants. So tomorrow I'll tell Lise I didn't believe her, but show it doesn't matter.

Hell, though, why do I have to get involved? *Again.*

122

Frank's Girl

*   *   *

"I feel so bad about yesterday! I'd completely forgotten about these friends . . ."

I'd rehearsed my sentence, a friendly "Don't bother making excuses," but I didn't get the right tone of voice, so its effect was lost and she probably didn't realize I hadn't believed her.

"Let's go and have lunch." I took her arm. "So"—my second rehearsed sentence—"how did you enjoy the evening?"

"Oh, it wasn't too much fun. We just sat around talking. Henri Picard was there. You know, the one who's written to you?"

She held tightly to my arm as she led me through the Latin Quarter, head down, serious. Perhaps she was telling the truth after all, and I'd overdramatized my disappointment, making unwarranted assumptions just because she'd travelled on for a farther station on the métro with Frank Harding. As we sat over the lunchtime normality of paper tablecloths, beer mats, and broken rolls of bread, I became more inclined to believe her; and determined, too, not to spoil the last day by feeling sorry for myself. As we talked, I observed the others in the restaurant. A couple of lovers, who forgot to eat because they kept looking at each other. French students, tourists, and locals who shook hands with friends as they entered. Our steaks, rare and with little pots of a butter sauce and French mustard, were better than a gourmet meal.

We talked about the future, our financial problems, the difficulties of academic life; our hopes for avoiding the type of conventional life we saw in our families. I told her briefly of my previous loves, and she told me of hers.

"I'm French, after all. We know all about love. But it's not often I actually . . . go with someone. The men friends I have, well, they're good friends, no more."

A. Colin Wright

I suggested I should skip the afternoon classes so we could go for a walk.

"Why don't we go to the Bois de Vincennes?" she said eagerly. "I've got to change before the banquet this evening, and we can walk from there to my place." She laughed at my enthusiasm. "Wait a minute, though."

She rolled up her long hair and tucked it into a jaunty sailor's cap she pulled from her bag—which turned her into a young girl, with a puckish strength of independence.

We took the métro not to Vincennes but to the other side of the park, so we could walk across. We strolled arm in arm by the lake, where I laughingly quoted to her from Lamartine's famous poem imploring time to stop for those in love: "*Oh temps, suspends ton vol! et vous, heures propices, suspendez votre cours . . .*"

Lise laughed, too, and resisted firmly when under the trees I tried to kiss her.

She told me she was more at home in male company than female, but had no regular boyfriend. "A lot of them tell me all their problems. Like Henri. But I've never really been in love."

She was interested in the arts, and in my thesis and the other things I was trying to write. And she wanted to visit me in England. "I'll come and see you, yes?"

After the park we went to her apartment, and she invited me in for coffee. Modern furniture, but instead of a bed there were only blankets piled on a mattress in a corner, under a photograph of her with her parents. Everywhere there were books and papers, and an album of constructivist pictures lay on the glass-topped coffee table. On the wall above, with several contemporary paintings, hung a nude pencil drawing of her lying on the couch.

I looked at it with curiosity: small breasts with prominent nipples, while her pubic area remained hidden.

124

Frank's Girl

"Oh, that's not very good," she said impatiently. "I don't know why I keep it there."

She skipped laughingly out of my reach when I tried to kiss her again.

As I walk back to the métro at the Château de Vincennes—it turns out to be much farther than I think—I'm elated at the success of this last afternoon, almost a reward for my making light of Lise not coming to dinner with me the night before. I'm aware, of course, that she's twice resisted being kissed—but how foolish to have assumed she's involved with Frank. It seems she keeps all of us at bay, choosing consciously and rarely when she wants to make love. Of course, I repeat to myself, I still can't be certain she was telling the truth about last night. I'm determined not to be fooled by her. Except that she had little enough reason to lie about it. There's perhaps a certain mystery about her, but it only makes her more attractive.

We throng around the restaurant's American-style bar in loud anticipation, outside a larger room where the banquet tables have been prepared. Julian, anxious as always for female company, has already found a table for four: for himself, Harry, Frank, and Lise.

"Go ahead," I tell her with pretended confidence: "I'll see you afterwards."

More olives. Except when forced to make stuttering, awkward conversation, I watch Lise sitting with the others at a window table that overlooks the river and Notre Dame, while I'm pressed against the opposite wall.

Sometimes I catch her glancing at me, but this evening her mood seems to have changed. I sense that she's upset and no longer wants to be

125

with me; that our afternoon was somehow the best time together. She's distinctly fidgety. Keeps turning to look around the room, sometimes gets up to speak to someone, even leaves for a while. There's something about her I don't understand, a kind of perpetual desire for something else. But at least if I've lost her, I'm somewhat consoled that Frank doesn't seem to be in the picture either.

After the meal she's sullen, complaining it wasn't worth the money. "We're only poor students, after all. I think our lunch was far nicer, don't you?" She produces a notebook: "Martin, write down your address so I can visit you, all right?"

I get her address, too, pretending not to notice she's saying goodnight to me. Then there's a suggestion for a group of us to go dancing at some discotheque close by on the Ile de la Cité. Lise is unenthusiastic, yet allows herself to be persuaded. I'd rather not go either, but I remember how two nights ago I left her unwillingly to go back to my hotel by myself. Now an innate obstinacy to pursue her to the end combines with a growing curiosity to find out what's gone wrong.

The room is dark, with flashing coloured lights, and the music unbearably loud, unending. There's little I can say to her in staccato phrases shouted between the beats of the music, and my dancing is clumsy. Frank is unconcernedly natural, conversing brightly with another girl, while Lise remains remote from all of us.

"Well, I think I'll be going then." Said to me privately, apologetically.

"I'll take you home."

She gives an awkward laugh, nodding at Frank. "I don't know." She turns towards him. "Are you taking me home?"

Evidently he's decided not to. He's clearly enjoying his new companion and, ever the opportunist, doubtless realizes Lise isn't going to succumb to him. "Goodnight, Lise," he says cheerfully.

Frank's Girl

*   *   *

We walk arm in arm across the bridge, with the dark river flowing beneath, towards the bright lights of the Place du Châtelet and its tall column in front of the grandiose Sarah Bernhardt Theatre; then into the métro station on the far corner of the square. Down the tiled corridor, divided by green railings that separate the departing and arriving passengers—unnecessary at this bleak hour—and onto the deserted platform. *Direction Vincennes.*

We stand by the diagram of the métro lines, waiting endlessly for a train, and our previous attraction has turned to a nervous irritation with each other. Lise, needlessly impatient, keeps complaining that at this hour the trains are so few, and I can't understand what's the hurry.

We sense the vibration from along the tunnel, but it's still almost a minute before the lights appear, and then longer until the sky-blue train is slowing in front of us on its whistling rubber tyres. As we sit in its bright emptiness, she says "So, Martin, you'll get out at the Bastille and then perhaps I'll see you in Canterbury in a few weeks' time."

She doesn't want me to take her all the way home, and we argue about it above the rattle of the train. A gesture of futile impatience from her as the Bastille comes and goes.

"So," she says when we get out at the Château de Vincennes, "you can turn round here and go back on the same train. It'll be quicker and save you another ticket."

It would be sensible of course, but I give way to my own stubbornness and just joke about it, following her up the steps to the street. I realize that we can take the bus, which at least will be better than that long walk. But when there's another interminable wait for the bus, she becomes even more irritable, almost insisting that I leave her—while I, in my obstinacy, laugh it off.

A. Colin Wright

Finally she says, so quietly that I have to ask her to repeat it: "Martin, I don't *want* you to come with me. I . . . I'm going to meet someone."

A momentary startled pause before I can pretend cheerfulness. "Why didn't you tell me before?"

"I thought you'd have understood."

I kiss her on the cheek and head back into the métro, just in time to catch a departing train, where I sit chuckling to myself at the unexpected conclusion. All of us running around her, while she played us off one against the other, and the whole time she had a secret lover anyway. If I hadn't been so stubborn, I wouldn't have found out . . . and now I feel a vague regret, thinking of the nude drawing of Lise and the makeshift bed she'll be sharing with some clutching man.

At the same time I'm not sure I believe her, and half suspect it was only a ruse to get rid of me. She told me earlier she had no one, and she had little enough reason to lie about it. But I continue to think of her having a secret lover all along, of how she fooled me, Harry, Julian, Frank.

In the empty, rattling train I realize that one thing bothers me. If she'd planned to meet someone, who couldn't have known she was going dancing after the banquet, where were they going to meet? If he'd been waiting in her apartment, she wouldn't have been so anxious about my going with her on the bus. But anywhere else and he would have been waiting endlessly, without knowing what time she was coming home.

Almost convinced it was only an excuse, I'm still trying to work it out as I get out at the Bastille. Then I realize that the métro station was the obvious place to meet. But I saw no one there. Or was her lover coming later?

I go into my shabby hotel and take the rickety, ornate lift to my floor. But a lover coming on a later train still couldn't have known what

128

Frank's Girl

time Lise would get there. The only ones who could have known were the four she'd gone dancing with.

"The *only* ones," I say to myself, puzzled, as I step out and fumble on the wall to find the light for the corridor. "Myself, Julian, Harry, *Frank* . . ."

I remember her impatience that the trains were so few. Someone who'd follow . . . A moment later I close the door behind me in my lonely room. *Again.*

Finally, bitterly, I understand it all. But you, Lise, why make a secret of it? What had happened between you and Frank that I didn't understand, and why the deception? I wouldn't have let myself get involved at all if I'd known you really were his all along. Was it an attempt to spare me, because you were attracted to me just the same; or was it simply a habit of lying because one's intimate life is supposed to be forever hidden from others? Or was it even—my one consolation—because you saw through Frank's easy charm and were perhaps a little ashamed about going to bed with him? He, of course, was laughing at it all, once again proving to himself his superiority; playing with the two of us, knowing he'd won before it even began. Although at least he hadn't deliberately caused the humiliation and despair I now felt, since he hadn't intended for me to find out. For him it was purely a private triumph.

Will you visit me in Canterbury, Lise? I wonder. And if you do, what shall I say to you?

The President Reminisces

(An unauthorized transcript of the President's informal speech at a private dinner with the Friends of the Union Club, before his television address to the nation)

You will all recall our nation's excitement when we heard that our starship *Exploit* had found intelligent life on the planet Dee. Creatures who, except for their tails, were remarkably like humans and who communicated in speech much as we do, albeit in a funny language. The degree of civilization there, it seemed, was not greatly inferior to that of Earth's African countries, and they welcomed our boys with that friendliness and interest that Americans have come to expect everywhere.

I was only vice president then, and little did I suspect that relations with that unhappy world would come to dominate my term of office when I assumed the presidency. The fourth planet of Sirius had long attracted scientists' attention with its earthlike size and appearance, except that seas covered a far greater area of its surface. Its atmosphere, too, was like our own, with oxygen and nitrogen, but lacking in carbon dioxide. During that first week, as the news flooded in, I rejoiced that we'd found a people to whom we could stretch out our hands in friendship, for undoubtedly they would need our assistance to bring their standard of living up to our own. I'm proud to have played a small part in the shaping of events—that I'm confident will turn out for the best, despite the present crisis—but of course, the major credit belongs not to me but to this great nation of ours.

130

The President Reminisces

There were problems from the beginning, for we must not forget we were dealing with an underdeveloped planet. And then, because of its rotation rate and the natives' metabolisms, everything happened all at once: Deeans simply live faster than we do. I don't know how many of you remember what they actually called their planet. I'm sure *I* don't. Rasty something, about fifty syllables long, a word no real American could possibly pronounce. Except for a few eggheads in the universities, that is, who figured it was designated in the natives' quaint writing system by signs that looked remarkably like the English letters DEE—which is what all sensible people started to call it.

In retrospect, I have to admit that my state visit there after I became president was an imperfect success. (This is all strictly off the record, by the way.) But free trade with Dee was one of my campaign promises, although obviously economic aid had to come first. So after granting Dee recognition, I sent our ambassador ahead to make arrangements and let the Deeans know who would be accompanying me: economic and scientific advisors, representatives of the media, and so on. With Americans so used to space travel nowadays, there's no point my describing the flight (which took only three days with our new Dow-Boeing 8000 starship), except to say that I'll never forget the view as we approached Dee, with its vast seas shimmering a pale blue like I remember from pictures of Earth's before they turned a brownish yellow.

There was a huge crowd at the starport (constructed in some haste by our engineers), and as I got out, there was an enormous cheer. One of the Deeans ran up the boarding ramp. He was a puny little guy, as they all are. You've all seen pictures of them with their cute long tails and outlandish clothes, which could have come from one of our community handout centers in the Bronx. Anyway, who can tell one Deean from another, or their men from their women for that matter? But now our fruitcake interpreter made a typical balls-up by introducing *everyone* rather than just me. Our mistake had been to take passengers: businessmen who were owed political favors and, for a reason I can't remember (since they're not an important lobby), some fags from the literary and artistic community. One

131

A. Colin Wright

of them was Doren Sanderson, whom I'd met once before without realizing what an asshole he was. I had to present him with some piddly award and pretend I'd read his poetry. He was standing behind me and the Deean went up to *him*, presented him with a few cheap gifts while performing some heathen ceremony, and there was another, louder cheer.

I took no notice and waved to the crowd, but there really had been a terrible mistake. They were cheering not me but that bastard Sanderson!

I don't mind telling you it was embarrassing. When we got into the starport, hundreds of Deeans rushed up, tripping us up with their tails—and again Sanderson was the one they were interested in, while I was ignored. It was only after he'd been carted off in some kind of primordial vehicle that I managed to find our ambassador and ask where Dee's president was.

"He'll be along shortly," the ambassador answered apologetically. "It's just that presidents aren't considered important here."

That's when I started to realize the kind of chaos that existed on this planet! While we were waiting—the Deeans had left to escort Sanderson—our ambassador explained that there'd been little interest in my arrival or in promises of aid, and even less in the media people, since Dee didn't have TV, newspapers, or movies. But it seemed they were crazy about poetry and could hardly wait for Sanderson's arrival, even if, not knowing English, they wouldn't have the faintest idea what he was talking about (as if English would have helped!).

Dee's president arrived eventually, having walked from the city and quite expecting that I and my advisors should walk back with him! Well, through our screw-head interpreter I told him I was president now and didn't intend to walk anywhere on a state visit, except for a photo opportunity. The interpreter finally managed to organize transportation for me—just a wagon pulled by some weird animals—although the others had to get themselves to the city.

132

The President Reminisces

I must say their president seemed quite likeable, for a Deean, and I settled on the name of Charlie for him. He took me to his *house*: a three-room boxlike affair, like all the others I would see there—comfortable enough, I guess, if you've never known anything better. Only I kept wondering when the state dinner was scheduled to take place, and I was edgy because of his lack of concern for time. As it turned out, I needn't have worried because it never *did* take place, and—now don't you all go telling anyone else about this!—I and my interpreter ate every day with Charlie in his kitchen: a slimy abomination he prepared himself on something resembling an antique twentieth-century barbecue.

I asked how he managed without a presidential residence, or a wife, since he was obviously a bachelor.

He gave an offhand reply, which my interpreter translated as "Well, there's not much to do, is there?"

"How's that?" I asked him. I'd learned from my advisers that, although Dee's land mass was smaller than Earth's, there was only one country and it was still larger than the United States, if you don't count our economic dependencies.

I could hardly believe Charlie's answer. Dee's basic laws and financial system had been established centuries ago, so that the planet ran itself by means of primitive computers. A small regulatory council handled any occasional problem that arose. Charlie had to chair this, but when I asked how long he was elected for, he looked totally clueless and there was a long discussion between him and the interpreter. I finally caught on that Charlie had simply been educated at some kind of Deean university for a position on the council, which he'd applied for like any other job. The presidency rotated: no wonder he was considered so unimportant! Well perhaps it was okay for the Deeans, and I guess I could have accepted that until I heard some of the other details. They had a crude monetary system, but every single person got the same wage as everyone else! There were no banks, no way their funny

133

A. Colin Wright

money could be made to increase in value. In fact, everyone somehow shared the planet's resources and production equally.

In all of this, I was starting to get a terrible suspicion. What they had here was a form of socialism! From that moment on, I could no longer feel the same warmth toward Charlie.

Later our experts confirmed that in this rigid economic system, the computers determined what kind of things people could or could not do with their money, and of course no one could own land or businesses. No one could own more than a few personal possessions, in fact. Oh, the Deeans in their ignorance were *happy* enough, but I understood immediately that they'd been so indoctrinated in the way the country was run that it never even occurred to them to criticize it. There was no overt restraint, no censorship of free speech, only because *they didn't need it*—but they were as lacking in freedom as if they suffered the worst forms of oppression!

It wasn't a good week. Quite apart from the alien primitiveness of it all, there were no receptions, nothing. And nothing I could do except stay with the president and share his cooking nine times a day. Well, on Earth I often have to put up with foreign junk, but even now it would be embarrassing to admit to the American people that the President of the United States had been forced every day to sneak back on foot to the starship for hamburgers and fries!

The departure was another disaster, with me having to walk while Doren Sanderson was driven to the starport by an even larger crowd of Deeans. For the whole three-day trip home he boasted of the fun he'd had, and it's nothing short of disgraceful that his name now stands in the *Guinness Book of Records* as the first human being to have sexual intercourse with an extraterrestrial. Once we got back to Earth, I let his publishers know that if they wanted to sign a billion-dollar contract for my memoirs, they were going to have to forget all about marginal books of poetry that didn't make money, and they were happy to drop him from their list.

The President Reminisces

I was glad to get home. I couldn't feel friendly any more toward people who, content though they seemed to be, were denied their God-given right of improving their lot in life and making money. The question, though, remained: how was it going to be possible to do business with them? Trade, naturally, was a necessity—and Dee did have the one commodity we badly needed. Of course, our demand for water had been partly alleviated by the accession of the twelve northern states to the Union, giving us their lakes and rivers, and then access to the northern polar ice cap itself. They had forests and uranium as well, vital to both our defense and our ever-increasing energy needs. But by the midterm elections, all these were becoming scarce again, and the water situation was getting desperate. Much of our space exploration had been undertaken in the hope of finding new sources of supply, and with the discovery of Dee, people were demanding a rational interplanetary resources policy.

I immediately summoned my top experts to my summer residence at Meech Lake in the State of Quebec, to consider what our policy toward Dee should be. Only Wayne Underhood dissented from the general view that we should start by sending massive aid. "No one can figure why socialism works there when it hasn't anywhere else," he said. "Yet they seem to be content. Why don't we just leave them to it?" Well, Wayne didn't retain his job long in *my* administration.

Others were more aware of the opportunities. Deean industry was underdeveloped, and our auto makers in particular wanted to set up production plants there, to replace the few antiquated vehicles we'd seen. We would have to build roads, of course, for theirs were insufficient: they relied on rail. Our aircraft manufacturers were most excited, for there were no airplanes on Dee at all, despite its suitable atmosphere. There were ships for coastal and river traffic, but we could certainly provide bigger and better ones. And we could help with the consumer goods they didn't have. Our entertainment industry planned to introduce television and movies as a more profitable alternative to the Deeans' serious, high-minded books that reflected only their primitive culture. And I suggested baseball. Sports, too, weren't organized on a planetary level.

A. Colin Wright

Education was obviously the first priority, and we decided to send English-language teachers so Dee could take its place in the universe alongside us. Well, as I recall, some joker suggested that we should make an effort to learn Deean, but I soon nuked that ridiculous proposal. We still have our cranks in this country, particularly disaffected pinkos from the former Canadian and Mexican states who have never really appreciated the material advantages of being American. Well, that's what democracy is all about, I guess!

So our aid program got underway, and by God it worked! It's true we were incompletely successful in educating the majority on Dee, despite our movies and TV shows demonstrating the superiority of our way of life. But an increasing number of enterprising individuals realized its benefits, so that private industry and business started to thrive, to our mutual profit. But by then Charlie's turn as president had come round again, and now he revealed his true dictatorial malice by trying to prevent this. The forces of democracy, though, were not to be stopped; and you'll recall how the entrepreneurs, assisted by our advisors, managed to take over the starport with its nearby coastal lands and declare their independence. And they did very well, too, because by developing an uninhabited area they discovered uranium, which we were happy to buy from them. How I laughed over Charlie's bad luck! So since then we've only been trading with this new country that we called Dee 2, and which has rapidly outstripped Dee 1 in its economic growth. We've taught them how to make proper houses, with all those little comforts necessary to superior beings; and I'm happy to say that on my second visit, I was received by Dee 2's businessmen in a far more appropriate style.

The water negotiations also went quickly, and it was one of the proudest days of my life when the first sparkling-pure shipment was transferred to the tanks constructed in the California desert. You all know how Dr. Cornelius Thornton of Cal Tech won the Nobel Prize for his pioneering work on the transportation of water through space. Soon the shipments were arriving regularly, and we were happy to supply military hardware to the Dee-2-ans in return. For alas, the troubles were brewing already.

136

The President Reminisces

In a few years we'd succeeded in introducing the principles of a competitive economy in Dee 2. We'd demonstrated the fallacy of a state run by computers, and had inspired them to establish a true market system, where they were free to do business and make a profit, and free to speak openly. Now they could finally challenge those evil ideas on the other side of the border, where the reds still resisted all change into the modern world. Unfortunately, though, their pernicious propaganda was not without effect. I personally was greatly saddened when—with temporary employment difficulties caused by a mild recession—some of Dee 2's free citizens decided to defect to Dee 1, giving up their freedom for an illusory security within a manifestly unfair system of equal wages for all! And it truly grieves my heart to think of that huge population living in oppression as they have for hundreds of years, without any of our advantages, under the dictatorship of Charlie and his gang. How mistaken I'd been in my first opinion of him, I don't mind admitting!

In the meantime, things continued to go well in our relations with the progressive part of that sorry planet. We supplied the weapons (of a type now obsolete on Earth), while the Deeans provided the water and uranium we needed.

Well, my presidency is approaching its end, and I was looking forward to the prospect of a well-earned retirement on my coastal estates near Havana. But of course I can't think of any personal plans until this present crisis has been brought to a final, happy solution.

I summarized it all at my press conference just the other day. It was faithfully reported by the media, and you all know how the Dee-1-ans illegally occupied the democratic state of Dee 2, using the pretext that Dee 2 was squandering the planet's water resources—regardless of the fact that they were bound to us by iron-clad interplanetary obligations!

We have tried all possible means to deal with the matter by diplomacy. For the first time ever, Deeans came to the United States to plead their case in American trade courts, which, by treaty, are duty

A. Colin Wright

bound to arbitrate in cases of interplanetary dispute. My own attorneys represented the Dee-2-ans, but the Dee-1-ans couldn't afford proper American counsel and had to represent themselves. And what ridiculous figures they cut, puny in size compared with humans and with their absurdly long tails! They claimed that Dee 2 had no right to sign contracts involving a common resource, although it's clear that Dee 2 owns the adjoining oceans and can do what it wants with them. The Dee-1-ans were, quite literally, laughed out of court!

But let me now conclude in the words of my television address, to be broadcast to this great nation shortly. Tonight I appear before you with great sadness in my heart, and so on and so forth. Ah, here we are. We have tried all possible means to deal with the matter by diplomacy. You know how our courts have ruled that Dee 1 has no legal right whatsoever to occupy Dee 2. But it seems the leaders of Dee 1 have little regard for law and are inflexible in their refusal to withdraw. Even as I speak, a tiny country with a small, courageous population is occupied by its larger, aggressive neighbor, which brazenly states that it's none of our business, when clearly security and justice everywhere in the universe *is* American business.

We have been patient long enough and can no longer ignore this flagrant violation of Dee 2's sovereignty. Of far greater import than the continuing supplies of water to us is the fact that the people of Dee 2 are no longer free! *They are not free!* Not free to pursue happiness, compete with others, and make money!

A few hours ago I gave our forces the order to move to the starpads for immediate launch, should the Dee-1-ans fail to meet our deadline for withdrawal. My interplanetary secretary, Dwight Shufflebottom, has also reported that he's secured the agreement of other members of the Allied Nations to send troops. I pray most sincerely that this war won't last long. Because of the distance and the sheer numbers of the Deeans, it won't be an easy task. But despite arms shipments to Dee 1 from other traitor nations on Earth, we have clear superiority. It is my certainty that right shall prevail

138

The President Reminisces

with, we hope, as little loss of (human) life as possible. I also give my word that selective strikes by our new superbright missiles will cause a minimum of collateral damage among the civilians of Dee.

In the meantime, we shall ensure the continued shipment of *our* water to Earth, taking all necessary steps to prevent the Dee-1-ans from poisoning it; for I fear that, lacking the morality on which this very country of ours was so gloriously founded, they are quite capable of such a despicable action.

It's a sad day, but it is our solemn duty to counter aggression wherever it might occur. In these last few hours before what seems likely to become our first interplanetary war, I pray for you all. To our forces I say God speed. There will, I fear, be losses, and even one American life lost is an unbearable price to pay. You know how anxiously we shall be waiting for your return. I call on you to do your duty, in the name of justice, interplanetary trade, and a better universe for all—in which, as on Earth, Americans will be proud to lead the way.

God bless you all!

God bless America!

The Jump

Matthew's skis hung heavily on his feet, grazing the tops of untrimmed bushes as his chair moved steadily upwards through the trees. He'd been following the irregular tracks below him in the snow, where one skier had left the trail for the more risky descent under the lift. "Oh Lord," he prayed, chuckling to let the Almighty know he was making a joke of it, "who wants us to be perfect in all things—help me to be a better liar."

He looked at the chair ahead, at the backs of his wife and son in their bulky jackets, Mary in green, Jonathan in blue and red. Their skis, hanging beneath them, slid like four nearly parallel lines across a crumpled backdrop of green-brown and white, until suddenly one line splayed outwards and Jonathan turned around. "Hi, Dad!"

Matthew gave his casual wave and then, in case his son's projecting ski should catch one of the pylons, he yelled to him to be careful. Mary made Jonathan face the front again.

He leaned back, determined to forget his problems in the sunshine of God's natural world, to rid himself of the thought that those lies— which had gradually become necessary in a minor way—might now lead him to major ones, which nothing in his life had prepared him for. He smiled, though. "I have no spur," he thought, with his habit of resorting to quotation—as if fictionalizing life's difficulties would make them more bearable—"to prick the sides of my intent, but only vaulting ambition, which o'erleaps itself and falls on the other."

The lift took him out of the trees and over a broad white trail, where a number of skiers were descending, shouting to one another, their skis whistling and clicking in the snow. On the far edge, where the chair entered the woods again, a boy had stopped and was scooping up the snow with his arms, gathering it into a pile. Matthew wondered why, but he was soon carried past him and, once again, only the solitary skier's tracks broke the snow amid the bushes and tree stumps below.

"Beat you down!" The straps on Jonathan's poles were already on his wrists before Matthew had skidded off the lift.

Beware the Jabberwock, my son—and they were off, Matthew thrilling to the sideways oscillation of his legs beneath him: *One, two! One, two! And through and through the vorpal blade went snicker-snack!*

Mary was left behind. Matthew risked a small jump but couldn't keep his balance and sat down on the snow, embarrassed at having fallen on his first run. Mary, checking to see he was all right, skied on past, concentrating on making her turns, her rear end sticking out in her bulky warm-up pants. He skied on more carefully but soon passed her and then Jonathan too, who'd stopped, chortling triumphantly.

Matthew waited lower down, under the lift-line. He found himself looking into the face of the young boy—eighteen, nineteen perhaps?—who'd just straightened up after dumping another armful of snow onto the pile he'd been accumulating. The boy smiled at him apologetically, brushing the snow from his arms. Aware of looking foolish perhaps but—Matthew was shamed into turning his own eyes away—with all of youth's enthusiasm for the wide world that awaited him.

"The service went very nicely, I thought."

A. Colin Wright

Mary sipped her hot chocolate, going over the week's events that she hadn't yet found the opportunity to talk to him about. Jonathan was still outside, having scorned his mother's suggestion that they should take a break after only five runs. Matthew, too, was impatient to get back on the slopes, but Mary had taken off her ski jacket and dumped it across the table beside them.

"You know what I heard Mrs. Miller say afterwards?" she went on, placing her free hand on his across the table. "'That Matthew Cummings is such a marvel—I've never known a man to do so much for others!' And you conducted it so . . . so meaningfully, as always."

"I fit that role very nicely." He added that slight touch of irony to his voice that he used so effectively. "But do you think a woman's soul can live on a talent for preaching?"

Suspiciously: "What do you mean by that?"

"It's a line from the play, that's all."

"Oh."

He was well aware of how all the church women twittered over him, and normally Mary's telling him about it brought him pleasure. At the same time, perhaps because knew there was an element of deception in it all, it depressed him. This occasion had been the annual cub service, which he, as Akela of the First Summertown pack, had conducted. His secret with all these things—in his Sunday-school class too—was to treat them in the same way as his amateur theatricals: as a performance he put on to entertain. The children loved him and their parents spoke of him enthusiastically, for he could always be relied on to do a good job of instilling those values that they, in the comfort of their tasteful suburban lives, could never quite manage to exemplify.

Mary squeezed his hand again, smiling. "I'm so glad I'm married to a husband everyone thinks so highly of."

Yes, he thought.

The Jump

* * *

This time the boy had got hold of a shovel from somewhere and the mound of snow was growing higher. Obviously he was building a jump, not satisfied with those that were already there on almost any trail. Jonathan memorized their every location and never failed to insist that his parents ski ahead so they could stop and watch him go over. Today Jonathan was restless, wanting to ski faster and explore without them, but, at the same time, not yet confident enough to do it alone.

They took a higher lift and skied some of the trails on the far side of the mountain, where there were spectacular views over the frozen lake below and into the misty distance of other peaks. One of them was patterned with the jagged artificial bands of white that indicated ski trails there too. Like another planet, Matthew thought, where people were doing the same as here, only the trails were different.

At odd times, as he looked out over the valley or was skiing an easy bit, he thought of the production that was to open the next weekend. For the first time he was acting with Janice Delauney. That might not have bothered him if it had been a different play, yet it had seemed an obvious choice for him to audition for Morell, and Janice, playing Candida, had been delighted. "You're a natural for the part!" she'd said. Which wasn't very flattering. Emotionally he felt closer to the poetic Marchbanks, but you had to be young for that role. Doubtless the women would rave about his performance as Shaw's cheerful, self-satisfied clergyman in love with his own wife. Like Prossie in the play, they'd idolize him for his eloquently convincing brand of Christianity. Which Janice had to foster on stage, easing his path with wifely devotion, while in real life she laughed at him for it.

The next time up, Matthew and Jonathan left Mary so they could try one of the expert trails. Steep descents made Matthew nervous but he attempted them anyway, taking them slowly and often side-slipping the more difficult parts, while Jonathan went on confidently, calling to his father to keep up. On a flatter stretch they came on a group of

143

A. Colin Wright

young people gathered around a jump, where they were practising aerial somersaults with casual proficiency. Matthew stopped to watch as one of them made an effortless approach, flipped right over as his skis left the snow, and landed with perfect control, skidding to a halt before climbing back up the hill again.

"Dad, can we burn down the Bunny Hop again and then go and eat?"

Matthew would rather have tried some other runs, but Jonathan's enjoyment was based on what he considered fun rather than on any sense of achievement.

They had to take the first chair again, which meant they could see how far the boy had got with building his jump. It was quite high now, but he was still shovelling, adding more snow at the sides and the approach. When they skied down past him, he was packing it energetically with the back of his shovel.

Matthew stared at the chocolate layer cake he shouldn't be indulging in and took a drink of his coffee. Rehearsal had finished, and he looked at Janice, thinking that in some ways he didn't like her very much.

"So what am I going to tell Mary?"

Janice made a gesture of impatience, looking at him with those eyes that were always highlighted by expertly applied mascara. She had black hair, features a little sharp, and pouting lips with just the right amount of lipstick. An irritatingly attractive woman, with a tendency to bluntly oversimplify human relationships. "Why don't you tell her the truth?"

The question was difficult to answer in any way she'd understand. So he simply used his shocked tone of voice, managing to convey irony

The Jump

and humour at the same time: "Tell her I'm going to Montreal with you for a weekend?"

"It's only a theatre workshop. It's not as if we're planning to sleep together."

No. He'd been seeing her secretly like this for months, but only to discuss the theatre. A betrayal of Mary only in the sense that he'd been sharing meaningful conversations with another woman. And even that . . . Well, Mary wouldn't have minded if it had to do with church or community work, and the meetings needn't have been secret. It was his new addiction to the theatre that was the betrayal.

"And," Janice went on, lighting a cigarette and inhaling with a gasp of pleasure, "think of all it might lead to."

He chose the safest interpretation of her ambiguous remark. "You don't think a producer like Marvin's really coming with the idea of looking for talented amateurs, do you? Anyway, that might be fine for someone like you, but there's no way a forty-five-year-old man with my commitments could ever do anything serious on the stage."

Slightly older than he was, Janice had gone through two marriages and numerous affairs. At present she was free of attachments, although he wondered if she hadn't perhaps singled him out as a rather unlikely prospect. The thought had first occurred to him when he was reading a lesson in church, and he'd felt himself blushing because of a quite unreasonable, tempting sensation of guilt. But no one had noticed and his rendition had been eloquent as always.

"You owe it to yourself," she said appealingly.

He smiled at the cliché. "When it's only encouraging an impossible dream?"

"A greater commitment to acting? That's not impossible. Won't Mary realize the workshop's important to you?"

145

A. Colin Wright

It sounded so simple. People like Janice could never understand how you became committed not just to another person, but to the view that person held of you. "She thinks the theatre takes me away from the important things."

Janice shrugged contemptuously.

"And then," he went on, using his final argument, "it's her weekend for volunteering."

"Her *what?*"

"Oh, once a month she . . ."

But Janice was shaking with laughter, not listening.

He looked up now as the green of Mary's ski outfit appeared at the table in front of him. She sat down and laboriously unbuckled her boots.

"In a happy marriage like ours," he began, joking aggressively to ease the transition from his thoughts of Janice to the actuality of wedded life, "there's something very sacred in the return of the wife."

Mary raised her head to stare at him. "I wish you wouldn't keep quoting at me from your confounded play." She stood up again. "Where's Jonathan?"

"He's gone for another run until we're ready." Their timing was wrong as always: Matthew had finished his lunch and was eager to get back outside, but now Mary would want him to sit with her while she had hers, so they could then continue skiing together.

She went to join the line for the cafeteria.

"That boy who's building the jump," she said when she returned with her soup and hot dog. "It's enormous. I can't see the point of something like that. Why doesn't he just ski the trails and enjoy himself?"

146

The Jump

"He's a young man with aspirations. What's wrong with that?"

Now she looked at him intently, but laughed as she sat down. "It's true, you *do* speak with your tongue in your cheek."

Quite literally. Apparently it was one of his mannerisms, which he used all the time: on stage, in Sunday school, with the cubs, in his university classes, even with individuals in private conversation. He'd told Mary a colleague had pointed it out to him, but of course it had been Janice. "Always to the left," she'd said, "curling it up in front of your teeth. You must have practised it once."

If so, he no longer remembered.

He'd always loved the semblance of freedom that skiing gave him: the speed, the open air, the brilliance of the sun on a day like this, the exhilaration of the descent. Brought up in England at a time when skiing was a hobby reserved for the rich, he still saw it as something a little daring, something he'd once dreamed of while never thinking it would become possible. Like acting. But he'd learned too late in life ever to be more than a reasonably good intermediate. From the chairs he'd watch with envy the experts who could rough it out over the steepest, toughest slopes, leaping around with a contemptuous ease he could never achieve on far less difficult trails. Those young kids hadn't even been born when he'd already been skiing for years. Jonathan now complained that his father wasn't fast enough, and sometimes it was a relief to ski with Mary, so he wasn't constantly forcing himself to keep up.

In the afternoon, they passed the boy and his jump several times. It was still growing, and he was working at it with a determination that seemed out of place, a fanatic desire to achieve something before nightfall. It is the cause, Matthew quoted to himself, it is the cause, my soul. He hoped he would see the boy when he finally made the jump. A few moments of glory—the accelerating approach, the somersault in the air with the whole world turned on its head, the firm contact of skis on the trail below—then

A. Colin Wright

a further rapid descent before turning them across the hill in a shower of snow, to the applause of the admiring audience.

Later, Matthew tried a more difficult trail. Alone, so he wouldn't have Jonathan showing him how to do it. From the lift it hadn't looked that bad, but it was steeper than he thought, the moguls had hard crusts of ice behind them, and it was impossible to keep turning without going too fast so that the skis ran away with you. He found himself skiing stiffly from one side of the trail to the other, side-slipping clumsily to find a patch of soft snow to turn in and then still hitting ice, clattering painfully down on his rear end and landing with skis in impossible positions for standing up straight again.

After one fall, he remained seated in the snow, getting his breath, taking time to admire the view. He recalled how, at cub camp in the summer, he'd fallen after catching his foot on something, and everyone had gathered round making a joke of it. He'd used it for his address at church parade: something about its being natural for humans to fall and needing the helping hand of God to lift them up. There, too, he was a success. The games for the cubs, involving role-playing with greasepaint he provided, their sketches and songs around the campfire in front of the huge wooden chair reserved for him—at first it had seemed a natural extension to his acting. Now he was heartily sick of the camps, but it was as inevitable that he should run them as it had been for him to audition for Morell, playing to Janice's Candida.

"It's your everyday life that's an act," Janice had told him once, unfairly. "Because you've wanted applause from everyone all your life."

A skier clattered past him, his edges scraping confidently on the ice. Slowly Matthew got up, tried to direct his skis between the moguls, and found he was careering full speed toward the trees. He saved himself by a sharp turn into the hill, in the snow at the edge, and then had to spend a minute or so extracting himself. Finally he managed to side-slip to a flatter part.

The Jump

At last the trail joined an easy one and he was on snow he could handle, his legs working efficiently again as he sped on down towards the bottom.

One, two! One, two! And through and through the vorpal blades go snicker-snack . . .

It is the cause, it is the cause, my soul . . .

Matthew Cummings so marvellous in his comings and goings, organizing, helping in the parish . . .

Bunny Hop trail now past the boy, who has finished mounding snow and is clambering uphill . . .

Janice Delauney, oh reason not the need . . .

Something very sacred . . .

Exhilarated by his fast run down, wanting another before the lifts closed, he skied straight to the chair and onto it, hardly stopping since there was no longer a line of other skiers blocking his way. He sat back in the late sunshine, looking at the tracks below him that had been there since the beginning of the day.

"At what point," he asked the Almighty, "did it become mere activity? And how can *you* put up with the sheer volume of *words*?"

Such metaphors as falling and God's helping him to his feet—it was so trite. But for a moment the silence of the woods around him; the chair taking him slowly upwards; the quiet beauty of God's natural world; the snow, still glittering in places, although much of it was already in shadow: all of it gave him a vague hope for the way life might still become.

There was no one reason for the change in him, if you could even call it that. No one event he could point to. Instead there were many little things, some of which he wasn't even sure he remembered. Playing Morell perhaps. A sentence in a book he liked: "Jesus Christ, the place is full

A. Colin Wright

of *Christians*," spoken with a contempt that startled him into realizing that churchgoers could be despised as well as ignored. And somewhere he thought there was another argument, stored away for his justification. It was the shape of an evergreen standing out from the other trees that reminded him of it as he was carried by. Going into church one day, he'd been handed a scrap of paper, a pencil, and a pin. The idea was to write down what you most wanted to thank God for and pin the paper on a piece of green cloth cut like a Christmas tree. Taken by surprise, his immediate, unprepared response was to write down "Janice." He didn't do it, of course, but found a less compromising way of expressing the same thing: "Acting." Mary's slip read "Matthew"; Jonathan's: "Mom and Dad." When later he read the others, all without exception referred to people's families.

He looked at the snow-covered trees around him, and then turned so he could see into the valley with the frozen lake and the other ski hill in the distance. He'd told himself repeatedly that to go to a theatrical workshop with Janice was entirely innocent. Oh, yes, it would probably turn out that way. He didn't particularly like her, and her insolent sexuality often made him angry. He didn't want an affair with her. But if the opportunity presented itself, he suspected he'd get into bed with her as a simple act of rebellion against that particular image that led people to say he was a natural to play Morell.

As the chair takes him higher, he's aware that God has answered his prayer, and the lie he's been looking for has been obvious all along. Mary will never accept a theatre workshop, but anything to do with religion or the church will suffice. Some theological seminar at McGill University, say. And how Janice will laugh at that, as she laughs at his cubs, his reading the lessons.

He sits with his tongue in his cheek, feeling it against his teeth, somewhat in awe at the enormity of the fabrication he's planning. The chair's approaching the point where the Bunny Hop crosses below. Relieved at having reached a decision, he recalls with satisfaction that he'll see how the boy has managed with his jump.

150

The Jump

Just before the chair leaves the woods he has a premonition of disaster. On the far side of the trail he can make out a pair of crossed skis planted in the snow at the jump's approach; as he's carried beyond the trees he sees a group of people gathered below it. At that moment two ski-patrol members appear on the slope above, bringing down a stretcher. The boy lies motionless, sprawled in the snow, skis and limbs at odd angles, and there's something wrong with his neck.

By the time Matthew has reached the top and skied down again, the boy is gone. Only the crossed skis remain, warning others of possible danger. He hurries to catch up with the patrollers, who are slowly guiding the stretcher with its huddled-up form towards the chalet, followed by a number of others in solemn procession. He's dead, someone tells him.

Later Matthew hears the story. How the boy had never attempted a somersault before. How several times an instructor had tried to warn him, but he was determined. How he'd stubbornly gone ahead all day building his jump. But when it was finally completed, he'd been too timid, had hesitated as he'd approached and jumped at the wrong moment.

He'd managed to flip over and do the somersault, but had landed on his head, breaking his neck.

Talking to Mary and Jonathan about it during the long drive home, Matthew couldn't rid himself of the thought of how the boy had spent an entire day working, building his own death.

The Trouble with Saints

My statue of St. Francis has never been replaced, but otherwise the village is much as I remember: more prosperous now that its villas, once occupied by Mussolini's bureaucrats, have been restored to their benevolent self-confidence. Tourists eat ice cream in the café by the harbour, but the local men still argue under stucco arches in the bar farther down Lake Garda, near the smaller port where I used to kiss Emanuela.

The statue was a few cobbled streets away, a larger version of those figures of saints with their brown sheen and whitish faces found in shops for religious kitsch. A path led up the hillside to a monastery, and St. Francis stood in a brightly lit shrine cut into the rock, eyes cast piously down and a hand raised in blessing. Each night, after taking Emanuela home, I used to stop and lay at his feet a pink flower from the bushes. Now I look at the empty niche, thinking that I'm the only one who knows why he's no longer there.

I'd talk to him of Emanuela; even, occasionally, of Clara. In one brief summer I had met and desired both, but it was to Emanuela that I said "I love you": little understanding in my youth that those words are seldom clear except as a vague contract interpreted differently by each partner. She'd lay her head on my shoulder, look at me with those mystified brown eyes, and whisper "*mio caro,*" while the knowledge that somewhere there might be a husband gave our love greater poignancy.

152

The Trouble with Saints

"No one knows I'm married," she told me that first night as we sat listening to the waves in the darkness, while my hand stroked her nipples inside her dress. "My father couldn't have trusted me if he'd known I'd married someone who wore a Fascist uniform."

The war had been over for more than two years, and I wandered across Northern Italy, justifying my search for adventure with journalistic pretensions, mailing bulky envelopes to editors in Toronto—although the only article I'd sell would be the one about Emanuela's father. It was him I'd come to talk to. A prosperous winemaker, he'd joined the Italian underground when he was fifty, allowing his villa to be used for meetings under the nose of Mussolini, who at that time ruled his collapsing empire from nearby Salò. I would come to admire Emanuela's father, seeing his deep affection for her in the way he spoke to her, while his shyness was even greater than my own. Because of this, our first meeting was difficult. And then, not used to interviewing people in my imperfect Italian and intimidated by the scowling maid who'd let me in, I hadn't known the right questions to ask.

He couldn't spend much time with me. "Mister Tony"—he hadn't grasped my surname—"could you return the day after tomorrow? I'm sorry, eh? Tonight I go to Milan."

He'd been telling me of a cheap pensione where I could stay when his daughter came in: a mischievous Botticelli nymph with impudent eyes. "Emanuela,"—he turned to her as he shook my hand—"please accompany our guest to the door."

"He likes you," she told me as she showed me out. "Don't be put off by his awkwardness." Her hand lingered in my own, her lips parting as though to say something more. But then she looked into my eyes, waiting for me to speak.

"Could you . . ." I began, aware that our bodies were almost touching. "Could you perhaps help me by telling me about your father too?"

153

A. Colin Wright

"Of course," she said, laughing, and we agreed to meet that afternoon.

But by four o'clock I still hadn't found accommodation, either at the Pensione Flora—which would have a room only two nights later—or anywhere else I could afford.

"I can invite you to the villa then," Emanuela said over a *cassata* and coffee in the newly opened café by the harbour. "Maria won't mind. She'll just grumble as always."

I looked at this delightfully brazen girl in front of me, thinking how she might make up for my disappointment with Clara.

So Emanuela went home to tell Maria, and we met again in the evening. Walking along the lake we joined hands, impatient to kiss and start exploring each other.

While raucous voices from the bar floated to us across the port, Emanuela told me about her husband. They'd had only a brief, clandestine honeymoon before Alberto, like other unfortunates after Italy's capitulation, had been mobilized by the Germans. Near Ortona he'd been taken prisoner by the Americans, but later escaped. That was all she knew.

"I can't tell anyone, I can't marry again—if he's dead, that is. I have to pretend I've never been . . . intimate with a man."

We walked back to the villa, through empty streets, kissing as we went. I'd left my suitcase at the pensione, but I had my pyjamas in my briefcase, which I had to put down awkwardly each time I drew her toward me.

She laughed after another long kiss and said "What are you doing fooling around with pyjamas?"

As we made love in her bed that night, she was an extraordinary mixture of provocativeness and self-doubt. Next morning, waking early, she turned on her radio, stretching across me so that her breasts brushed

154

The Trouble with Saints

over my lips. It was a programme of classical music, some of Grieg's lieder with their swelling crescendos, and I eased myself into Emanuela as the chords on the piano led into his famous love song, "*Jeg elsker dig.*"

"I love you," I translated the words into Italian as her hips beneath me moved with my own. "I love you, in time and eternity."

Perhaps I really believed it would be that way. But when her father returned I had to move to the Pensione Flora, and Emanuela couldn't come to me there because she knew the family who ran it. She didn't hide the fact that she was seeing me, which took courage in the Italy of those days. Her father, with his gauche kindliness, seemed to approve of me, for even if I had been too young for the war I was still Canadian, one of the allies. But now Emanuela and I could only meet on our bench, kissing passionately in the darkness.

"Help us to be together," I'd pray to St. Francis each night after I'd left her, knowing he understood that I wasn't traditionally religious. Patiently I'd explain to him that churches and saints were important in my life only because, if you're interested in Italian art, they're unavoidable.

In those days I dreamed of becoming a great lover. It didn't turn out that way, and in the intervening years, and during my marriage, I've come to understand that few of us turn out to be a great anything, and that most of our loves are little ones, fearful of being hurt, not wanting emotional commitment without a lifetime guarantee.

In love with Emanuela, I was embarrassed to recall my stupidity over Clara not long before. My failure with her hadn't been my fault and I no longer blamed myself, but how could I have dreamed of love with her when her one commitment was to God alone?

I'd met Clara in Padua, where I was staying in a Hotel Agape—named appropriately for Christian rather than erotic love. I was standing

155

A. Colin Wright

in St. Anthony's Basilica beside his sarcophagus, built into the back of an enormous altar.

"He'll grant your request, I guarantee it."

I turned to see a dark-haired girl, like a Tiepolo cherub, I thought. I started to object that I wasn't one of the pilgrims who had arrived in busloads as I was going in, but was there only because the Scrovegni Chapel with the Giotto frescoes was closed. But, looking at her smile and dark locks of hair, I stammered instead: "I . . . I guess he's my patron saint."

She indicated that we should line up behind the black-shawled women waiting to touch the sarcophagus, which was covered with letters giving thanks for favours received. I read them thinking that Italians who'd gone through the war probably needed to believe in miracles. Yet to me it seemed miraculous enough that I'd been spared the effort of having to approach an attractive girl, so I too said a prayer of thanks, feeling foolish as I watched her lips move silently while she pressed her forehead to the marble.

"So your name's Antonio?" she asked me over coffee.

"Tony, yes."

"Mine's Clara Gentile. Really. Can you imagine a nicer name?"

It suited her: kind, pleasant, gentle.

"One day God will call you too," she insisted. "I guarantee it."

I had no desire to be called by God, but to talk to her about religion seemed the obvious way to get to know her.

As she took me on a tour of medieval Padua, she told me her only passion was to see Christ in his second coming and—brushing aside my attempt to mention more earthly passions—assured me it would be soon.

"And will people recognize him?"

156

The Trouble with Saints

"Absolutely. Because we're told he'll come in glory. And I know I'll see him: either in my lifetime or at the moment of my death."

Strolling through cobbled streets, by the market with its thirteenth-century Palazzo della Ragione, she said she had a guardian angel beside her, protecting her from danger. Believing I was an unconscious pilgrim (I laughed at that!) she showed me almost every church, always stopping for a prayer. But she had a sense of fun and showed no disapproval when I argued that one should enjoy the pleasures of this world.

"I'll pray for you," she said with a laugh. "You'll come to God, I guarantee it."

She invited me to dinner the next evening. She had only two rooms and a miserable kitchen, their walls covered with reproductions of religious paintings. I learned she was a teacher, giving most of what she earned to the church. But whenever I tried to ask about her personal life, she kept returning to her religion—and to the Pope, whose every utterance, she maintained, reflected God's truth. In vain I argued that one could hardly put much faith in the Pope after the Concordat with Nazi Germany and Pius XII's pro-German attitudes in the war.

"He had to choose between terrible alternatives," she defended him. "As for the Fascists . . . well, at least they stood up to the evil of Communism!"

For this reason she'd given a grudging assent to Mussolini. Those in the resistance, she explained, were sincere but had been duped by the Communists. Her brother was one: "I try to make allowances for him, but he's given me so many problems. My conversion to Catholicism caused even more of a rift between us." Before I could ask about this, she continued: "Of course, the Fascists betrayed us. But we're told to love our enemies."

I disagreed with most of what she said, but she argued charmingly, refusing to sit in judgement over others. "Only God can do that."

A. Colin Wright

When, unwisely, I tried to kiss her, she dodged me, and we parted laughing.

I returned several times. Her cooking was abominable, which I don't think she even realized. Irritated by her unquestioning belief, I found her attractive just the same. Perhaps, I suggested, she was the only saint I'd ever met. She made a joke of it: "All I need is credit for a few miracles!"

St. Anthony, Clara had told me, had been a disciple of St. Francis, so when a few weeks later I came upon my statue, I was constantly reminded of her saintliness. I'd left Padua disappointed. I was looking for a woman, not a saint, and it seemed to me there was indeed this guardian angel standing beside Clara. She perhaps had the radiance of God, but it set her apart from other mortals. I sensed in her a personal joy I might have envied, but I could never get close to her because she'd never speak of herself, except in terms of her faith. Nor could I talk sincerely about my own sexual nature and deepest longings because, although she accepted them, she saw them as failings to be prayed about and dismissed.

When I told St. Francis about this he only winked, saying we all had different purposes in life.

That very day I met Emanucla. I plunged into my affair with her all the more recklessly, finding at once the abandonment that love demanded, our bodies moistening for each other at the slightest touch. But after I took up residence in the pensione, we knew all the passion of despair. October became November and, with only our bench to go to, we had to dress more warmly, our hands stretching under more layers to caress those enticing places we longed for. If we brought each other to a climax, I had a cold and clammy walk home, with St. Francis laughing at my discomfort as I stood before him.

158

The Trouble with Saints

"Help us to find a way," I begged him, while he gazed down inscrutably.

One evening Emanuela's father invited me to dinner.

"He hopes you might want to marry me," she told me. "But what can I do, when I'm married already? For that all to come out . . . I couldn't hurt him that way."

He stammered during the meal, apologizing for not inviting me earlier because of his difficulties since his wife had died. Afterwards, he reached for a leather-bound book.

"D'Annunzio," Emanuela told me. "He feels reading poetry is a way of sharing with his friends."

He was embarrassed. "Not if you don't want . . . But to help you write about—eh?—the paradox of the Italians that led to Fascism. Eh?"

My Italian wasn't up to understanding poetry. But as he read, I couldn't help being moved by the flowing, musical cadences.

"Yet Gabriele D'Annunzio, who created such beauty"—he paused in distress—"wanted to be a hero, wanted glory for Italy. To wield the sword as well as the pen. 'Not to plot, but to dare,' he wrote."

Emanuela giggled. "And that he didn't know which pleased him most, to spill blood or to spill sperm!"

Her father chuckled to hide his embarrassment. "Violence, sensuality, decadence, heroism. Fine in poetry, but . . ." He was interrupted by the doorbell. "Maria's in the kitchen, get it will you please, Emanuela?" He went on: "But when it comes to life around you . . . eh? It's easy to blame the Germans, but Italians too . . ."

Emanuela returned and handed me a telegram. "Forgive me for opening it. Your name didn't show in the window."

159

A. Colin Wright

I read the words "TONY PLEASE COME CLARA"—sent to the only address I'd been able to give her.

"How many others are there?" Emanuela asked as she showed me out.

When Clara met me at the station in Padua, I walked by without recognizing her, and she had to run after me. She wore a scarf over her head, but the shining black locks were gone. So too, I realized, was the rest of her hair.

"Why, why didn't you come as soon as you got my telegram?" she sobbed.

I hadn't realized how important it was. Why me, when I seemed so incidental to her life? Few people had telephones then, and there was no way I could have called her. I'd spent the next day trying to explain to Emanuela and, by the time she'd come to an unwilling acceptance of my irrational feeling that I should do as Clara asked, it was too late for the last bus. I could only send a telegram saying I'd arrive the next evening. But it wasn't the loss of Clara's hair that I would have prevented.

"Last night," Clara told me, "I . . . was raped."

She led me through those familiar streets, crossing herself each time we passed a church, but walking so fast that I had no chance to ask what had happened. Not until we got to her apartment did she finally start to talk, her tears dripping onto a plate of spaghetti she'd prepared, knowing I'd be hungry, but had let boil so long it was barely edible.

Even then she seemed to avoid the most important thing. "Tony, I must tell you something. I'm Jewish."

She took off her scarf, revealing only a slight stubble covering her scalp. It occurred to me that I might have guessed it from her appearance, but I never think about such things.

160

The Trouble with Saints

"I changed my name. To something I liked better."

Choosing 'Gentile,' I thought, with all the solemnity of a sacrament. Of course: Italian for both 'gentle' and 'gen*tile*.'

"But it was during the occupation. My parents were deported. My brother Giuseppe attributed it to cowardice. It wasn't cowardice, I swear! I was safe. Like many Jews I was hidden by Catholic priests. It was then that I saw God, became converted. My parents . . . were unlucky."

I was still impatient to know what had happened, but she needed to tell me in her own way, crying the whole time.

It had started three days before, when Giuseppe had come to see her and they'd got into an argument about his Communism. "Why I even bothered with him, I don't know! He only thinks of himself, having a good time, showing his friends what a man he can be."

She couldn't make him understand how she had to oppose the forces of the Antichrist. He'd become violent and stormed out, but returned later with some friends.

"I shouldn't have let them in, but I couldn't cast aside my own brother! They'd been drinking, called me a Nazi, accused me of betraying my parents. If they'd known what my conversion cost me! Then they shaved my head, as though I were a collaborator." She ran her hands over the stubble. "But that," she sobbed, "was nothing! Vanity, that's all. The next day, at mass, I met this student I know, Enrico. But when I told him what they'd done, he hardened his heart. He told his friends, some of them Christians, but some neo-Fascists too. But good boys, you know! All they could think of was revenge and what weapons they could get hold of. 'Love your enemies,' I kept saying to them, but they wouldn't listen. That's when I sent you the telegram."

"What did you think I could do?"

"Oh, with an outsider . . . They would have respected you. You can talk to people in terms they understand." Clara shook her bald head with

161

A. Colin Wright

quiet despair. "Last night, you didn't come. I knew they were planning to find Giuseppe and his friends. They used to fight at school too. I was afraid someone would get killed because of me! And they were supposed to be Christians!

"I didn't know what to do. Find them and try to stop them, or not get involved, which was cowardly. I spent over an hour in prayer, and then I felt yes, God had heard me and I could leave it to Him. Only then I started wondering what might be happening. 'Beware of vain curiosity,' we're told. If only I'd heeded that! Instead, I decided to go to Giuseppe's and find out."

I was beginning to see where the story was leading. But where, Clara, was your guardian angel?

"A voice kept telling me 'Go back,' but I *wanted* to find out. Curiosity, that was my sin, and how God punished me!"

She told me she'd found about ten of them at her brother's apartment, and there was blood all over the place. But she soon realized it had mostly come from a nosebleed, and they were now drinking. There'd been the usual brawl, and then, honour satisfied—"That's so important!"— they'd got into Giuseppe's stock of wine.

"Nothing terrible had happened, and I could only kneel and pour out my gratitude to God." She smiled as though still remembering to be thankful, and then started crying again. "Lord, do with me according to Your good pleasure and do not reject my sinful life, known to none more fully and clearly than Yourself."

I took her hand, happy at least to fill the role of comforter.

"But the fighting had excited them and they were *proud* of themselves. They wanted to glorify in their sin by doing something worse. My praying seemed to make them more excited, and I realized they were looking at me with lust in their hearts, even my brother. Even Enrico. They started taunting me, trying to get me to drink their wine, and when I wouldn't, they grabbed

162

The Trouble with Saints

me, pushed me to the floor, stuck the bottle into my mouth so I had to swallow or be choked. 'This is my blood which was given for thee,' I heard Enrico say. Defiling the Blessed Sacrament! 'And this is my body,' came another voice. They had my legs apart, and I felt someone clawing at my underclothes and forcing himself into me. All I could do was shut my eyes and try to keep from choking on the wine they kept pouring into my mouth."

I recalled how I'd imagined making love to Clara myself: passionately, but not like this. It occurred to me that for once she was speaking about herself, but almost with detachment. As though, afraid of breaking down, she'd rehearsed the words.

"After a while I remember thinking that it didn't hurt so much, although I knew I must be bleeding. They . . . took me in turns. And . . . after a while it didn't seem so bad. I could just observe it all and think, Madonna!, all this is happening to *me*."

I was silent, uneasy.

"In the past I'd denied myself so much," she went on. "What they were doing was terrible, but there was even a certain curiosity within me, to know what it was like, can you imagine? Then they weren't holding me down anymore. I remember sitting up and taking off my clothes to keep them from being torn or getting more blood on them. But I knew it was an excuse, that I wasn't really concerned about the clothes. I knew I should be in despair, but some part of me . . . I can only put it like this . . . was enjoying my shame and humiliation. 'Blessed are ye when men shall revile you,' I found myself thinking. I was proud that I was a martyr and that none of it was my fault! Only it began to change. I began to do everything they suggested, terrible things. Not from pleasure, I don't even know why, perhaps just to be able to *say* I'd done them. Things I thought I'd driven from my imagination by prayer and fasting."

"You're only human."

A. Colin Wright

"Alas," she quoted again from somewhere, "'a perverted pleasure overcomes the mind that surrenders to the world, and counts it a delight to lie among the brambles.'" She looked at me with defiance. "Giuseppe was the last. Bruises on his face, a cut over his eye, and his lip was bleeding as he kissed my neck, my breasts, even my . . ." She indicated with her hand. "Then he seemed to stay inside me forever, becoming part of my soul. Now I'm damned, I thought. Now I know Satan. I didn't care. My brother, my own brother!"

That night, in a makeshift bed on the sofa, I kept going over it in my mind. I knew that Clara in the next room was wakeful too. I was torn between thoughts of what had happened and, I admit it, a newly aroused eroticism, a desire to make love to her myself: gently, happily. I was betrayed by my own timidity. I didn't want her to think I was *like those others*, and so I didn't even show the natural affection that might have comforted us both.

I returned to the village feeling guilty. It occurred to me that no one would see it as my responsibility if Clara became pregnant, and yet, at the same time, I thought I might welcome such a responsibility. Yet as the bus skirted the lake, taking me past D'Annunzio's ornate villa, I realized that it was still Emanuela I wanted. Clara would always represent for me Christian love, agape, while it was the pagan eros I longed for.

I'd rarely stopped to talk to St. Francis in daytime, but now I needed to compose my mind. I had another problem too: my money was running out. Should I do the logical thing and return to Canada, or prolong an impossible situation with Emanuela?

St. Francis promised to find a way out of my dilemma, and I walked to the villa telling myself to expect a miracle.

The Trouble with Saints

Emanuela answered the door, kissed me, looked at me with those mysterious eyes, and then took my hand and led me into the living room. "It's finished. My husband's alive."

"You've seen him?"

"I'm going to Bologna next week. He's in prison." Her voice rose in anger. "He sent a message to my father! I had to tell him everything! Alberto's coming out soon and needs somewhere to go."

For a moment it seemed like a bad melodrama, and I barely restrained a desire to laugh.

"Alberto's a petty crook! All this time I could at least think of him as a hero. He ran away from the Americans with one of their soldiers and lived by the black market. He never *bothered* to come back. Until now, when he needs money."

"And you?"

"It hurts," she said. "I'm married to him. You know what that means in Italy?"

She could see nothing but emptiness for us ahead. "All we have is physical," she said, "which isn't enough. There's not even a way to sleep together. Nothing's the same."

Her father, when I said goodbye, shook his head. "Eh, Mister Tony. I'm sorry, eh? I'd have been happy . . . But how could I have known? Eh!"

It was dark when I left, walking to our bench, where I sat listening to the waves. Then I walked on to where St. Francis was waiting. "Thanks!" I spat at him. "You were going to answer my prayer."

"I did," he said with his usual serenity. "You asked me to find a way out of your dilemma."

A. Colin Wright

"But that's not the way I wanted! You were no fucking use!"

Still he gazed piously down—at an earthenware pot in which someone had arranged some of the flowers.

I've never been a violent man. Never have been able to spill blood. Spilling sperm is more in my line, although, if truth be known, I've spilled little enough of that in my wretchedly cautious life. But, faced with emptiness where once there had been dreams, all I could do was indulge in a futile gesture of despair.

I picked up the pot, dumped the flowers on the roadside and, infuriated at the mocking radiance of his face, thrust the pot against it. The statue didn't have the inner strength I imagined. A crack appeared in one shoulder, darted across the body to the opposite hip and—slowly, so that I almost wanted to catch it and hold it in place—head, torso, and raised arm slid down, then toppled forward to the ground, where the whole thing broke into several pieces.

I was dismayed, wanting to destroy the evidence of my crime, and at the same time elated. Casting the pot aside, I started grabbing the pieces of porcelain and throwing them down in a fever of destruction; toppling the base of the statue as well, so that it too shattered onto the road. The light in the niche went out. I was horrified at myself but I couldn't stop. Seeing that the face was still intact, I took the larger pieces and threw them at St. Francis's eyes, nose, lips, bombarding them, kicking them, crunching my heel on the slivers I eventually reduced them to.

St. Francis lay dying, bleeding. Then I saw it was my own blood, from a gash in my hand.

I heard later that Clara became a nun. She wrote to me occasionally, assuring me that she prayed for me, and I hadn't the heart to reply that it didn't seem to do much good during those troubled professional years. Six months ago her Mother Superior wrote, telling me Clara had died from

The Trouble with Saints

cancer: a long letter saying how she'd been loved for her saintliness, and ending with the sentence "She had the radiance of God." Did she finally see Christ in his glory at the moment of her death?

Perhaps that had something to do with my returning to Italy—something I'd been thinking of ever since the breakup of my marriage. With no more dreams of becoming a great lover, I'd be happy to settle for one woman to love. With the tourists I eat ice cream in the café by the harbour, reading headlines that tell of atrocities committed by the Red Brigade. At night I sit on my bench, listening to the waves in the darkness and telling myself that Emanuela must be out there somewhere. Times have changed, and nowadays we could perhaps have lived together without worrying too much about her husband. I walk to her father's villa, try ringing the bell, but the house is as empty as the shrine where the statue once stood.

I go to find it again, praying it was only a dream and that St. Francis will still be there. But there's nothing except for the empty niche and the pink flowers growing close by.

Tomorrow I'll go to Padua, to the Giotto frescoes in the Scrovegni Chapel, and to the Basilica of St. Anthony where, with the believers, I'll line up to touch the sarcophagus.

Perhaps I'll pray to Clara.

Clara, Clara, please send me a miracle. I beg you with all this stupid, idiotic heart of mine! I would like to have believed. Why did I always deny it? All you need is credit for a few miracles, so I can pray to you. Not even that I may find Emanuela. It's too late for that, I don't deserve it, but that one day there will be someone to love again.

Make Someone Happy

I can't approve of John. He's been a conscious and unrepentant sinner since I've known him, and it's unlikely he'll change. Yet every day I pray God will forgive him for continually breaking the seventh commandment, since I very much doubt he breaks any other.

I met him nearly ten years ago, when I was driving from my parish in St. Hubert to the Kingston area, where I used to help with a church-sponsored camp. I was well beyond Montreal when a huge truck pulled out ahead of me, forcing me to slam on my brakes. I got by, but I was shaken enough to stop at the service station on the 401 just across the Ontario border.

I walked into the restaurant, telling myself I shouldn't let the incident spoil my enjoyment of God's world on a sunny morning. But the truck must have pulled in after me, and I'd just sat down at the counter when I saw this gigantic guy with bulging muscles coming at me.

I muttered a quick prayer, but he was already addressing me in a curiously gentle, deep tenor voice. "Excuse me, Father, I seen you drive in. It ain't my usual stop, but then I think, why not say I'm sorry for cutting you off? This car come in from the side, see."

Make Someone Happy

A couple of truckers behind him guffawed, while he eased himself onto the seat beside me. "A coffee for my friend here," he called to the waitress.

People don't often call me "friend" when I'm wearing my dog collar. He was in his mid-twenties, I judged, about half my age, and with childishly blue, smiling eyes. The dark-haired waitress was impressed with him, for she turned around and almost dropped a plate.

"You must be John," she said. "I'm Brenda. I've heard of you from my friend Cathy in Morrisburg."

"Nice to meet you, Brenda," he said, offering his huge hand. "I heard you're saving to go to Europe in the fall? Cathy told me all about you, except how beautiful you are."

Brenda giggled, briefly touched his arm, and went to serve someone else.

"Morrisburg's my usual stop," he explained to me. "Cathy . . . well, she's real fun."

Brenda came back and started telling him about her planned trip to Europe. Smiling at me as well, he listened attentively, just saying "really?" or "no?" as though it was the most wonderful thing he could imagine. "You take lots of pictures now and show me afterwards, eh?"

When I left, he interrupted the conversation to accompany me to the door, holding it open for me. "We'll meet again," he said, shaking my hand as though afraid of being too rough with me. I drove away thanking God for the beautiful morning.

At camp I thought of John, even speaking of his friendliness in one of my addresses. And then, on my way back, I ran into him again, at the Morrisburg service centre this time, where a redheaded waitress—Cathy, obviously—was fussing around him. Over lunch he told me about

169

A. Colin Wright

himself with an innocence that suggested he found everything in the world endlessly fascinating. Women in particular intrigued him, and he found it a source of wonder that they were always throwing themselves at him.

"I like it, of course," he said. "It makes me feel good that people like me too. And then . . . well, Father, you know how it is."

I mumbled something. It was a line I sometimes heard in the confessional, but the fact is that, although I'm occasionally troubled by the sins of the flesh, I *don't* know how it is. Even when I was younger, women were never attracted to me the way they were to John.

He told me, without boasting, about some of the girls he'd slept with. His frankness surprised me, because most people either adopt a false kind of reverence with a priest, or are at pains to keep the conversation on a morally neutral level—except for the few who are aggressively provocative. John spoke to me as he would to anyone else, so that I could relax and not constantly feel I was on duty.

He talked of his girlfriends' problems and the things they could teach him that were beyond his personal experience. He was particularly in awe of the ones who were better educated.

"The things they study in them colleges. Wow! I can't even understand the words they use. But they enjoy talking about it, and—who knows?—some of it might rub off." He added that he was always careful about not getting any of them pregnant. "I mean, that makes it difficult for a girl."

I didn't want to give him any encouragement, but at the same time I felt that one of my little moral sermons would be inappropriate. I've never really understood what makes men attractive to women. In John's case, was it his size, his muscular physique, his deep voice—none of which I possessed—or was it more?

"Do none of your girls get jealous?" I asked.

170

Make Someone Happy

He looked at me in amazement. "Jealous? Over *me*? Why? They know I'm not much of a catch."

"You accept them as they are." I tried to intellectualize it. "And they accept you as *you* are."

He couldn't quite grasp that. "Na, they're just having fun, like I am. Anyway, ain't jealousy one of the seven deadly sins?"

On our way out, he headed for the gift shop. "Hold on, will you, Father?"

I strolled around the shop while I was waiting, looking at some of the junk people spend their earnings on. Mostly I thank God that I'm spared the frenzied pursuit of money and idle entertainment—the so-called good life that so many are ambitious to achieve—but my isolation from what others consider important in the world can sometimes be a burden for me. John disturbed me not so much by his sinning as by his innocent enthusiasm for things that I'd long ago had to renounce—not without some relief.

He came over with a plaid woollen scarf. "There's this girl who works in an office in Toronto," he said. "Not a girl*friend* or anything. Her dad's out west, her mom's dead. Not very happy, not many friends, poor kid. Think she'll like this?"

The scarf wasn't cheap, and I said I was sure she would.

"Jenny's one of them quiet types. Not pretty, no one bothers about her. I *love* taking her presents. She gets so excited, can hardly wait to tear the paper off. It gives me a kick just to watch her."

I met John several times after that, since I was going back and forth to the camp all summer. The other truckers treated him with a mixture of humour and respect. They laughed at him because he wasn't interested in cars, possessions, or even baseball and hockey, but his reputation with

171

A. Colin Wright

women gave him enormous prestige. They thought him something of a simpleton. When they argued over how to make a buck on the side, John would sit there shaking his head, as though it were too great an effort to figure it out, but they'd admit that his friendliness brightened their days.

"John's different," one of them told me. "Like last Christmas, he gets out of his cab and the parcels spill all over the road. Presents he's taking to everyone he knows on the way."

I wondered whether John believed in God or went to church. But really, I didn't want to know because, if he said he didn't, I'd feel an obligation to discuss it with him. I knew I was being neglectful in not pointing out that his conduct was sinful but, when I saw how genuinely happy he made others, all my imagined sermons dissolved into air. I was beginning to think there were things he could teach *me* about loving one's neighbour.

It turned out anyway that John went to church in the north end of Montreal and sang in the choir. He told me so after I met him climbing out of his truck, singing to himself in his rich tenor voice.

"I lift my voice to the Lord and think how beautiful heaven must be," he said as we walked towards the restaurant. "I don't go in for prayer much. And I often don't understand the sermons. But when I sing, I just get the feeling God's there, even if I can't explain it to anyone."

With the end of summer, my trips to camp finished, so I didn't see John for a while. I don't want to give the impression that I was unconcerned about the way he was living. I was bothered by the thought that many of my own parishioners would have been aghast at his sexual licence, while showing little of his natural Christian charity. I kept praying that his various escapades would be forgiven, and wondered whether he even confessed them, but I tried to reassure myself that it was a problem not for me but for one of my colleagues.

Make Someone Happy

I next met him the following summer, when he was about to go on a two-week holiday that, he told me, he always spent with his mother in New Brunswick. He wanted to know what I thought of an idea he'd been considering.

"That poor kid"—he was talking of Jenny—"hasn't any place to go for her vacation. What would you think if I invite her home? Just for a holiday, eh? It's one of them big old houses on the ocean, so she won't be in the way. Swimming and walking. Be a change for her."

I knew by now that he only asked about things he'd already decided, so I didn't point out what would have been obvious to anyone else: that other people would misinterpret his motives. But it was no one's business but his, and the invitation seemed typical of his usual generosity.

Our paths didn't cross for the rest of the summer, so it was another year before I saw him again, in the service station at the Ontario/Quebec border once more. He came over as soon as he saw me, his broad face beaming—although he stopped to wink at Brenda in a way that suggested they'd become better acquainted since I'd met him two years previously.

The first thing I noticed was the wedding band on his finger. He could hardly wait to tell me about it, while Brenda, who'd obviously heard the story before, looked on from behind the counter.

Jenny, he told me, had been thrilled at his invitation home, although she'd been worried about what people might think. ("Let them think what they like! They enjoy it and everyone's happy.") She'd loved the old house on the Bay of Fundy and had gone for long walks along the shore every day, showing her gratitude by helping John's mother in the house, with a quiet efficiency that impressed the older woman.

John was delighted that it had all worked out and that the two women got along. For most of the time he left them so he could go out with other girls in the village, not expecting Jenny to make any more demands on

A. Colin Wright

him than he did on her. Every evening he'd ask her politely about her day, tell her of his own doings and whom he'd been with. When he planned to spend the night with some girl and not be back until morning, he told her about that, too, while hiding it from his mother. His mother, though, was puzzled. Since John hadn't explained his relationship with Jenny, she thought that at long last he was planning to get married. When she discovered he'd been with another girl all night, she was understandably shocked.

She tried to ask Jenny, who became embarrassed. So she finally decided to tackle John, who only now explained he'd invited Jenny home only to give her pleasure.

"You mean you had no intentions toward her?" his mother asked.

"Of course not. She's a nice girl, that's all."

"And what about the neighbours? And what do you think *she's* thinking? Don't you see she's in a difficult position here?"

That hadn't occurred to him. "Gee! You mean that others could think . . . ? That *she* could? Yeah, I guess you're right. Hell, I'm sorry I upset you. I just thought you'd be happy to have her here."

"Of course I was happy! I thought you were going to get married. That's what I've wanted all along. Haven't you noticed how devoted she is?"

"Well, I guess she's grateful."

"John," his mother said earnestly, "why *don't* you marry her? She'd make you a good wife, and I wouldn't have to worry about you all the time."

John had known for a long time that his mother wanted him to marry, but he had never taken it seriously, assuming there was no hurry. Now he remembered her hints about having grandchildren and understood it wasn't as trivial as he'd supposed. "It would sure make you happy, eh?" In a moment, he made up his mind. "Of course I'll marry her if you want." His enthusiasm almost overwhelmed him. "I'll ask her straightaway. No,

174

Make Someone Happy

tomorrow. I promised to take Marie to the dance tonight and it would disappoint her not to go."

As John told it to me, his mother threw her arms around him and reached up to kiss him, while he lifted her off her feet and whirled her through the air.

Then he went to the dance with Marie. He told everyone he was engaged. They all toasted him, and he felt he'd made them happy too. Even Marie didn't seem to mind when he assured her they'd still be able to have fun together whenever he came home. They were kissing in the back seat of his Chevrolet at the time, and John hadn't the heart to refuse when she wanted to make love.

He went to see the local priest and made all the arrangements for the wedding. "Here," he then told Jenny, giving her some money, "get yourself a pretty dress. Mom will help you choose. Not something I'm any good at."

"A dress?" she asked. "What for?"

"Well, everyone needs a dress to get married in, don't they?"

I can't make it sound the way he did, and perhaps he was exaggerating about forgetting to ask Jenny to marry him until that moment. But perhaps not, for John's never been one to do things in the conventional way. Anyway, a month later they were married.

"We went back again to New Brunswick for it," he told me. "A glorious day it was. Everyone singing and having a great time, and her dad flies in from out west. Wonder I never thought of getting married before. Jenny's real happy, particularly since our little girl's come along. Two months old and a real beauty already. We call her Joy. I tickle her with my finger and she looks up at me and laughs. And I never seen my mom so contented."

A. Colin Wright

I almost fell into my usual congratulatory speech for such occasions, but I stopped, feeling that the words weren't appropriate. I was pleased for him, but I suspected that by using the same old clichés I'd be making John's marriage the same as anyone else's. That, may God forgive me, I didn't want to do. Why was I secretly disappointed, when I should have given thanks? I am, of course, totally committed to God and the church, but I've always realized that for me it's partly a refuge, a way of avoiding things that, deep down, I'm afraid of. Did I harbour a hint of regret for that other life, which can at times be so very beautiful and desirable, and perhaps not so very wrong?

As we were about to leave, Brenda came over and put her hand on John's shoulder. "When am I going to see you?" she whispered. I pretended not to hear.

John chuckled, while a broad smile spread across his face. "Next week," he said. "My schedule won't be so tight. I'll do my best."

"At my place? You'll call me?"

"Brenda's a nice kid," he told me as we went out. "She's taking a course at one of them colleges. Just to hear her talk about it makes me think what a great place the world can be."

I still meet up with John every summer. He and Jenny have three children now, but he's always the same, as friendly as ever and still in demand at various places along the highway by girls who want to get in on the action. Don't ask me to explain it.

I asked him once if Jenny knew he was unfaithful to her.

"Of course," he said, surprised. "Why deceive her? All the lying—what's the point?"

"And doesn't she mind?"

176

Make Someone Happy

He frowned. "She has the kids, and she knows I'll always stay by her and look after her. And I love her so much."

"You love them all!"

He grinned. "So how could I disappoint all the others? Why refuse a bit of happiness when there's so much unhappiness around? And I admit it does me good. Broadens my outlook. People, they're . . ." He searched for the word. "They're an education, aren't they? And women give you a different outlook from men. They're more fun. It gives me a kick to see them happy."

I still couldn't approve of his attitude. I wanted to point out the problems it could give rise to, ask him whether it wasn't mere self-indulgence, and whether his view of love mightn't be naïve. Was it lack of courage that prevented me, or the feeling that he wouldn't understand? Surely it was my Christian duty to challenge him? But then who was I, a celibate who'd struggled for years with those troublesome desires of the flesh, to try to advise *him*? I recognized that this was only an excuse, for it's part of my calling to advise others, whatever my own experience has been. And I do worry about his soul, and about my own responsibility for him. Today, now that everyone's concerned with AIDS and other diseases, I worry as well whether he takes proper precautions, for I could easily see him being careless because he's persuaded himself it might spoil things for his partner.

Not long ago, for all his care, he did get one girl pregnant and she had a baby boy.

"It's made it tough for her," he told me. "I give her what money I can. Might as well spend it on something worthwhile, eh? 'Take no thought for the morrow,' ain't that right?" Before I could challenge his misuse of the quotation, he went on: "Let me show you what I bought for the kid." He produced a parcel full of clothes. "He's a tough little bastard, that one. Going to be like his father."

177

A. Colin Wright

The last thing I heard was that the baby's mother was sick.

"What would you think," he asked me, "if I take her and the baby home to stay with Jenny and the kids, so we can look after the two of them for a while?"

Seven Minutes' Silence

"As we remember the glorious heroism of those comrades who once were with us," Father André says for the fifth or sixth time, trying to drag it out, "we recall our own many and selfless sacrifices of those dark and terrible years."

Jacques Coustoulin looks at the town-hall clock and whispers to Annette Lieutaud standing beside him. "He's mistimed it. It's only eight minutes to eleven!"

"You remember how we timed it to the second when we blew up the munitions train?" Annette says, her voice wheezing. At sixty-seven, she has asthma. "How many *boches* did we kill?" She laughs, her medals jingling as she heaves her still ample breasts. Once, Jacques recalls, they stood out proudly, a prize he competed long to uncover. Then, after the war, Annette married someone else.

Past seventy now, he would rather be playing *boules* than standing here in ragged formation with the others on the dusty town square. Only six of us left anyway, he thinks. In the past forty years most have died, or moved to cities like Nice, Cannes, Marseilles. It's not as if their medals, shining proudly from their annual polishing, still mean anything. Playing *boules* on the square he'd known all his life—tossing heavy metal balls, aiming carefully for the jack or smashing other shots out of the way—

179

A. Colin Wright

was far more real for Jacques nowadays than memories of tossing hand grenades. And yesterday: what a victory it was.

The curé drones on, consulting his watch between sentences. The mayor, a pen-pusher with glasses who wasn't even born when the war ended, looks round at the spectators with self-satisfied importance as he clutches his wreath and waits for the speech to end. At eleven o'clock precisely he'll place it at the foot of the war memorial, a bugler from the youth band will play the "Last Post," and the usual two minutes of silence will begin.

But the town-hall clock shows only 10:55 when, with sudden relief, Father André pronounces the words "So let us now keep silence in memory of those of our brothers in two world wars who died that we might live."

His watch must be wrong, Jacques thinks. That would never have happened with the old mayor, who could rise to any occasion and would have spoken himself to fill in time. But the present one, an outsider from Toulon, is caught off guard. After a few seconds' hesitation, he walks forward with the wreath, shrugs as though to say it isn't his fault, deposits it at the memorial, and stands awkwardly to attention.

Jacques shuffles to attention with the others. Léon Pichotin and Henri Poitevin in front of him salute. Annette doesn't, and Jacques decides not to either. The bugler plays two notes of the "Last Post," but stops when he sees the bandleader gesticulating and pointing urgently to the clock. Father André, however, has hung his head in prayer and the mayor still stands at attention in front of the memorial.

"Seven minutes' silence?" Pierre Matheron mutters from behind Jacques. He must have decided to salute, for he adds: "When's the last time you had to hold a salute for seven minutes?"

By 10:56 Jacques is already finding it difficult to concentrate. He's aware that since he was a Resistance leader no one has had any use for him, except

Seven Minutes' Silence

during these ceremonies designed largely to make the mayor feel important. Still, he makes an effort to rehearse the names of his dead friends.

Only now he's aware that something else is wrong. The silence is no silence at all. No one has thought to stop the weekend traffic crawling past the square in a steady stream towards the coastal resorts in this exceptionally late autumn. Drivers are hooting impatiently because pedestrians are standing in the road. All because of the mayor, Jacques thinks, who, for all his show of intellect, has done nothing about building a bypass to the town.

"Have they no respect?" Even the normally unflappable Annette is upset, wheezing indignantly so that her medals jingle again. "When I think of how my parents were shot . . ."

Behind her, Michel Giraud swears softly. Jacques wonders if Michel's still angry with him for making that old joke about being the youngest. Eighteen at the start of the war, Michel would have been in the army like Pierre, but was rejected for some medical problem he was ashamed to talk about. So he joined the Resistance instead. Still the youngest at sixty-four, even nowadays he feels the need to prove himself to the others.

Pierre Matheron has been sulking all morning since Michel virtually accused him—again!—of being a coward, of sitting out the war years in England, as though he hadn't fought desperately, first at Dunkirk and then on the beaches with the returning French forces in 1944. All morning Pierre's been repeating the story of how he neutralized a German machine-gun emplacement with a grenade, killing all of its occupants, outside Colleville-sur-l'Orne.

The traffic is as loud as ever, making a mockery of these painfully long minutes of remembrance. Yet Léon Pichotin, in front of Jacques, holds his salute proudly, as though unaware that anything's wrong. Léon hated the German occupiers with a fanatical intensity, and the happiest moment of his life was when their group ambushed the munitions train

A. Colin Wright

and he bayoneted two of the guards along the line. Now he recalls that killing, the placing of the charges, and the whistle of the approaching locomotive. Henri Poitevin, standing to Léon's right, was wounded in the same incident, losing his right arm (he now salutes with his left). He's visibly annoyed, and his one good arm must be getting tired—only it's a matter of pride with him not to let it droop in front of the others. Jacques sent him that night with a message to the railway signalman, whose assistance was vital to the success of the operation, and for which he was later shot. A German guard opened fire and shattered Henri's elbow, but he got through all right, despite the pain.

A large tourist bus rolls into the square and stops. By 10:57 the local gendarme has finally thought to halt the traffic. One by one the other drivers turn off their engines, but the bus's continues to throb loudly while its exhaust splutters like a machine gun.

"Just like the *boches*!" Pierre Matheron says from behind, and spits.

Jacques turns his head and, over the heads of the spectators, sees on the side of the bus the words: *Reisegesellschaft Horst Rappich, A. G. Europarundfahrt.*

"Germans!" Michel has seen it too.

The bus driver has got out and started arguing with the gendarme, and there's no mistaking the hoarse, guttural sounds that issue from his mouth. Didn't they all, during the occupation, hear similar voices shouting at them often enough?

Jacques can't catch what the driver's saying, but he can just about understand the words on the side of the bus. Horst Rappich Touring Company, then Europe . . . Europe what? Abandoning all pretence of keeping the silence, he asks Annette.

"Europe Round Tour," she translates.

182

Seven Minutes' Silence

In front of him, Léon Pichotin's neck turns red as he jerks his head toward the bus. "It's disgraceful! Not only has the whole ceremony been a mess, not only have we all been made to look foolish"—he seeks for something else to nourish his habitual temper, and finds it—"not only is there no damn silence here at all, but now the Germans are on our square again, trampling all over Europe!"

Jacques continues to watch the driver, who's left his engine spluttering as he gesticulates angrily at the gendarme. He has a beer belly now, but in features, manner, everything about him, he's identical to the lieutenant who arrested Annette's parents. And inside, sitting by the front window, isn't that Major Keller, who was in charge of the execution squad? Behind him sits the young SS Corporal Hans Dietmar. Well, the boy on the bus is too young to have been alive then, but he's the same type all right, with blond hair, a mocking smile. And behind him is a fat, ugly woman: the Commandant's wife, whose photo, on the one occasion Jacques was in his office, hung on the wall opposite the portrait of Hitler. Then a bald man with an obsequious smile, ex-Gestapo obviously. There's another man, too, sitting at the back, only older, like themselves, quiet, respectful. But the others: how dare they come and make fun of an Armistice Day service!

It's 10:58, and the supposed silence, shattered by the bus's engine and exhaust, drags on. The mayor and Father André stand, oblivious.

"But surely someone has to do something." Léon Pichotin repeats Jacques's words that had caused him to join the Resistance in the first place. But what can he do? Only turn his head aside and spit.

And there, lying in the dust of the square between Henri Poitevin's feet, is a large metal ball that someone must have left behind after yesterday's game. Léon looks at the bus and then down at the ball again, judging the distance. He's played *boules* all his life: his toss is accurate and powerful.

To Henri, whose one arm is drooping in spite of himself, it's a welcome relief when he hears Léon's loud whisper next to him: "Can you get that *boule* for me?" He reaches down and gives it to him, hesitating

183

A. Colin Wright

before he feels obliged to salute again—which is a mistake. He badly needs another excuse to exercise his muscles.

"How about it?" Léon continues with his usual bravura. "Let's fix the bastards! All of us. At eleven o'clock precisely, when the clock strikes, right? Pass it on."

Jacques Coustoulin passes the message on to Pierre and Michel at the back with considerable misgivings. He's as angry as the rest, but what can they do? In the Resistance he often had this problem. Hotheads like Léon always wanted to plunge ahead, kill for the sake of killing, while he, Jacques, had to judge what their group would achieve, what their chances of success were, and whether the results would be worth the inevitable reprisals. And now it's no longer wartime, after all. But he still feels a responsibility for the others that he hasn't enjoyed for forty years, something to cherish, and he can't take the decision lightly.

"There are only six of us," he says gravely.

"Plus all the other people on the square!" Michel Giraud responds sarcastically, seizing the opportunity to contradict him. "You're getting old, Jacques! I'll lead the way if you won't."

"Think it's a job for a youngster like you, then?" Pierre Matheron growls. He adds: "We need to take them from both sides. Léon and I in the front, you and the others round the back."

Léon says nothing, but starts tossing the *boule* in his hand and catching it.

"How do you know the others will follow?" Annette asks innocently.

"They will," Henri Poitevin says, dropping his salute and stretching his shoulders, "if I go and tell the bugler to sound the 'Cavalry Charge' instead of the 'Last Post.'"

184

Seven Minutes' Silence

Still Jacques delays, as the hand on the town-hall clock edges towards 10:59. He's never been comfortable with hasty decisions, but Henri has to be sent now or not at all. And what Michel says is true: he's getting old. A last, unexpected chance to show his leadership; yet his natural instinct is to say no, for what good will it do?

"Come on, Jacques," Léon urges. "It's years since any of us have had a good fight. That's all it would be. We're still men, aren't we? Let's show 'em!"

A louder explosion from the bus's exhaust startles all of them. "Shall I go and tell the bugler?" Henri asks again.

"The mayor won't like it," Annette says, with an unexpected little laugh.

He won't like it at all, Jacques thinks. "All right then." He nods to Henri: "A good fist fight, but no more. Leave the *boule* behind, Léon."

"Are you crazy? When it's the only weapon we have!"

Henri leaves while the others stand waiting for the clock. Only Pierre Matheron and Michel Giraud, who isn't to be outdone by an ex-army man, still salute. Even the mayor is shuffling now, wondering perhaps whether to end the silence on the hour or wait for the further two minutes.

In the background the bus still roars, its exhaust still splutters, but the driver's no longer talking to the gendarme. Perhaps, as always, the overbearing German has got his way, Jacques thinks. But then, miraculously, it suddenly moves forward again and cuts its engine.

The silence is unnerving. What are the *boches* up to? Léon keeps tossing the *boule* in his hand.

It's like waiting for the train to appear. The guards disposed of, the charges laid, the plunger raised, ready to be pushed in when the locomotive's in the middle of the bridge . . .

185

A. Colin Wright

The hand on the clock moves closer towards eleven. Checking with the second hand on his own watch, Jacques Coustoulin wonders—as he did then—whether Henri will get through. He can't see. And what will be the end of it all? In the past he trained himself never to go back on a decision, despite his doubts, unless the situation changed. Now it suddenly occurs to him that it's only been in such moments, waiting for action, doubting, aware of danger, that he felt most truly alive. There's been nothing in the peacetime years to compare with it. But now—isn't the whole thing crazy?

He looks again at his watch. Fifteen seconds to go. The bugler, he sees, anxious to get it right this time, has stepped forward and raised the bugle to his lips in anticipation. Has Henri delivered the message or not?

"Jacques!" An urgent whisper from Annette: "Look!"

He looks where she's pointing. The bus has moved forward sufficiently so that the back of it is now visible as well. In the rear window is a white oval with the letters: *CH*. He reads *Reisegesellschaft Horst Rappich, A. G.* once more, but between that and *Europarundfahrt* are two words in smaller letters: *Zürich, Schweiz*.

"Oh my God," he says, as the town-hall clock hiccups, preparing to strike. "Heaven help us, they're Swiss!"

Léon's toss is deadly. It ploughs into the ball closest to the jack, knocking it halfway across the square. The day is theirs. They've beaten their opponents fair and square, even with the mayor playing on the other side to balance the teams.

"*Particularly* with the mayor playing on their side," Jacques mutters to Pierre Matheron, as they all head towards the bar. "It seems that even novices from Zurich can play better than an intellectual from Toulon."

Seven Minutes' Silence

Pierre links arms with Major Keller who, delighted with the nickname, has insisted on keeping it all afternoon: when he served in the Swiss army, years ago, he never got higher than the rank of corporal.

"So you were in life insurance?" he asks Pierre in quite good French, although with that comical Swiss accent. "I too, I too!"

Léon walks behind with the bald ex-Gestapo agent, a retired bureaucrat from the World Health Organization in Geneva, who during the war was a member of the Swiss Committee for National Defence. He has an astonishing sense of humour and a repertoire of foul jokes.

The young blond boy—Danish, as it turned out—hasn't been able to stop Henri Poitevin talking since politely asking about his arm.

"Oh yes, I got through with the message all right," Henri explains to him. "Whatever the cost, you have to do your duty, which not everybody appreciates nowadays. And of course, there's no sense of discipline anymore," he adds, thinking of the bugler that morning, who refused outright to play anything other than the "Last Post" and said he didn't know the "Cavalry Charge" anyway.

They go into the bar, where a number of the bus's passengers have remained since lunch while others have been walking around the town. Annette Lieutaud and the fat woman from Lucerne sit telling each other about their grandchildren and comparing photographs.

At the table next to them the bus driver looks up cheerfully as Michel Giraud returns. Earlier, Michel managed to get the bus towed to his garage, and he's just been on the phone to his mechanic. "It'll take another hour," he says, sitting down. "It was lucky I could get hold of him."

The driver laughs, his beer belly quivering. "Thank God we'll be able to make Nice by tonight after all! It was good of you to open up for us. The bus started acting up last night. And then this morning I couldn't get it into that gendarme's head that if I turned it off I'd never get it started again."

A. Colin Wright

Good fellows, these Swiss, Jacques Coustoulin thinks as he sits down. And they were prepared to defend their country against the Nazis too.

"We're the toughest army in Europe," Major Keller is saying with pride. "Only for our defence, of course, but just let one foreign soldier step across our frontier and we'll make the bastard jump all right. I came across this guy in the war, you know, when I was on border patrol. Plug him first and ask questions afterwards, that was the way of it."

"Same with me many a time," Pierre Matheron answers him. "A grenade's the best. Toss one properly and watch the bodies fly!"

"And there was that train," Michel comes in, not wanting to be outdone. "The locomotive turned right over and went rolling down the embankment. Then the boxcars started to explode."

"One guy was blown to pieces right before my eyes," Léon boasts. "His head came right off his body, and boy did he look surprised! Serve him right, the bastard!"

"And Annette Lieutaud, she was a demon with a sten gun."

And in bed too, Jacques recalls sadly, with her unexpected little laugh.

Nothing's the same anymore. In those days we were real men, not like the intellectuals in spectacles who pretend to run the world today. Listening to the others as they indulge in their memories—the Swiss men competing too—Jacques is depressed, getting old perhaps. Things had turned out all right that morning, fortunately. The "Last Post" had silenced them. Even Léon, seeing that the bus wasn't German after all, had dropped his *boule* with a shrug of disappointment, and they stood in quiet meditation for the final, legitimate two minutes until the bugler played the "Reveille." Everything was as it should be, and the war, after all, was over.

188

Seven Minutes' Silence

I'm tired, Jacques thought. Too tired even to tell my own war stories with the others.

One older man, sitting apart from the rest, is the first to get up when Michel Giraud announces that the mechanic has finally fixed the bus, which is now ready to leave.

He doesn't take part in the handshakes and laughter all round. A Swiss national for many years now, he was once a young lieutenant, torn away from a doctoral thesis on Martin Luther to fight alongside comrades who, except that they spoke a different language and were brought up with different ideas, had little to distinguish them from those here in the bar. He did his duty without thinking about it. He killed others, since they were the enemy. They killed friends of his, and he took lives in exchange. He had to arrest members of the Resistance as well, in towns like this that he can no longer remember, and he wasn't too disturbed by what happened to them during later interrogations. It was no business of his, and they had it coming to them anyway.

In the bar he listened to the war stories of the others. He used to hear the same ones, it seemed, from people on his own side as well. He too had won medals. But he didn't mention that.

He just kept very, very silent.

Bethlehem

"Tom, he'll wake up James."

Oh shit, now she's going to fuss. Stretch your arm out from under the covers; turn the clock towards you. The phosphorescent hands have lost most of their glow, and it takes a few minutes to make out the time in the darkness. Five thirty.

"What's he doing?"

Stealthy shufflings from the hall. Peter must have snapped off his alarm instantly, but you heard it of course. They were up to something last night: "Daddy, are you a heavy sleeper?" James, not old enough to be casual about it, had repeated his brother's question twice, laughing. Then Peter asked about Grandma too.

"Oh, dear! It's too early, they know that. They'll be up late tonight too. It really *is* too bad of him!" Elizabeth has raised her head from the pillow and turned towards you: "What are you going to do about it?

Edge one leg out of the bed and grope with your foot for your slippers. "Merry Christmas anyway."

Grunt. "Merry Christmas."

Both feet out, and now the covers.

190

Bethlehem

The night light in James's room reveals a huddled form in the bed, still asleep, despite an alert silence. Bathroom and guest room at the head of the stairs are reassuringly normal.

Peter's door, with spindly letters scotch-taped onto it that read "Private Keep Out" is closed as if a secret is hidden behind it. His bed is empty.

"I don't know where he is," you say as you get back into bed, doubting you'll be allowed to enjoy the warmth of the covers on top of you for long.

"In James's room, that's where! Did you look under the bed? Tom, if he wakes up James, he'll be impossible in the evening. Why can't they just wait?"

A floorboard creaks.

"Peter," you call, "what's up?"

Subdued silence. Then a grudging: "Nothing, Daddy."

The toilet flushes. "Oh no . . ."

A snort of disapproval from beside you and the more distant click of the guest room door. "Is anything the matter?"

"Now Mother's awake!" Elizabeth says.

"Daddy, I've got a nosebleed."

Two minutes later, long complicated sentences explain a plan to take sleeping bags downstairs and sleep there to celebrate Christmas.

Impatience stirs beside you. "Get back to your room, Peter. Go to sleep and don't you dare wake anyone particularly James before seven."

"Honest, Dad, we weren't going to open any presents. It was going to be a surprise, just for fun; then this nosebleed spoiled it."

191

A. Colin Wright

Decide, Tom, you think, before Elizabeth's logic sends Peter back to his room.

"I don't s'pose," Peter begins.

"Mummy says you mustn't wake up James."

"Then d'you think just I . . ."

"Then James will be disappointed." (And Elizabeth will never agree, Christmas or not.)

"So can we?"

What you knew you'd say all along: "Go on then."

"And can I wake up James?"

"I suppose so."

Enthusiastic thanks as he runs to wake his brother.

Now it comes. "Tom, that's not fair! James'll be so cranky tomorrow. I'll be busy, Mother'll be in a bad mood, they won't sleep . . ."

"It *is* Christmas."

But you get up again to supervise, insist on sleep and no opening of presents, no getting up before seven. You consider putting a flame to the wood already laid in the huge stone hearth, but you decide they'll be warm enough until morning. Wood is short this year.

Stairs again creak underneath as you go back up.

A face peering around the guest room door: "What's the matter?"

"Nothing, Mother, just a scheme the boys had."

You prepare to placate Elizabeth, but she's already turned over in disgust and is almost asleep again. Other noises now as Mother, too,

192

Bethlehem

attends to a call of nature. Try, Tom, not to listen apprehensively for sounds from below.

"You asleep, James? It's so warm in my sleeping bag like, you know, animal skins wrapped around me. Dark shapes in the living room: awesome, a different world."

"We mustn't talk. Daddy said."

"It's Christmas, though. Special."

Bundles under the tree. "Should we put its lights on, so we can see it shining in the darkness? They wouldn't understand, but Daddy didn't say not to. Would have though, if he'd thought of it. Still, this way we can imagine we're somewhere else, like that first Christmas. Yes, this way it's more enticing. That sounds nice. Funner. Daddy says not to say funner but more fun. Who cares?"

A light—how come?—from the star on top of the tree. Like things that sometimes move in my bedroom, making weird noises, changing their shapes. There are people who have powers. "Just your imagination," Mummy would say. "Go to sleep."

"The star's shining."

"Peter, I'm scared."

"It's all right, James." Mustn't show that I'm frightened too.

"But there's a light. The star. I thought we had a Santa there anyway."

"It's getting brighter."

"Peter, it's moving!"

Off the tree now, towards the stone archway of the door.

A. Colin Wright

"Peter, I'm scared!"

"No point being scared, James, of things you don't understand."

Sitting up and watching curiously as it moves out into the dining room with its long wooden table and benches on either side.

"Come on!"

"Where?"

"We have to follow it, stupid! Look, James, I don't understand anything about this either, right? I just think we should."

It's not too cold as we crawl out onto the bare wooden boards.

"Peter, wait for me!"

"Hurry up then."

"Wait up!"

Through the kitchen with its large earthenware pots and hanging wineskins, sliding back the heavy bolts and out into the yard, where the star's now taken its place in the sky.

"It's really a supernova. That's a star that suddenly explodes and shines very brightly."

"But why does it explode?"

"Or perhaps it's Jupiter."

The snow underfoot isn't cold at all. There's the Big Dipper overhead, and Orion and Taurus.

At the bottom of the yard where the star's shining, there's a whole crowd of people. "Undesirables," Grandma would call them, "far too rough to live on Chipwood Park Crescent." And animals, all kinds, the old

Bethlehem

Tobias oddly quiet, not even growling at the sheep and the cows, although normally a squirrel's enough to make him take a fit.

A light inside the shed.

"It's the baby Jesus, isn't it, Peter?"

"No." (I know more than you, James.) "It's just the people who came to stay last night, and the girl who was . . . pregnant? . . . has had her baby. Oh, but perhaps . . ." (Don't spoil it for him) "I don't know. We'll see."

It's difficult to explain.

Disbelief: "Now tell me again about your dream."

"We started following the star, you see."

"And it led you . . . ?"

"It moved across the sky through Orion."

"To the northwest, then?"

"But you must have seen it too."

Obviously they haven't. They don't believe us, shake their heads, exchanging glances. And yet if he'd at least looked . . . Thinks perhaps we made it all up. Or is there anxiety in his eyes as well?

"What time was it when you first saw it?"

We tell him.

Decision. "Go then to Bethlehem. And when you've found him, come back and tell me about it so I may come and worship him too."

*   *   *

195

A. Colin Wright

"Oh, little town of Bethlehem, how still we see thee lie. Above thy deep and dreamless sleep the silent stars . . ."

You pronounce the words clearly, looking down so that James can try to follow. Six years ago you used to sing it to him to send him to sleep, often to all three of its tunes. Peter sings loudly on the other side of you, holding his hymnbook high in front. Elizabeth and her mother, in fur coats, sing with respectable moderation.

"Yet in thy dark streets shineth the everlasting light; the hopes and fears of all the years are met . . ."

Fears?

Grandma this morning looked on with benevolent satisfaction as the ritual stripping of wrappings began. "All right!" from Peter, as he opened the first parcel. James wanted to open all his presents at once, tearing paper furiously, while Peter examined more carefully, taking his time. Beginning to show a measure of adult restraint about his enthusiasms.

"Oh-h-h! Do we have to go to church?" (James.)

"That's what Christmas is all about" (Grandma). "We have to go and worship the baby Jesus, don't we?"

"Can I take something with me?"

"May I."

"As long as it doesn't make a noise."

"But the cows were making a noise last night and the sheep and the angels, they made a noise." What had Peter meant by that?

"While mortals sleep, the angels keep their watch of wondering love . . ."

Were you Peter's age when you crept into your parents' room at night, trying not to wake them? It was to be a surprise. You'd written

Bethlehem

"Christ is Born" on your blackboard and wanted to take it in so they'd see it in the morning. So black and cold when you edged out of bed, took the easel, and moved with creaking slowness down the hall and into their room. One step at a time through the darkness, mysterious like another world, taking an age to get to the bottom of the bed.

Suddenly a gasp, your mother was awake. Stand still, hold your breath.

An urgent whisper: "Jim! Jim, wake up, there's someone in the room!"

"It's all right, it's only me."

Embarrassment, disappointment, shame at failure. It wasn't the same after stumbling explanations.

In the morning your father, pulling on socks to go downstairs and make up the fire, barely commented. Your mother, later, hugged you. "Thank you for your little announcement."

"And praises sing to God the king . . ."

She'd been frightened at first.

"Don't be afraid that you're pregnant. Being alive and bearing life is God's gift. Your child will be great and holy."

"But I don't know who it was."

"It's God's will just the same, for God in his omnipotence wills everything to be."

"I thank the Lord for all he has done for me, his poor servant. How strong he is, wiser than the coteries of men, looking after those who hunger for understanding and turning away those whose minds are blocked with inherited prejudices."

197

A. Colin Wright

*   *   *

Evening now. A commercial on the radio says all that's necessary: "Don't be a Scrooge this Christmas." Do your bit for the economy and buy. A man was arrested for denouncing the Santa in a large department store and causing a disturbance. The children appeared to have enjoyed the ensuing fight.

You've played with the kids most of the day, put toys together, made repairs. Grandma squints, trying to thread a needle, only somehow the thread won't go through the eye. She and Elizabeth have worked to make sure everything's as it should be, and now sit in tired gratification. Only once:

"What can Tom have been thinking of to let them get up and come down at five o'clock?" (Five thirty, Grandma, you always get it wrong!) Then she'd left in the middle of a long joke Peter wanted everyone to hear, because the turkey had to be seen to.

Why are you so depressed? In your own childhood, with happy unawareness of what rents and mortgages really meant, your one joy was to play Monopoly with everyone. Remember how they always had to be cajoled? "It takes so long." "Well, for an hour perhaps, all right two, you have to have a time limit." "We'll stop for the King's speech" (Queen's now). Or worst of all: "All right but we'll shuffle the property cards and deal them out, that's quicker." But not playing properly, less fun. In real life they never deal the property cards.

And now: "What do you want to do that for, dear?"

"Grandma, I asked Mummy, not you!"

"Don't be rude, Peter. Grandma's right anyway, why do you want to go outside now?"

"I want to see if I can find Jupiter. I'm reading about it in the book Daddy gave me. He said I could see it tonight."

198

Bethlehem

"What I meant was it's visible tonight, not necessarily that you could go out and look for it. I doubt . . ."

"But I want to show it to James!"

"I don't think they should go out, Tom, Elizabeth. They'll both freeze to death. There's always another night, the stars are always there."

"Jupiter's not a star, it's a planet, and it's not always there! And sometimes it's cloudy."

(And sometimes a star explodes. And me and James—oh, James and I—weren't cold this morning.)

"No, Peter, not tonight."

"But it's Christmas. And if you can't look at Jupiter on Christmas Day if you want, what's the point of being alive at all?"

"Such a shame for the children."

"Spoiling their fun like that, I just don't understand it."

"This isn't the true meaning of Christmas! It's only a way to make a profit. Santa doesn't exist, children, it's all lies."

"We can't have that kind of thing going on here. Someone fetch the police!"

"Oh, I know none of you will listen. I'm just a voice crying out in the wilderness."

"You're in the Bay, mate, that's where you are."

It used to be Sears.

"He's crazy. Just look at him. Rags, not even dressed properly."

"Commercialism, hypocrisy all around you."

199

A. Colin Wright

"Spoiling Christmas for us all, it shouldn't be allowed."

"It's been a big day. Goodnight James, Peter. Lights out."

"James, you asleep?"

"No, Peter."

"Should we go and say goodnight to . . . ?"

"Yeah!"

"Mummy and Daddy won't like it. But you can't always do what other people tell you to. They ought to know we have other business sometimes."

Creep slowly downstairs, hold our breaths each time a board creaks. I can hear their voices in the living room.

"You'd think they'd at least get married for the child's sake. But no, the old, tried ways aren't good enough for them."

We mustn't giggle or they'll hear us. Exciting, awesome. They never understand things like that.

"I can't think why you allowed them to stay in the shed. What will the neighbours think?"

"Shh!" Out into the yard, where the star's still in its place over the shed they're talking about.

"Adults are so stupid!"

"You shouldn't say that, Peter."

"Perhaps we'll be like that someday too."

200

Bethlehem

"I wish I was grown up."

The star shines more brightly as we approach.

Not everyone thinks it's a supernova.

Pulling the curtains you're puzzled by what seems to be a star out of place. Could it be the reflection from the kitchen light on the shed window? Or perhaps it's only Jupiter low in the sky. No reason to go out and investigate. "Oh, morning stars together proclaim the holy birth . . ."

" . . . about to give birth. Not even married. And he's no more than a common carpenter."

"They say he's not the father, Mother. Apparently it was some god or other."

"Well dear, that's the kind of nonsense the Romans might believe in with all their gods, not us. And did you see the broken down old Jeep they came in? Oh, I know they have to come here to be taxed, but there's certainly no room for them here. Why doesn't Caesar Augustus do something about it? What do we pay our taxes for anyway? And how you allowed them to stay there . . ."

"I felt sorry for them."

"Well, dear, they shouldn't be staying in this household. You have to be so careful nowadays. Do you know what one of the servant girls told me? One of those ruffians was here again early this morning, you know that agitator they've just arrested? One of his crowd. Wants to change everything like they all do. Only this one must have been scared, pretended not to know him."

You almost open the curtains again.

"What are you doing, Tom?"

201

A. Colin Wright

"Nothing."

There probably wouldn't be much to see. If you looked, really looked, out of the window, perhaps you could manage to see Jupiter. But the lights in the living room, the reflections from the tinsel-covered Christmas tree with a Santa on top, the plush carpet still littered with gift wrappings, the comfortable furniture and blazing fireplace, the merriment of Christmas: all this makes it difficult to see out of the window anyway.

"For goodness sake come and sit down instead of dancing about."

The flaming torches in the palace, the sumptuous gold and silver dishes covered with victuals, the rushes strewn profusely over the floor, the dazzling young breasts of the serving girls who are yours to command: all this makes it difficult to see beyond your own power and glory.

"My lord?"

"All the male children, under—oh, let's say two years old. Order your men to seize them and kill them. Be sure you don't miss a single one. I don't trust what the strangers said. Perhaps there's a threat somewhere to our lifestyle."

James and Peter lie dying. John's head lies in the platter while a potentate's eyes cannot leave it despite the dancing girl he desires. Birth in Bethlehem, what sufferings will you cause us? A lot of good-for-nothings challenging the accepted order. Show no mercy on them. If they can't have respect for the authorities, cause trouble, rock the boat, they got what's coming to them.

"That's another Christmas come and gone. I've always loved Christmas. The old, eternal tradition. It's too bad some people don't celebrate it the way they used to."

"I know, Mother. And it's getting so expensive anymore."

Bethlehem

"Are the children asleep?"

"I think so. They were tired out."

You wonder whether, outside, the stars really do still speak of the wonder of the universe. One brighter than all the others, supernova, Jupiter, or whatever, perhaps still shines for anyone looking that way. Might others even, in different galaxies, perceive it too? It's unlikely, though, that there are others in the universe besides ourselves.

A creak on the staircase.

"Peter, what's the matter?"

"Nothing, Daddy," as they creep back up.

"Not another nosebleed, I hope?"

"Oh dear, when are those children going to grow up?"

You hear a giggle: "They'll never believe us."

Evidently they've reached the head of the stairs.

"Let's not tell them, then!"

How silently, how silently, the wondrous gift is given. You smile as James starts to laugh hilariously, with his child's ability to forget everything except what, to him, is important.

White Nights

Malcolm sat in the tiny hotel cafeteria—here they called it a buffet—watching the glass doors for Natasha to come in. Last night, he thought dreamily. Could we really have told each other we're in love? Her sudden confession, as he gazed out from his room over the broad River Neva, had astonished him, but now he needed to hear her say the same again, before the others started arriving for breakfast.

Leningrad, he thought, the end of their Russian tour. He recalled with a sense of strangeness how in Kiev and Moscow he'd been planning to go to bed with Sylvia, one of the other English painters in the group, a serious artist like himself. He'd singled her out, though, more for her sense of fun and cheerful acceptance of the failings of Russian hotels, while the others only complained. For two weeks she'd responded with laughing interest to his innuendoes about what would happen when they reached Leningrad, where they'd finally been promised individual rooms instead of having to share. But five nights ago everything had changed, when an interpreter from the Artists' Union had joined them.

They were to leave Moscow by overnight train, the Red Arrow. On a poorly lit station platform, beside dull red coaches with silver Cyrillic lettering, Natasha shook his hand in a way that prevented him from approaching too closely, yet all the while looking directly into his eyes. He had been unprepared to meet someone beautiful. Or at least, he supposed

204

she was beautiful, for the intensity of her gaze prevented him from really being aware of her features. The power of observation he prided himself on deserted him, and he felt, irrationally, that he'd find it impossible to capture her on canvas. Her profile, when she looked down at her list, was almost classically Greek; but trying to observe her when she turned towards him again, he found himself looking only into those shining grey eyes. She spoke his name with a lilting emphasis, telling him who'd be sharing his sleeper for the overnight journey. Then she was already shaking hands with Sylvia, who had dark curly hair, full lips, and a sensual figure, but was lacking the mystery he sensed in Natasha.

Sylvia had noticed his momentary confusion. "She's wearing a wedding ring," she said pointedly as she followed him down the corridor, looking for her sleeper. "She's the type of woman one doesn't fool around with."

Sylvia was probably right, but as he got out onto the platform again, to fetch the suitcase he'd left there, he once more found himself seeking Natasha's eyes. "A new person had appeared on the esplanade," he recalled from Chekhov, whom he'd been reading in preparation for the trip, "a lady with a little dog." How did it go? "If she's here alone without husband or friends, it wouldn't hurt to make her acquaintance . . ."

He was to share a sleeper with the same elderly landscape painter he'd been with so far, while Natasha was with Sylvia in the next compartment. As the train glided from the station, the four of them stood talking in the corridor, observing in the fading light the dull uniformity of concrete factories and apartment blocks which, as the city was left behind, gradually gave way to birch forests and wooden houses with elaborately carved tracery around their windows.

"We'll be in Leningrad for the White Nights," Natasha told them. "It never really gets dark there in summer."

Like other Russians they'd met, she spoke enthusiastically and in excellent English about her country and everyone's hope for Gorbachev's reforms. She said little about her own life, and Malcolm learned only that she had a ten-year-old son, whom she'd left with her mother while she was away. In any case, he found himself listening more to the cadences of her charmingly accented voice, which rose slightly in pitch when she ordered tea for them all, speaking Russian for the first time. Then they were interrupted by the woman conductor as she went back and forth along the corridor, serving tea in steaming glasses from an electric samovar at one end.

Finally they retired to their compartments. Undressed in his bunk, with the lights extinguished and the older man snoring below him, Malcolm was aware of the strangeness of it all: a country he didn't know, the steady motion of the train, and a woman he wanted to find out more about. But just five days remained until he had to return to life's routine.

"A lady with a little dog," he thought. The story's main character seemed rather like him. Malcolm had been married once, but he wasn't successful enough as an artist to support anyone, and when he painted he tended to forget everything else. He sometimes slept with his models, but he never found this as meaningful as the paintings he made of them. It was only on holiday that he looked for something resembling romance. He'd expected it to be that way with Sylvia: a brief courtship, followed by a pleasant but undemanding intimacy of a type that so many wanted, and then a parting without regrets or complications. But he doubted it would be that way with Natasha.

He looked up hopefully as someone came into the buffet, but it was only Sylvia. "Hello, there," she greeted him, as she joined the queue to order. He still found her voice inviting, while she was now obviously disappointed that he hadn't pressed his pursuit of her to the conclusion they'd both expected.

How familiar this buffet had become, he mused: the hissing coffee machine; the plates of cheese, salami, or red caviar and pats of butter; the

White Nights

bottles of mineral water, vodka, and Georgian wine. But—he glanced at Sylvia again—it was Natasha he wanted to share it with. Just two nights ago they'd been sitting at this very table, laughing about how the prices were printed in purple ink on cardboard tickets, but were all collected together at one end of the counter so you couldn't figure out which items they referred to.

"And the descriptions are written in Russian," Natasha had added with that little laugh expressing her desire to please. "The hotel's only for foreigners, and yet foreigners can't read them! That's the way we do things here."

His reminiscences were interrupted as Sylvia unloaded her dishes onto the table in front of him. "So today's the last day," she said, pulling out a chair to sit down. "And later this morning Natasha will leave us at the airport for our return flight to London. Where you'll forget her."

It wasn't true, but inevitably he'd cease to feel this longing for Natasha, so demanding now precisely because it wouldn't last. There wasn't enough time. A few days of passionate intensity had to compensate for all those others, when the only thing that seemed real was an endless succession of bare canvasses to be transformed into something that represented for him the intangible purpose of life.

"And I can make time for you in London, if you want." Sylvia touched his hand, laughing. "You don't have to take everything so seriously!"

"True." But looking at Sylvia as she squeezed a piece of lemon into her tea—pleasant, but with none of the magic so lacking in his life outside his painting—Malcolm knew that when he was working he'd find no more time for her than for anyone else.

Yesterday he'd had breakfast here with Natasha. She'd come in after him, smiling shyly as she waited at the counter. "I've brought you your second cup," she said when she joined him. "And a chocolate."

A. Colin Wright

"You'd make a good painter," he complimented her, unreasonably happy that she'd noticed his habit of buying one of the individually wrapped chocolates to go with his second cup of coffee. "Most people aren't that observant."

"Oh, I'm too caught up with all the little details of life," she said in an attempt to hide her obvious pleasure at his comment. "Looking after my family. My husband. He's an engineer, but he appreciates art too."

"You love him?" he risked asking.

She hesitated. "He's very much in love with me. He's very kind to me, looks after me. And Sasha, my son, he's the whole world for me." She went on: "A girlfriend of mine had a son who was killed in Afghanistan— he was doing his military service—and I cried for a week, knowing how I'd have felt in her place."

Sylvia, as she ate her breakfast, was talking about her life in London. I'm in love with Natasha, he thought, partly because she's from a different world. Because she comes from a story of Chekhov's; because she can feel sympathy for Russian soldiers killed in Afghanistan whereas I have only ever thought of them impersonally, as aggressors. But what could she possibly see in me, an aging artist who's always failed at long-term relationships?

He had started to grow close to Natasha, it seemed, on the very first evening, when their group had gone to the Kirov Theatre—the Mariinsky, she called it, using the old tsarist name—to see *Die Fledermaus*. The operetta was chosen for them, presumably, because it was light and well-known enough to make few demands on their comprehension. In the baroque opulence of the theatre's first balcony, they'd quite accidentally sat together. Each time there was a well-sung aria or an amusing scene on the stage below, he was aware of Natasha turning towards him to smile into his eyes. At first this embarrassed him, although he soon realized it

White Nights

was a Russian habit that differed, charmingly, from the English one of staring determinedly ahead. When he started smiling back he found he was sharing the performance with her in a way that brought a growing intimacy without their even saying anything.

For their daily excursions she always sat at the front of the bus, while he sat just behind her, aware of the same kind of shyness that came over him when he was about to tackle an important picture. He didn't even sketch her, although others had their pads and pencils out at every opportunity. They went to the usual tourist places. The Hermitage, where the guide bored them with overdetailed explanations, so that several of them wandered away; but he was too conscious of Natasha, walking not far from him, to concentrate on the pictures. They went to the Russian Museum, where she talked so interestingly to him about the Russian nineteenth-century realist painters that they arrived back late for the bus. They strolled with the others by granite-lined canals and along the crowded Nevsky Prospekt; took a hydrofoil on the river; visited artists' studios, where they all got a little drunk because their hosts thought being hospitable was more important than showing their works.

Then there was the Salvador Dali exhibition. Natasha was excited about it since, as an official delegation, they could get in straightaway, while most Russians had to wait for hours in long queues. Along one wall of the gallery hung whimsical ink and wash drawings on mythological subjects, and Malcolm was immediately attracted to a highly erotic picture of three naked girls, who turned out to be the Three Graces displaying their charms to Paris.

"I wouldn't be able to sleep at night if I had that hanging over my bed," he said to Natasha to see her reaction.

She blushed, laughed, and said "You see the kind of thing we've been missing in the Soviet Union for so long? Until recently, any gallery

A. Colin Wright

showing that would have been closed for pornography. And that one"—she pointed to the next picture—"would be even worse!"

It was a depiction of the Birth of Venus, who was shown emerging from frothy dark blue waves spurting from an enormous penis scrawled in black ink.

"Can you understand how marvellous it is to see such works after the years of puritanical . . . ?" She left her sentence unfinished, and he couldn't be sure whether it was because of intense feeling or sudden modesty.

That evening, they all arrived back late at the hotel after a rather dreary reception, and she agreed to go with Malcolm to the buffet for a goodnight drink.

"Will you let me paint you?" he blurted out while they were sitting there.

She looked at him seriously. "If we ever see each other again, yes." Then she became confused, perhaps understanding intuitively that he normally painted nudes. "But there's no chance for you to paint me on this trip, is there? And besides"—she gave a coquettish laugh—"I'm not really like Venus or the other goddesses, you know."

It was their most intimate moment so far. But he couldn't imagine actually taking off her clothes and making love to her. Even to picture her naked—whether or not she'd be as beautiful as those young girls, or Venus rising from foaming waves of semen—seemed sacrilegious.

When they went upstairs, Natasha walked down the corridor ahead of him. At the door to his room—hers was farther on—she shook his hand in a hasty goodnight, guessing perhaps that he was trying to summon up the courage to kiss her and not giving him the opportunity.

*　　*　　*

210

White Nights

Sylvia, who had already finished her breakfast, was now talking about whether to go and start packing. He had no idea what else she'd been saying. Other people were coming in, too, chatting in loud English voices. But why hadn't Natasha come yet? I'm searching for her like the hero of Chekhov's story, he thought fancifully, just waiting for the time when she'll appear again.

The night before, they'd all gone to the ballet, only this time Natasha's seat was on the opposite side of the stalls from his. But they kept looking at each other, and once she acknowledged him by closing her eyes and then raising her head, smiling as she opened them. A distinctively Russian gesture he'd noticed before. He knew they'd see each other at the farewell party back at the hotel.

But then, with everyone milling around the buffet, there was no chance to be alone with her. He hoped she'd stay behind when the party finished, but she stood up with everyone else. In the corridor upstairs they all headed for their rooms. Saying goodnight at his door, she left her hand in his for a moment, but her withdrawal of it was quite firm. Perhaps, like Chekhov's heroine, she was conscious of the fact that she had a husband.

He closed his door behind him and, as always, went to stand by the desk in front of the window, gazing at the wide expanse of the river below with its stately bridges. The sky was still a faded pinkish blue, and tonight he made no attempt to close the curtains, which in any case covered only three-quarters of the window and made little difference to the eerie twilight in the room. The majestic Winter Palace on the opposite bank, the city's domes and spires clearly visible in Leningrad's White Nights: none of this, he thought, will exist tomorrow. Slowly he turned to go into the clumsy bathroom with its heavy square tiles, to brush his teeth in the old-fashioned washbasin without a plug—thinking how on other such trips he usually ended up going to bed with someone pleasant. Now, he wanted simply to be with Natasha; to sit and talk to her, discover something of her elusive inner being before she too receded into the past.

A. Colin Wright

In his pyjamas he returned to the window, leaning his elbows on the desk and watching the play of light on the river below. We could lie down together so I can hold her, and it needn't go further than that. But no, that couldn't happen . . . and the extraordinary thought came to him that, while sex had often seemed to him a way of communication, it was now preventing him and Natasha from being together. It was impossible for her to come to his room without implying a willingness to go to bed with him, which—because of her husband, perhaps, or her official position with the group—she wasn't prepared for. How could he tell her he wanted not so much the intimacy of her body as the simple intimacy of shared emotion?

He made no attempt to wipe the tears from his cheeks, knowing that such moments, however maudlin, represented what was best in life. From childhood on, he'd been taught not to give way to his feelings, and even now some inner voice told him he was being unmanly. Voices from his adolescence joined in. "Sloppy romanticism," said his grammar-school English teacher, while his classmates chanted the accepted story about Russian women, who never said anything except "You can have my body, but you can never have my soul."

"It's her soul I want," he thought. As a painter, fortunately, he didn't have to define what that might mean.

But as he looked out at the mysterious northern city on its dreamlike river, something extraordinary happened. Turning his head in the direction of the sea, he saw that the most distant bridge was moving. Parting in the middle and lifting its two arms, until he could clearly see open space between them as they pointed towards the sky. He closed his eyes and opened them again—and this time the next nearest bridge was doing the same. Magically, a third opened, and then a fourth, quite near, and soon the broad river lay open like a pathway to infinity.

At that moment the telephone on the desk in front of him started to ring. He stared in disbelief and then picked it up.

White Nights

"Hello?"

There was a moment's silence, and then her lilting, accented voice asked timidly "Malcolm?"

"Yes?"

"It's Natasha. I wondered . . . have you seen the bridges?"

"I thought I might be dreaming."

"They open every night for ships to come up the river. People often stay up to see them during the White Nights. I forgot to tell you. Isn't it beautiful?"

He didn't know how to respond. "Would you like to come over so we can watch them together?"

Her little embarrassed laugh: "No, we can't do that."

"I . . . I was thinking of you."

"Malcolm, tomorrow's the last day, and I just wanted to say that . . . I must tell you or you might never know. I think I'm a little bit in love with you."

His happiness took his breath away. "Can't we see each other? We could go downstairs . . ."

"No," she insisted. "You'll try to kiss me, and I'll want you to kiss me, and it will just be a brief romance for you. I love you, that's all I wanted to say."

Already she'd put down the phone. He stumbled to the bed and flung himself onto it, tears springing from his eyes in his unexpected joy. Lying on top of the pocket-like sheet enclosing his blanket, he looked up at the tiles in the ceiling. A mysterious room where a Russian girl had just told him she loved him.

213

A. Colin Wright

Only he hadn't told her he loved her too. He got up, opened the hotel folder on the desk to find out how to reach her room, picked up the phone, and dialled the number.

"Hello?"

"I'm in love with you too."

"Malcolm," her voice rose happily. "Don't you think it's crazy, our talking like this? It's a dream. I couldn't ever say it to your face, it would make it too serious, but here on the phone: I love you, love you."

"I loved you from the moment I saw you at the station. I'll always love you." He noticed that he'd written "Natasha" on the pad in front of him, and he underlined it twice, starting to shade in the letters and draw patterns around her name.

They talked for an hour or more. She told him of her childhood, her studies, her private disappointments; her grandparents in the south of Russia, the hiking trips she'd been on in Siberia, her love of nature, the animals she'd seen there. He spoke of his failure at marriage, his passion for painting, his attempt to capture the essence of life while critics saw him only as a mediocre realist.

"You can have my body, but you can never have my soul." Laughing, he told her about the old cliché. "And that's what the critics say of my work. They see the body, but not the soul I struggle so hard to uncover."

"Do you believe in God?" she asked.

"Yes. While you probably . . ."

"I too. Russians have always been deeply religious. There's nothing else left for us."

The bridges closed, one by one. He and Natasha finally said goodnight. He returned to his bed and immediately fell asleep.

*   *   *

White Nights

"Good morning," she says simply, sitting down beside Sylvia.

"I thought you weren't going to come."

"I didn't sleep."

She's unusually silent, and there's little enough time before they have to leave to finish their packing and bring their cases downstairs. There's no opportunity to speak to her alone.

In his room, Malcolm piles everything from his desk and drawers into his suitcase, closes it wearily, and goes to the window for a final look at the river. Trucks and buses crowd across the bridges in the bright sunlight of a Leningrad morning, and it seems impossible that last night ever happened.

On the bus, he and Natasha sit together in near silence, afraid to acknowledge words that might not have been said at all. For a moment he holds her hand.

At the airport, she has to deal with tickets and then say goodbye to all of them. Shaking hands with him, she says only that she hopes they might meet again, smiling and looking into his eyes.

In the plane rising over the pale blues and greens of the Gulf of Finland, Malcolm reflects that the last five days are over forever. For an hour or so he observes the changing coastlines of Sweden and Denmark; then, all too soon, the distinctively curved shape of East Anglia lies below him. A long descent into the tired familiarity of London ends with his arrival under clouded skies, followed by the usual wait for baggage in a crowded terminal before he's heading for the Underground and back to his studio in Wandsworth.

Unpacking his bag, he sees that in his haste that morning he unthinkingly put the hotel folder in with the other papers from the desk. He sets it aside and goes to get lunch. That afternoon he busies himself

A. Colin Wright

with the routine things necessary for his comfort before he can start painting again.

It isn't until evening that he finally opens the folder.

In front of him, on the hotel writing paper, is Natasha's name with patterns around it—and above it is a drawing of her, sketched in a few simple lines while he was speaking to her on the phone. Behing this drawing is another one, and then—hastily he starts to turn them over—others still. There's even one of her with a little dog—an unconscious tribute to Chekhov—and an attempted nude study, which causes him to smile guiltily as he remembers how, before saying goodnight, they finally admitted they might like to make love. That drawing, of course, had been influenced by Dali.

He looks through the sketches again more slowly. They have a spontaneous charm precisely because they're unpolished. If he can manage to recreate that for his next exhibition, he might be able to express not only his love for Natasha, but his fascination with the whole of that mysterious life outside him that he's forever trying to capture.

"I love you, Natasha," he whispers, knowing he doesn't have to define what those words mean—until the time, perhaps, when he'll return to Russia.

In the meantime, he'll repeat them every day while working on a series of small canvasses to express his unachicvablc longing for the divine.

The Comedy of Doctor Foster

Doctor Foster went to Gloucester
In a shower of rain.
He stepped in a puddle up to his middle
And never went there again.

Those who maintained that Dr. Foster's demise was the result of a pact he'd made with the devil were, quite frankly, mistaken. They were members of the congregation of St. Joseph's Church, Wittenberg, Ontario, and they had cause to remember Dr. Foster with some alarm. But the people of St. Joseph's didn't know everything, or even—with the exception of the rector—very much at all. As they said, "There's no smoke without a fire," but it wasn't hellfire that Foster was involved with.

It's as well to set down the facts. Foster was not on his way to Gloucester but merely to Toronto. It wasn't raining at the time, but was one of those days in midsummer when warm sun alternated with violent thunderstorms, and it had rained shortly before he set out. The "puddle" was one of those insignificant rivers along the 401, in which Foster's car landed after going out of control. He died instantly, and thus not only did he never go to Gloucester—Toronto—again, he never even reached it. His name, however, certainly was Foster: John Foster, B.A., M.A., Ph.D.

The rhyme? Well, some malicious person scrawled it on the wall of St. Joseph's the day before the funeral, and it was later suggested as a fitting epitaph for Foster's tombstone. For Foster will never be forgotten by that long-suffering congregation, whose only option over the years had

A. Colin Wright

been to show Christian endurance towards the man. The obituary notice in *The Wittenberg Torch* stirred up further animosities. "Written by one of his colleagues," Major Austin told everyone he met, "praising the originality of his thought or something. Which only goes to show the preposterous ideas that are taught to young people nowadays. I read it until I got to the part about Foster being an expert on Nitchy." (He meant Nietzsche.) "Nitchy, I ask you!" The remark fell flat, as nobody else, except for the rector, was sure who Nietzsche, or Nitchy, was.

Twenty-four years earlier, when Foster had first come to the nearby university, he already had a reputation as a scholar. He also published novels, under a different name, and was a competent amateur artist too. ("Something must have gone wrong since," the rector's wife would later say. "Even I could paint better than that.") In those early years, as a few old-timers remembered, Foster was one of the pillars of the community, and of St. Joseph's in particular. True, he had his oddities. Then in his fifties, he was divorced and so not quite respectable. He read books that couldn't be approved of. He showed a singular indifference to the niceties of parish behaviour by attending church in baggy trousers and a jacket with patches on the elbows, and those who sat near him maintained he ostentatiously left out certain sentences from the Creed. But he attended regularly, and no one paid him much attention.

And then it started. In the summer of 1960 to be exact, twenty-two years before Foster's death. He was looked after by a Mrs. Wignall, who came to clean for him twice a week. No harm there, for she was a good soul and likewise a respectable member of St. Joseph's. But she fell sick, and Foster used that as an excuse to replace her—with a blonde creature, a foreigner, in her twenties or younger, and with a figure . . . Well, the male members of St. Joseph's would, in their jocular, broad-minded moods, describe it with whistles. What's more, she lived in. Now no one could prove anything, but they talked and shook their heads. Some even sniggered. Only they couldn't interrogate the girl directly, or have the pleasure of snubbing her, because she didn't come to church at all. Foster, when tackled discreetly on the subject,

The Comedy of Doctor Foster

laughed the whole thing off. But already there were murmurs about such things being a threat to the moral fibre of the community.

Actually, the rector met the girl and reported that she was charming, intelligent, and seemed happy working for Foster—and refused to speculate further on their relationship. Others were dissatisfied, saying the rector wasn't sufficiently on guard against sin. (That was the old rector, of course, and there have been two more since, but all of them stood up for Foster, even when it became obvious to everyone else that he was an evil man.) Anyway, later that year the girl was obviously pregnant. Foster seemed cheerfully unrepentant and just answered "yes" when someone asked him about it. No shame at all, and now people started avoiding him even in church, which he didn't seem to mind.

The girl finally went away somewhere and never returned. Foster carried on as usual, or rather, worse than usual. It was one thing to live in sin with an outsider whom nobody really cared about, but quite another to seduce the organist's wife. Oh, the affair didn't last long, and the stupid woman soon went back in tears to her husband, but the effect on the congregation was shattering. The more so because, even after her husband took her back in loving forgiveness, she refused to show repentance or to say a bad word about Foster. She seemed almost willing to run to him again and, for all the wrong he'd done her, to offer him the other cheek (or whatever part of the anatomy was involved).

Now Foster began to get objectionable. He'd always sworn a little. Now he swore a lot. He pretended there was no such thing as "good" or "bad" language (except when it was ungrammatical): just that certain language was appropriate for some contexts and not for others. When someone objected that swearing was morally reprehensible because it took the name of the Lord God in vain, he countered by asking why it was all right to say "my God!" or "heavens!" and not "Christ!" or "Jesus!" Or why, in Spanish, even an archbishop could use Christ, the Virgin Mary, and all the saints thrown in as a simple expression of surprise, and no one took it amiss. When someone else claimed that swearing reduced everything to

A. Colin Wright

the unpleasant aspects of life, he asked what was unpleasant about shitting and fucking, adding that he enjoyed both.

"It's not the *meaning* people are afraid of," he'd explain, as though the worthy members of St. Joseph's were mere students, "but the sound of it. And that, ladies and gentlemen, is nothing but magic: belief in the power of the word."

Foster didn't swear indiscriminately, rejecting this as debasing the vitality of the language, which had to be used with precision. He did indeed swear with precision. He was vulgar with precision. Called things by their names with precision. Once in church, after a piece of unusual metaphysical nonsense in the rector's sermon, he farted with precision.

He told Constance Nightingale, a neurotic spinster in her forties, to take her pants down and have an affair. Then, worst of all, he seduced the eighteen-year-old daughter of one of the tediously married sidesmen. He became a problem. The rector couldn't turn him away from St. Joseph's, and in any case he was convinced the church was for sinners rather than the righteous (a sincere if naïve man, the rector). And, over the next two years, Foster had even greater success.

"St. Joseph's is becoming a congregation of cuckolds," Major Austin commented with his usual bluntness—causing the rector, the only one who knew that Joseph was actually the patron saint of cuckolds, to suppress an inappropriate chuckle.

Before Foster's break with the church, the majority of the congregation had come to hate him. They could have forgiven him nice, respectable sins. They could perhaps have forgiven a certain sexual licence, provided it was discreet, as a kind of childish last fling before he entered his golden years (or old age, as he indelicately called it). What they couldn't forgive was how he threatened all their cherished ideas.

220

The Comedy of Doctor Foster

"Of course I'm a threat," he would roar. "Why is it that Christians have to be so goddamn dull? Do you think Christ wanted a religion of ass-sitters? I'm more Christian than all of you. Read Kierkegaard!"

"Kierke-who?" asked Major Austin, who was deaf. "Is he swearing again?"

More offensive than anything was the fact that Foster was so obviously enjoying himself. Whereas the others were supposed to be living in God's grace, it was Foster who was happy; Foster who, they said, couldn't really believe in religion at all.

Why did he come to church? The answer was supplied by the Harrisons' eighteen-year-old son. They were a pleasant couple, but their son had "got" religion and had recently written a letter to the *Torch,* saying he was seriously disturbed about the moral standards of the community because a striptease was being performed in one of the local hotels. Anyway, he'd just entered theological school in the university and thought he knew everything.

"Obviously," he said, "Foster must have sold his soul to the devil. And he's making witches of all his . . . paramours."

Although the idea was ridiculous, there was a spark—a very tiny one—of truth in it. And it caught on because of a comment Foster made the very next Sunday at coffee hour, after the boy who'd got religion started to talk about stories of pacts with the devil.

"That's all nonsense," Foster said to the boy with an odd look in his eye. "Have you ever stopped to consider the idiocy of making a pact with the devil? Why the devil? When God is omnipotent, why not ask Him to grant your requests? More effective, and incomparably better as life insurance."

"Man's desires are often evil," said the boy who'd got religion. "God can only work good."

A. Colin Wright

"That's simple-minded theology, young man." Foster was now the serious professor. "God is omnipotent, the sole source of power. Man cannot limit God to his own ideas of good and evil, which are hopelessly muddled. God gave man the world to enjoy, and the desire to do so. Won't He, then, grant man his *true* desires?"

"Not if they're evil."

"In my experience, man's desires are evil only when they're petty and shortsighted. Don't you think that God might grant them for the love of man, rather than this far-fetched devil creature who wants souls to torture? Are not man's true desires just the natural demands upon life that God has given him?"

"So what are they?"

"To experience and know God's world to the full. To share love with all, both spiritually and sexually . . ."

The boy pounced. "Spiritually yes, but sexually no. We're told to renounce the flesh!"

"Are you sure that's what Christ tells us?" Foster asked. "He says only that the flesh profiteth nothing—in the sense that human power is helpless as compared with spiritual power. Oh, I know that church-sanctioned Christianity has always insisted on the renunciation of human desires as the ultimate virtue. I disagree with the church."

"But that's terrible," twittered Constance Nightingale, who'd joined them. "How can you possibly disagree with the church?"

Foster didn't deign to reply.

"Then," the boy went on, "there's no such thing as evil?"

Foster reflected. "What's evil is man's attachment to *pseudo* desires, which seem important only because, unless you have God's help, they're easier to achieve. Making money for its own sake is a pseudo

222

The Comedy of Doctor Foster

desire. The real desire is still for other things, excitement, adventure, security—which in itself is only freedom from fear. If you can have *them*, your true desires, then money itself is unnecessary. Stealing is similarly evil, because it arises from this pseudo desire for money. Love of material possessions is evil—didn't Christ himself say that?—because it's so much easier to flaunt your luxurious houses than to live, which involves risk. Fear can be evil. Love of power over others, violence, and murder: all are evil, but again they're pseudo desires that compensate for a lack of love and wanting just to be recognized by others—which we all desire but find difficult to achieve."

"But stealing other people's wives?" the boy asked.

Foster dismissed the objection. "A wife isn't a possession to be stolen. If you consider sex as wrong, but made permissible by limiting it to couples with property rights over each other, then obviously sex with anyone other than your spouse is wrong too. A position the church has adopted since the days of St. Paul"—Foster walked out of church during the reading of certain epistles—"while ignoring the far more insidious sin of coveting one's neighbour's possessions, which our whole advertising industry encourages. If on the other hand you consider sex as a natural, God-given expression of communion and enjoyment, to be shared as Christian love is to be shared—and who would dream of making that exclusive?—then the only 'wrong' is the hurt caused to others. But that is based on a human *vice*, jealousy, which in turn is based on fear."

A few of the more thoughtful who were present were uncomfortable, but the majority were horrified, particularly the boy who'd got religion. Foster concluded by saying that God united flesh and spirit; that He was as much at home with paganism as with church Christianity, in both of which there was evil as well as good; and that these ideas could be found in any number of writers.

"Blasphemy!" Major Austin snorted. "Religious anarchy, sexual anarchy, moral anarchy! Why, if this fellow continues making such a noise

A. Colin Wright

about things, he'll scare everyone away and where will our property values be then?"

"Blasphemy," echoed Constance Nightingale. "Rather wicked, don't you think?"

"Blasphemy," said the boy who'd got religion. "Can he be excommunicated or something?"

"Blasphemy?" said the rector doubtfully. "I suppose so."

"He's obviously in league with the devil," the boy continued. "Did you notice how he talked about making pacts? I tell you, he's sold his soul."

At this period, Foster was doing a lot of writing, and painting too. Not many knew about it, because the people of St. Joseph's didn't know everything. One might have wondered how he found time to sleep, for his sexual romps continued as usual. And he still taught in the university, where he was adored by his students (even though they found his standards too exacting); loved by some colleagues, who regarded him as a genius, and hated by others, who considered him subversive. His life, it seemed, would burn out from its very intensity, but in fact the opposite was the case. He was in perfect health, tremendously vital, and creating picture after picture, writing page after page.

"Fucking woman after woman," Major Austin said.

"Horace!" his wife remonstrated. "You're not in the army now!"

His ideas, though, did have some influence. Gradually a group of supporters—mainly younger men and women—grew up around him. The things they perpetrated were beyond belief. Drunken orgies and obscenities of all kinds. The boy who'd got religion attended a number of Foster's parties to try to exert his influence to stop them, and reported on all the disgusting details. He asked the congregation to pray for their lost brothers and sisters, and for him, too, for all the humiliations he had

224

The Comedy of Doctor Foster

to endure at Foster's house. The congregation's prayers had a positive outcome: the boy was miraculously cured of acne.

And then, insult of insults, this man who'd so impracticably preached against the evils of money suddenly received a great deal of it, from the publication of the first book written under his own name. The novel was outrageous and had an immediate success with the non-discriminating public, which lapped up any kind of perversion. The critics hailed the novel too; and the following year it was put on the Canadian literature course in a number of universities, but the members of St. Joseph's didn't know about that. Anyway, with the publication came money. Which to everybody's consternation Foster spent, frivolously, on his riffraff friends. Nothing went into life insurance or pension plans, or into any kind of solid investment. Nothing was given to the Progressive Conservative Party. Foster didn't even consider improving his house or putting in a swimming pool, which might have raised the tone of the neighbourhood.

"No, they'd only have orgies in the pool then," Constance Nightingale said, giggling, to everybody's surprise.

But then, thank God, Foster went away altogether.

The rector at last found the courage to ask him to stop coming to church.

Foster understood immediately. "I won't give you any more trouble, Hugh," he promised.

The rector grinned. "I've never had such an exciting time. Between you and I"—Foster interrupted to correct his grammar—"I get pretty fed up with the triviality of some of them, as you said once."

"Pissed off, were the words I used."

"Well, er, pissed off then."

A. Colin Wright

"I'm going away for a while anyway. I'll be back, though. You won't get rid of me entirely."

That business over, they passed onto other topics, as two friends. But since both were religious, in different ways, it's not surprising that religion was a central topic in their conversation. And somehow they started to discuss the nature of heaven.

"Do you want to know what my dream of heaven is?" Foster asked.

The rector nodded.

"I dream first of a cottage in a clearing in the woods, by a broad river with a sandy beach. With sunlight, not too hot, and no mosquitoes or thorns or things like that." He smiled. "Because I like woods and rivers, but not the mosquitoes. Or perhaps there'd be mosquitoes, only they wouldn't really bite, or the thorns wouldn't really prick. Rather they'd produce brief scratches of almost unendurable pleasure, just so you'd know that everything was real, more real than this world that surrounds us. And the rest of heaven would be an infinity of beautiful places to explore and discover. Forests, mountains, snow, sun, beautiful cities, a land where all could have the simple joy they most desire. Humans would have access to God's omnipotence and omniscience, to learn and, in the fullness of eternity, to discover the secrets of the universe. They'd be able to travel at will within it—oh, to see and comprehend it all!—but always to return to their one spot in heaven to gaze on its beauty and know, *know,* of the rest of the infinite beauty around.

"There'd be libraries, institutions of truly higher learning, art galleries, concert halls, for who can conceive of heaven without art and music? People would perform, and create, as they do on earth. All that's best of humans would be there. And all that's worst as well, for they must not be ignorant and need to know the bad too. So there'd be museums of horror, vice, pettiness. Of course there'd be no war, no conflict except for earnest dispute. No sickness, no politicians. Not even any social scientists,

226

The Comedy of Doctor Foster

thank God. Doctors, I suppose, yes—but to study the inner physical workings of man.

"And then, most important of all, we'd be resurrected in our young, healthy bodies instead of our old, ailing ones. Death would be an awakening out of sleep into the reality of life. Or perhaps we wouldn't even notice death. Life would be forgotten like a dream it's not worth making the effort to remember. In our wonderfully real bodies, our appetites and desires would still exist: for food, sex, and all the pleasures of life. Only now it would be with all the vigour and passion of first youth. Lovemaking would be there in its most voluptuous, most erotic, and most spiritual form, for now there'd be no jealousy, no fear of being displaced in another's affections. One would meet again, know and explore—completely, carnally—all one's old loves, as well as those one never had time or opportunity to know on earth. Whenever one wished, one would know where one's loves were, whom they'd be with. One would rejoice that all are joined in a common love of God, who uniteth all things, in whom is the sacred and profane, the humorous and the serious, the joy and the suffering, the beginning and the end." He paused. "But there would be solitude as well, for humans have need of solitude to create."

"The God you speak of isn't the Christian God."

"Not that of the Christian church, at any rate," Foster said sadly.

And so Foster went away, and life became more peaceful for the members of St. Joseph's. He would return again after many years, but in the interval, with things in the parish back to a normal observance of religious proprieties, he became a mere conversation piece, to be remembered even with nostalgia. How could a man behave in such an extraordinary way, or hold such disturbing ideas? Was he really in league with the devil?

A. Colin Wright

There was, of course, an explanation. The people of St. Joseph's didn't know everything, and they would have been surprised to learn that, before it all started, Foster had quite seriously considered making such a pact. To that extent, the later rumours had some validity. The problem was that he didn't know how to go about it. He was a highly intelligent man and didn't for a moment believe the devil would appear before him, horns, tail, and all. But he'd studied the devil as a literary figure and recognized him as a valid symbol of man's aspirations for knowledge and experience: in revolt against a God who, in the thoughts of some, would prefer man to remain innocent and ignorant of evil.

It was knowledge and experience that Foster wanted. He was already a scholar of no small reputation; he'd published his novels and painted pictures that hung in a few of his relatives' living rooms. But he knew that his achievements were minor. His scholarship was sound but inessential; his novels had been published under another name because they were trivial; and his pictures . . . Well, what was wrong with them was precisely that they *could* be put up on his relatives' walls, alongside pictures of forest streams, lakes, mountains, or sentimental women and children that had been bought at Zeller's. "He's artistic," one of his aunts would tell her friends, unaware that the word was used to describe people who produced flower arrangements or such with no comprehension of what art was all about.

That wasn't what he wanted, and he was miserable. Unable to endure the high-minded snobbery of his colleagues or the inanities that were the daily life of the members of St. Joseph's—and being uninterested in the fact that his neighbour's three-year-old was now toilet trained, which everyone else seemed to regard as the most important piece of news since the day it became known that old Mr. Krapowski was no longer toilet trained—he was isolated from others, lonely. Which wouldn't have been so bad had he not craved some intimate contact beyond the superficial level, while at the same time being tormented by simple sexual desire. The two were linked. A great deal of "experience" for him meant sexual experience, for he was well aware that this was one way of coming close to another

The Comedy of Doctor Foster

human being without the meaningless exchange of information that took place in other social situations. For sexual experience understood in such a way, masturbation was a poor substitute, and in any case seemed somewhat ridiculous in a fifty-year-old man.

And so he thought of a pact with the devil. Not with smoke and magic circles and incantations, not at first. Foster, although he knew a lot about witchcraft in a literary sense, didn't take it seriously. No, he realized he needed to change his life, to rid himself of his old inhibitions and attitudes, and he saw a pact with the devil as a symbolical representation of that change. But how was he to go about it? Even if the devil were only a symbol, he had to make it into one that was real for him. So finally he decided to devote himself to the mumbo jumbo of magic—not because he thought spirits would arise before him, but in order to convince himself of what he was doing. For this he had to study many obscure works, whose authors in some cases might simply be charlatans. He joined a group of devil worshippers, whose practices he found grotesque and ridiculous. But he put up with it, feeling in his soul that he was an outsider, although the others welcomed him as a convert, and took it for granted that he shared their beliefs in the same way as the members of St. Joseph's took it for granted that he shared theirs.

The night came for his first practical experiment in summoning the devil. He'd removed the rug and most of the furniture from his living room, leaving only a couch and chair, and now he brought in the other things he needed: candles, candlesticks, chalk. It didn't take him long, and he then lay down on the couch and went to sleep.

He didn't know what time it was when he awoke. He lit the candles, placed the candlesticks in their preassigned positions on the floor, and started to draw on it with chalk, beginning various incantations as he did so. "Bloody fool," he thought. "What good will all this do?" He worked eagerly, though, enjoying it. The procedure was complicated, involving some foul-smelling liquid he had to prepare. He couldn't remember everything, but was sceptical enough not to think it mattered.

A. Colin Wright

Finally he came to the words that were meant to summon the evil one. *"Venez, venez, seigneur, venez!"* he pronounced, wondering why the devil should respond more readily to French than to English, and whether it made any difference if the French were Parisian, Old Norman, or Québécois.

Nothing happened. Of course. But to make sure, he repeated the French in different dialects and then checked his chalk figures. He'd made a mistake. So he got down on his knees to correct it, murmuring further incantations, but sticking in a few swear words because he was annoyed at himself for being so ridiculous.

"What the devil are you doing there on your knees, you stupid runt?" came a voice from behind him.

Startled, he turned around, put out his hand, and stared at the stranger. "Say, then, who art thou . . . ?"

"Oh, cut out all that crap," the other interrupted. "You don't really believe in it, do you?"

Foster hesitated. "No, of course I don't."

"Good. Then turn on the light and come and sit down on the couch like a human being."

Foster did so, looking at the guest, who was a shortish old man of about eighty, with long hair that merged into a beard, and dressed in a white robe. A bit like Karl Marx in a nightgown. "How did you get in?" he asked.

"Through the door, you idiot, how else?" The man was looking around with an expression of distaste. "Pretty sparse place you have here. Why don't you get some decent furniture? Make it comfortable for your guests. And what's that revolting smell? Oh, that liquid over there. Pour it down the drain, for God's sake."

Foster did as he was told, and then returned and sat down on the one chair. As he looked at him, the old man's irritable appearance softened.

The Comedy of Doctor Foster

He was still stern, but kindly too, trustworthy. Strength and knowledge was there, sadness and humour. No longer like Karl Marx, now that the irritation was gone. Younger perhaps. Or older. Not really how he'd conceived of the devil at all.

"But then I'm not the devil," the man said. "You should be ashamed of yourself believing in that nonsense."

"Only as a symbol," Foster justified himself.

"Oh, as a symbol, I'll grant you he serves a purpose. But he's one-sided. Much as your church God is one-sided too."

"Who are you then?"

"Come, Foster, you know who I am."

Foster was embarrassed. "God?"

"The trouble with that word," the old man said, "is that people misunderstand it. They think of me as the God they've created in their image. The half-potent God, able to do only what their limited minds think of as good rather than evil. Let's call me something else, shall we? To prevent confusion. What would you suggest?"

Foster thought. "Yahweh," he said.

"That will do splendidly. Sufficiently pre-Christian. Close enough to paganism without entirely suggesting my sole purpose is to strike people with thunderbolts. I like it."

"Is that your usual appearance?" Foster asked with curiosity.

"I've no appearance, you dunderhead," Yahweh said, getting irritable again. "I merely chose the form I thought you'd most appreciate." Suddenly he let out a roar of laughter. "And you've got to admit, it's better than those Santa Clauses or sickly sweet pictures of Christ they're fond of putting in children's books and on church walls." He became businesslike.

A. Colin Wright

"Now, tell me why in the name of thunder you were trying to call up the devil?"

"To make a pact with him."

"To renounce God, to get the devil to serve you for twenty-four years, and in exchange to give him your soul for eternity, I suppose? I must tell him that the next time I see him. He'll die laughing. Between you and me, he's getting a bit sick of all these pacts."

Foster was puzzled. "But who is the devil then?"

"Didn't I tell you? I am."

"You said you weren't."

"I'm not."

"How can you be and not be?"

Yahweh laughed. "I'm omnipotent, that's all. I *am*. And that includes I'm not. Don't worry about it. You're making human categorizations."

"And then you're God too?"

"That's right."

"And Christ?"

"Me too."

"And Buddha, and Mohammed, and . . ."

"Oh, do stop going on and on! It's all the same anyway, what difference does it make? I *am*, and am *not*, all of them."

Foster was sarcastic. "Is there anyone else that you're not? Or that you are?"

The Comedy of Doctor Foster

"Yes," said the other. "Or rather no. I'm you too, and not either, or hadn't you noticed? Or at least you when you're not pretending to be someone else."

"This isn't getting us anywhere," Foster said gloomily.

"Sure it is," Yahweh exploded, "if you try understanding rather than just thinking! You disappoint me. I expected more from you. But tell me, why did you try to summon up the devil rather than me? When I'm the source of power, wasn't that rather stupid? What can he do that I can't?"

"Well, I guess I thought what I wanted was evil. No, that's to say, I didn't think it was evil, but that God would. And that therefore God couldn't grant me my desires."

"That's simple-minded theology, Foster. You're confusing me with your church God again. I'm omnipotent, not half-potent, I tell you. I can give you anything you want. And what's more, I'm the only one who can."

"But will you?"

"Of course," Yahweh said happily. "Love to. Provided you tell me your real desires."

"And the conditions?"

"Not important. All this stuff about selling souls . . . Your soul will be mine anyway." He intoned flatly: "'As it was in the beginning, is now and ever shall be, world without end, amen!'" Businesslike: "Now, let's make a list of what you want."

Foster, at least, had his list prepared. "Fame," he said, "so that people will love me. Riches, so that I may travel, live riotously, and have the means to acquire knowledge and be independent. Power, to get people to do what I want. Creativity, to do something of what you can do. No,

233

A. Colin Wright

I don't want omnipotence, it won't be fun if it's not difficult. Joy and suffering, because one can't create without them. And immortality."

"Hold on a minute, can't you? I may be omnipotent but I can't write that fast. Let's sort these out a bit. How about we just put down love instead of fame? That's what you really want, isn't it? And although you forgot to mention it, you want to love others too. We'll throw in a bit of fame along the way, but deep down you know it's not the important thing. Can we cross out riches? You'll get money now and again, but what you want is travel, independence, experience, knowledge, and riotous living. By that you mean sex, I suppose."

"Yes. You see I think sex is the greatest form of human communication . . ."

"Oh, be quiet! Of course it is. Don't start explaining the world to *me*! Okay. No problem, at least for your lifetime. The generation after you will have to be far more careful than you will, because of a devilish virus getting loose somewhere. Now power. You don't really want to boss people around and feel important like a tedious prime minister? No, you want love again, to be an influence for the better in the world and, for all you give the impression of thinking only of yourself, the satisfaction of doing something positive for your fellow humans. Right? Creativity, joy, suffering—that's all excellent. Wise man not to ask for happiness, the sop of those who want to live like robots. Immortality you have already. Now what can we add? Knowledge we have, but how about a bit of wisdom? And courage in being yourself. You'd better keep a few vices too. The people of St. Joseph's will be happier if they have something to hate you for. So keep your arrogance, your lack of courtesy. We'll add a solid dose of vulgarity, too, and outspokenness. Let's stir things up a bit. Now, is that the lot?"

Foster was delighted. "More than I expected."

"Fine. One thing: you'll keep your loneliness, and an inner emptiness that can only be filled at the time of your final union with me. On earth, one can't have wisdom without it."

The Comedy of Doctor Foster

"And when will I die? Do you want me to sign a pact?"

"You and your confounded pacts. Of course not. You have my word. And I *am* the word. I suppose you want me to give you twenty-four years of life too? It doesn't make much difference when life's eternal anyway. Just let me know when you feel like a change."

"I never imagined you could give me all that," Foster said. "I mean, the church is so set against a lot of it."

"The church has a sin of its own," Yahweh said, not without sadness. "It's called respectability, which is a form of fear. And you thought I should be a respectable God. Me, Yahweh! Ha! The sole source of power. The creator of all things. The beginning and the end. Alpha and Omega. Me, who designed man to be Lord of the opposites, as one of your German writers so aptly put it. You recognize the quotation, I hope?"

Foster nodded.

"And no doubt," Yahweh said, getting up to go, "you'd like a little bit of skirt to spend tomorrow night with? Intelligent, beautiful, and sexy, right?"

Foster, by now, was more courageous. "Yes, and she should be . . ."

"Spare me the gruesome details, please. I know your tastes. I gave you them, remember?"

Foster looked at him and laughed. "You old bugger, you!" he said slyly.

Yahweh burst out laughing again. "That's the spirit! Never be afraid of me. Tomorrow Mrs. Wignall will be sick. Get rid of her. You'll find a better applicant for the job."

"I don't know how to thank you."

"Oh, say the Magnificat a hundred times or something. Live, damn you, live!"

235

A. Colin Wright

They shook hands, and Foster found himself lying back on the couch again with the lights out.

When he awoke, it was morning. After breakfast the phone rang. He told Mrs. Wignall he was sorry she was sick but that he wouldn't need her again. At the office of *The Wittenberg Torch*, where he went to place an ad for domestic help, an attractive foreign girl next to him asked if she could have the job. He agreed, and they arranged for her to come and settle the details that evening. Margrit was even more attractive without clothes on, and the details were settled in bed.

And so began the time of riotous living that the people of St. Joseph's found so outrageous. But there was a deeper side to it, of which they were unaware. There was pleasure, yes, but combined with it was an overwhelming sense of gratitude towards Yahweh. Foster was in awe at the enormity of the gift he'd received, the living manifestation of which was this marvellous girl, whose sexual inventiveness made his own fantasies seem as limited as those of a boy before puberty. It was the awakening of first love all over again. Unknown to anyone else, it was Margrit who initiated Foster into the orgy, on secret weekends when she'd take him to uninhibited places of hedonism.

The affair ended after she got pregnant. It was she who insisted on leaving. "Are you one to be bound by the ties of fatherhood and family life?" she asked him. He admitted she was right, remembering what Yahweh had said about loneliness—although he would still see her, and his son, from time to time.

So he took his new mistresses at St. Joseph's, and then gradually found a group of friends growing around him, so that the orgies now took place at his own house. Qualitatively they were different from other groups of swingers that were popular in those years. Theirs was a close society, which shared intellectual and artistic interests as well. The people of St. Joseph's saw only the immorality, but knew nothing of the discussions,

236

The Comedy of Doctor Foster

the musical and literary evenings, the amateur theatricals (some of which included sexual acts, performed with taste and love). But there were the drunken Dionysian revels too. Life in this group was far from idyllic, for the idyllic is one sided. Rather, it was often bestial, the participants lusting vulgarly after those who, shortly before, had been the recipients of tenderness, love, and respect. Crude fellatio and cunnilingus were the norm, for is not the wet and slobbering sucking of another's genitals, held with legs apart for all to see, the very epitome of earthy, animal sex, compared with which tender, blushing intercourse is ridiculously genteel and polite? For here both barbarism and civilization reigned together in a harmony of opposites.

Foster individually adored his partners and was adored by them. Some, of course, were jealous or possessive and suffered from his refusal to bind himself exclusively to any one; but, in this suffering, they experienced an essential part of humanity. He, too, had to struggle with the same self-doubt, for he was human as well; and, as the group grew, he was aware of the competition of other, younger men. He suffered from his own human imperfection, and gave thanks for it.

The orgy of the senses carried over into his painting and writing. He would regurgitate onto canvas in the morning visions that were still coursing through him from the night before, his tubes ejaculating paint, his hands palpitating, kneading the forms before him; and then, in repletion, he would paint a watercolour of utter tranquillity, working patiently on the finest detail, inspired, one would say, by the peace of God which passeth all understanding. It was the same with his writing. In his passionate outbursts he had no time for anything but a tape recorder; then he would patiently transcribe in longhand and work for days correcting and shaping. What he produced was both violent and eternally still, blasphemous and deeply religious, sensual and spiritual. The members of St. Joseph's found it outrageous, the critics were divided over it, but it sold: on the one hand, to those who immediately understood and loved the genius behind it; on the other, to those who craved cheap sensationalism.

A. Colin Wright

And so Foster earned money, until the day came when he left Wittenberg. His life, since his dream about Yahweh, had been full of action. He'd had no time to consider whether he was happy or not, which didn't matter, and very little for calm, lonely reflection, which did. He went to a tiny village in Austria, where he lived unostentatiously, with none of the uproar that had surrounded him at home. The members of St. Joseph's would hardly find it credible that he went each morning, except Sundays, to the ornate baroque church and spent up to an hour in mute contemplation.

"Are you repenting for your past sins?" a village girl asked him one morning.

"No!" he said emphatically. "I'm taking time to savour my life. To rest my soul."

She laughed. "That's too complicated for us here."

The girl became his mistress, and they lived together for over a year. They would walk in the mountains, breathe the air, look down at the villages, and up into the heavens. They would make love in the meadows, expose themselves naked to the goats and the cows, who looked on indifferently, chewing and producing their milk. They would laugh, and cry too.

And yet he knew that she couldn't understand him, no more than anyone really understood him. As always, he was condemned to be alone.

He had to think how to explain it to her. "The animal principle," he said at last. "With you it's become a beautiful dream, emotion, purity. The sensual has become spiritual, and very lovely it is too. But that alone is in*human*. Humans are just as full of lust and passion, of animalism. Of sordid, exciting desires. The spiritual must become sensual again. Sex, pure animal sex, has to have its due."

"Is life no more than sex, then?"

238

The Comedy of Doctor Foster

"Much more. It includes all that can be appreciated when the urge for sex is stilled. Yet, in another sense, life *is* sex. Sex creates life, in every way. It's the passion to live. Without it there's colourless self-denial, only angels and harps. The cows producing their milk." He paused. "But sex is death, too, for all of life is a process of dying. Is not each orgasm a small death?"

Bewildered, she just shook her head.

In the meanwhile, life was there before him, even if he often felt it wasn't quite real. How much less real, though, was the sedentary family life of many of those around him? For the first time, his feeling of sorrow for them outweighed his more usual contemptuous indifference.

He expressed his sadness in another book, and then he travelled on to other cities, leaving the girl behind. She was a happy memory, part of the fabric of his life, but only one of the cross threads, essential for the pattern but not running from end to end. And equally, he was only a cross thread in her life, which was woven in another direction, with the threads stretching away into other fabrics. Life in its entirety was a multidimensional construct of different tapestries, some bright and coherent, some irretrievably tangled, some consisting of nothing but a few twisted threads, some torn off and broken.

In Italy a cross thread was broken for him, painfully. He was in the south and had circumvented local prejudice sufficiently to attract a dark-haired innocent nineteen-year-old. Unfortunately, the son of a family friend considered himself betrothed to her and, following custom in such matters, burst into Foster's hotel room with a machine gun and sprayed the bed with bullets, killing the girl. Foster, ludicrously, was getting rid of a used condom in the bathroom, or he'd have been killed too.

In a moment he was back in the room, where the boy was weeping over the girl's naked, bloodstained body. He offered no resistance when Foster took the gun. They stood and looked at each other, blind convention staring in hatred at its insolent challenger. In the boy's look was all the

A. Colin Wright

fury of a man who knew he was right, had justice and honour on his side. Society itself, even the law, would support him and give only light punishment. Foster hesitated, shocked by his responsibility for this death, caused by his defiance of convention. Did it matter that the convention was evil? Should one simply submit? He looked at the girl's body, oozing red and ugly. Why hadn't Yahweh forewarned him of this? This was bestial, too, a thousand times more so than any of his orgies, where the senses ran riot. He was horrified and yet fascinated. This too was life: the very horror was part of it.

He couldn't bring himself to pull the trigger as the boy left. He sat in silent respect for the girl until the police came, and there followed the interminable inquiries and formalities. The neat documentation by the living of the incomprehensible fact of death. Unable to understand it, they got rid of it by giving it a certificate, as though granting a passport for travel to a foreign country.

We will not follow further Foster's travels, for his life was such that it would be possible to give only a superficial view of it. It could be made into an adventure story, with stirring deeds and times when Foster feared for his life, but the adventures of his soul would be lost. It could be made into a morality tale, for Foster performed good deeds to help others, but he would prefer them to go unrecorded. It could be made into a pornographic story, for sometimes the revels continued, but, in Foster's world, pornography had no meaning. A love story, a story of violence: all this it could be, for Foster, who thrived on life, thrived on opposites.

At long last he returned to Wittenberg. "He's coming back, have you heard?" the whispers went round St. Joseph's.

In eighteen years the parish had changed, for the children had grown up. There was now a certain antipathy between the old-timers (represented by Major Austin, now churchwarden, and old Miss Nightingale, honorary president of the altar guild), and the under-forties, who felt the world was passing St. Joseph's by. Their spokesman was none other than the man who'd once got religion. In eighteen years he'd married and raised six children, and had turned into an extraordinarily liberal personality.

With the arrival of Foster, the old-timers considered it their duty to warn everyone of the danger; while the under-forties tended to laugh and think the older ones had probably misjudged Foster. There was tension before anyone had even seen the man. The rector, always well-meaning, tried to reconcile the two sides, pointing out that Foster had become sufficiently well-known as a painter and writer to bring Wittenberg some fame.

"We'll have a great man in the congregation, even if he's as difficult as some people say. But he could have changed. And think of the example St. Joseph's could give the world. Let's welcome him, show the power of the church working with such a man." The rector was getting carried away by now. "How magnificent if we at St. Joseph's could give back to the church a true, repentant sinner!"

The man who'd once got religion shook his head. But others allowed themselves to be convinced, willing at first to show Christian forgiveness and accept their prodigal son with open arms.

If only Foster had been a repentant, prodigal son! Instead, he ignored them. Turned down their generous invitation to become a sidesman. Didn't come to church, even though the rector went to see him and came away hours later after a very friendly chat. It was all the more galling, because various celebrities started to visit Foster to pay their respects. Writers, artists, scholars. Well, the people of St. Joseph's didn't know everything, but they certainly knew the glamorous movie star who visited him. But did Foster let his friends, and this actress in particular, meet members of the congregation, or bring them to public functions where they could give a few autographs to the children? Of course not. St. Joseph's felt justly slighted.

A. Colin Wright

"I suppose he's having an affair with her," old Miss Nightingale said with prim satisfaction.

It became known that this indeed was the case. And when a few of Foster's former devotees started to return and the odd orgy took place, general indignation broke out again.

"He's still in the service of the devil," Connie whispered excitedly. "Perhaps he's the devil himself."

The others had forgotten this rumour, and the man who'd once got religion, remembering how he'd started it, looked embarrassed. But Connie Nightingale had become stubborn in her old age and went around repeating the same thing to everyone, with picturesque details—remembered from eighteen years before—of everything that supposedly went on now. She seemed particularly incensed at the celebrities who came to pay homage.

"Can't understand it," wheezed her ally, Major Austin. "In my day famous people had more sense."

"Now don't get upset about it, Horace," his wife commanded. "It's bad for your asthma."

The orgies, in fact, were nothing in comparison with the old days. Foster had mellowed. Everything was more discreet, less antagonistically obtrusive. Foster was in his seventies and looked it: worn out, Connie said, by a life of excess (although she herself was younger and looked worse). In this she was, quite frankly, mistaken, for Foster was in excellent health. But he'd had a good life, and the excesses no longer seemed as necessary as before. For the most part, except for the occasional encounter in bed with an attractive woman, he preferred just to write or paint quietly, with less élan. His works no longer had the youthful brilliance, but instead a calm maturity; so that they were prized by literary and artistic connoisseurs, but no longer appeared on the bestseller lists.

242

The Comedy of Doctor Foster

But the old-timers of St. Joseph's didn't know everything, and they tried, particularly Connie Nightingale, to make out that it was worse than before.

"A servant of the devil, right here among us," she said on one occasion, with an expression of diabolical cunning. "We can't put up with that. We must *do* something."

The younger ones looked at her strangely, thinking that since Foster's return she'd gone a bit dotty.

"What have you in mind?" someone asked. Connie only smiled.

The next day she went to call on Foster. According to what she told everyone afterwards, he invited her in, beat her, undressed her, tied her to a chair, and raped her. "And then he just threw me out into the street," she concluded.

The last was probably true, but no one at St. Joseph's believed that even a man like Foster would rape Connie Nightingale, and the under-forties thought the whole thing hilarious. She'd apparently expected them all to go to Foster's house and tar and feather him, but, when nothing happened, she visited him again. This time, she reported, he did even worse things. More laughter, even from old-timers. Soon people got used to the sight of her toddling off to Foster's house, although he'd learned not to answer the door if he could help it.

Although this was clearly her fault, some of the old-timers found in it a reason to blame Foster. "It's witchcraft!" Major Austin exploded. "Seen something of it in Africa, you know. The woman's infatuated with him." As she got stranger and stranger, others repeated Major Austin's comment and suggested that here was the traditional case of the devil turning a decent woman into a witch.

Thus Foster once again found himself cast in the role of the devil. Actually, the under-forties rather enjoyed having a devil in their midst. And to be frank, the old-timers enjoyed it, too, for here was someone they

A. Colin Wright

could legitimately hate, a scapegoat who could be blamed for everything that was wrong. When Connie Nightingale was taken off screaming to a hospital from which she never returned, there was gleeful talk of demonic possession, with Foster the instrument of her undoing.

"The whole world's going to the devil," Major Austin complained. "If I just had him in the army! What's happening nowadays?"

"The world's changing," his wife said. "It'll never be the same."

"Thank God too," said the rector, alienating them both.

What suddenly united St. Joseph's and turned young and old against Foster was the publication of his last book, in which it was obvious that the characters were drawn from members of the congregation and from the faculty of the university. The book was extraordinarily apocalyptic, in which they were all shown neither as welcomed into heaven nor thrown into hell, but as condemned to return to earth. The more sensible commentators pointed out that the characters were created with sympathy. This was not the old Foster who'd looked down on everyone, but a man of understanding, who regarded with genuine pity those who, for whatever reason, had been forced to live out their half-lives in the shadow of St. Joseph's or the university. But the faculty members, considering themselves intellectuals, were incensed. The atheists thundered against Foster's naïve religiosity. And as for St. Joseph's—well, the congregation couldn't abide his pity. Even the more moderate members (who, in the prime of their middle-class upward mobility, had been treated more harshly in the book than the old-timers) sided with the conservatives. Except for the rector and the man who'd once got religion, they all began to hate Foster.

"Impossible man!" they said. "We've got to get rid of him!"

"Devilry! Witchcraft!" Major Austin shouted. "Remember Connie Nightingale?"

"How do we get rid of him?" the others asked him.

The Comedy of Doctor Foster

"I'll tell you! We must . . . I think we should . . . Oh, hell, hang him on a post and bang nails into him!"

"Do you really mean that?" the rector said severely.

For once Major Austin looked sheepish. "No, of course not."

The next day came the news of Connie Nightingale's death. Most would have done no more than shrug if it hadn't been for Foster. He shrugged, too, when he was told the news. Said she'd been dead for most of her life anyway. Said terrible things, showed no respect. It was heartless, when he was responsible for turning her into a witch. A vile man. An odious man.

"No, no, no," said the man who'd once got religion. "He was only being honest, don't you see?"

They didn't. But the problem solved itself.

Foster was sublimely indifferent to the arguments going on around him, and he set out that Friday afternoon for Toronto in a blissful mood. He'd finished a painting and, unlike those times when he'd been restless at the thought that he might not get new inspiration, he felt there was no need to paint or write anymore. He had to take the painting to Toronto, however, to a colleague whom he'd promised it to. It was one of those days in midsummer when warm sun alternated with violent thunderstorms, and there'd been a shower just before he set out. He enjoyed driving, since it brought a feeling of peace and an opportunity to think. As he reached the 401 and turned onto it to head towards Toronto, he realized twenty-two years had passed since the dream.

"Another two years to put up with St. Joseph's," he thought, "to make twenty-four. But what was it He said? As long as you like, just let me know when you want a change. Do I want a change?"

He didn't notice as the car left the road, hit the bridge abutment, and plunged down a hillside into a small river. But there was no feeling of

A. Colin Wright

surprise when he found himself walking along its bank. The car was farther back, he supposed, but he didn't turn around, because all that was a mere dream that he'd left behind. The river, broader now, stretched on enticingly around a bend. It was exciting, needing exploration. And now the sun was fully out, a sun that warmed him pleasantly, and he was tempted to take it into his hands to find out what it was made of. He was naked, his body younger, firmer, full of life and power. Nothing like his body of . . . How long ago was it?

He walked on, eagerly, to the bend in the river. Forests on either side. Trees vibrating with life, and animals he could sense among them. How magnificent to be alive. What was it all about? He didn't know, but he would find out. Round the bend in the river was a group of young girls, all naked as well, splashing and playing in the clear water, laughing as he approached. He waved to them as he walked by, feeling strength in his loins and a powerful desire for them all. Who first? he wondered idly. A gleam came into his eye as he realized that an enticingly rejuvenated Constance Nightingale was among them. My God! What a figure she had, and yet in his long sleep she'd seemed so dreary. Or so he supposed, for he couldn't really remember. He glanced again at the women, passed on, and his desire for them subsided. There was time enough for all of them, and for all the other wonderful things he wanted to do. He recalled something about books he'd written and wondered if they were in the library here. Probably, but why bother with them? There was a universe to explore, and plenty of time.

Without looking back, he strode up the hill—oh, how pleasurably the mosquitoes bit and the thorns scratched!—towards his cottage in the woods.

"Hello, you old bugger!" he said as he opened the door, to the figure who awaited him.

246

Praise for Sardinian Silver:

"This novel is without a doubt as good as one of Graham Greene's . . . Astute readers might be reminded as well of the Alexandria Quartet, by Lawrence Durrell . . . Of particular note is Wright's ability to elicit the morals and mores of 1960's Sardinia . . ."

—Chicago Center of Literature and Photography

"Writers like Wright help map out the rugged landscape of masculine desire and yearning in a concise and evocative prose that subtly lifts the curtain on the softer parts of manhood . . . that countless men have been trained to leave untouched and unexplored . . . This is a novel . . . all about a Sense of Place."

—US Review of Books

"Sardinian Silver is an engaging, entertaining read . . . a sobering, yet amusing reminder of the emotional fragility that lies within us all."

—Apex Reviews

"The writing is clear and concise and, while fiction, often has the feel of a memoir. Sexual encounters are tastefully handled, sometimes comically so, largely because of the youthful romantic idealism of the characters. As an added bonus, the story often reads like a travelogue and you may find yourself searching the Internet, as I did, to learn more about this island in the sun."

—Peter Klein, Allbooks Reviews